It was possible that they wouldn't find Steel Eyes at the journey's end. Yet there had been no arguments over the course of action. And no second thoughts once they had begun.

Magus was a plague on all their houses. It was said that his artificially prolonged life had allowed him to master everything there was to master. That he knew everything there was to know. That this mastery and knowledge had elevated him to a higher level of existence. To a kind of junkyard godhood. He had become his own creation, a malevolent deity whose dark schemes and willing soldiers victimized and degraded a desperate world.

The companions had taken on the mission because they all knew some things were worth dying for, even when the odds were slim.

And ridding the Deathlands of Magus was one of those things.

**Other titles in the
Deathlands saga:**

# JAMES AXLER

# DEATH LANDS®

## Apocalypse
## Unborn

A GOLD EAGLE BOOK FROM
# WORLDWIDE®

TORONTO • NEW YORK • LONDON
AMSTERDAM • PARIS • SYDNEY • HAMBURG
STOCKHOLM • ATHENS • TOKYO • MILAN
MADRID • WARSAW • BUDAPEST • AUCKLAND

First edition June 2008

ISBN-13: 978-0-373-62592-5
ISBN-10:      0-373-62592-8

APOCALYPSE UNBORN

Wild, dark times are rumbling toward us, and the prophet who wishes to write a new apocalypse will have to invent entirely new beasts, and beasts so terrible that the ancient animal symbols of St. John will seem like cooing doves…in comparison.

—Heinrich Heine,
1797–1856

# THE DEATHLANDS SAGA

This world is their legacy, a world born in the violent nuclear spasm of 2001 that was the bitter outcome of a struggle for global dominance.

There is no real escape from this shockscape where life always hangs in the balance, vulnerable to newly demonic nature, barbarism, lawlessness.

But they are the warrior survivalists, and they endure—in the way of the lion, the hawk and the tiger, true to nature's heart despite its ruination.

**Ryan Cawdor:** The privileged son of an East Coast baron. Acquainted with betrayal from a tender age, he is a master of the hard realities.

**Krysty Wroth:** Harmony ville's own Titian-haired beauty, a woman with the strength of tempered steel. Her premonitions and Gaia powers have been fostered by her Mother Sonja.

**J. B. Dix, the Armorer:** Weapons master and Ryan's close ally, he, too, honed his skills traversing the Deathlands with the legendary Trader.

**Doctor Theophilus Tanner:** Torn from his family and a gentler life in 1896, Doc has been thrown into a future he couldn't have imagined.

**Dr. Mildred Wyeth:** Her father was killed by the Ku Klux Klan, but her fate is not much lighter. Restored from predark cryogenic suspension, she brings twentieth-century healing skills to a nightmare.

**Jak Lauren:** A true child of the wastelands, reared on adversity, loss and danger, the albino teenager is a fierce fighter and loyal friend.

**Dean Cawdor:** Ryan's young son by Sharona accepts the only world he knows, and yet he is the seedling bearing the promise of tomorrow.

In a world where all was lost, they are humanity's last hope....

# Prologue

Colonel Graydon Bell took his first breath in more than a century. Compressed air rushed down the plastic tube in his throat, inflating his collapsed lungs. Simultaneously, microbursts of electric current jolted his brain stem, sending his naked body into convulsions, slamming elbows, knees, and forehead into the sides of the narrow, stainless-steel cryotank.

His restarted heart pounding in his ears, Colonel Bell clawed at the base of his skull, tearing away the tangle of electrical leads. This ended the violent spasms, but he continued to twitch and shudder; his knees buckled under his weight and he slumped to a squat. The ballooning pressure in his lungs felt like a chain saw splitting him in two. With trembling fingers he pried out the nose plugs and exhaled. Minutes passed while he gasped and gulped canned air, struggling to regain the rhythm of his breathing.

As suffocation panic faded, Bell fumbled for the edge of the pliable adhesive that sealed shut his eyes. He peeled the protective material from brow and cheeks, then cautiously raised one eyelid. Not cautiously enough. Light speared into long-dormant nerves with such force that he nearly bit through the oxygen tube.

Mewling, he made brief forays into that place of impossible hurt. Repeated exposure was the only way to reinitiate his optic nerves. Through streaming tears he could see the cryotank's vacuum lid had opened, and on the ceiling above it a bank of fluorescent bulbs flickered erratically.

Bell yarded the intubation hose from his throat and let it drop, hissing, to his feet. The sickly sweet taste in his mouth was from trehalose, a sugar that was the key to successful reanimation from cryodeath. Prior to his immersion in deep cold, his tissues had been infused with this naturally occurring antifreeze. Trehalose kept the water in his body from turning to ice crystals, which would have ruptured his every cell, turning him upon defrost into two hundred pounds of slunky garbage.

Bracing his arms and back against the wall, Bell used his legs to slowly straighten, fighting the cramps that seized his thighs and buttocks. When he looked down at his corpse-white body, he saw wasted muscles, every rib showing, tendons standing out like load-maxed cables. Red starbursts of exploded capillaries dotted his skin. Galaxies of them.

Freezer burn.

The first stirrings of memory returned—the jumble of terrifying images and sensations sent Bell's heart racing. Lurching stiffly forward, he grabbed one of the rungs in the wall and started pulling himself out of the cylindrical coffin. He moaned as he climbed, panting hard between steps.

As Bell straddled the rim of the cryomodule, he was slammed by a wave of vertigo. He shut his eyes while the deserted laboratory spun around him. He held on with both hands until the dizzyness passed, then crawled onto the attached steel platform.

The cryotank on the other side of the access gantry had not opened, yet. Rivulets of condensation peeled down the module's gleaming sides, and its defrost unit gave off a steady hum. Reanimation in progress. From where Bell lay, he could read the tank's LED indicators. The internal temperature was 89.9 degrees Fahrenheit, and rising. Heart restart was still fourteen minutes, sixteen seconds away—a delay due to the fact that there was more of Dr. Antoine Kirby to thaw. Fifty-two pounds more, to be exact.

Still dazed, Colonel Bell dragged himself down the gantry stairs on his behind, dropping from one tread to the next, until he reached the lab floor. When he tried to get up, a stabbing pain in his gut doubled him over. Falling to hands and knees, he threw back his head and projectile vomited. Expelled trehalose syrup drew a ten-foot-long stripe on the polished concrete. He heaved until his stomach knotted and blood mixed with bile dripped from his chin.

The cryolab's computer control consoles were twenty feet away. Unable to stand, he crawled hand over hand until he reached the nearest desktop, then hauled himself into an ergonomic chair. On the counter before him were framed photos, color portraits of two beaming families, both of them his. Five children, ages six to sixteen, produced by two marriages. The boys and girls had inherited their father's firm chin, wide-set brown eyes and extraordinary intelligence. They were the joy of his life, the wellspring of his inspiration. When Bell looked up at the mission chronometer, the atomic clock that measured elapsed time to hundredths of a second, an icy hand pushed into the center of his chest and gripped his heart. Suddenly he was shivering again, teeth chattering, bones clicking, vibrating like he was going to shake apart. He pulled a thermal blanket from a drawer and clumsily wrapped himself in it.

Chronologically, Graydon Bell was 135 years old.

Everyone he had ever loved was dust.

And they had died unaware of his desperate all-or-nothing sacrifice to save them. Bell had thrown himself upon the anvil of death, anonymously, selflessly, unsure of resurrection, but confident that the threat facing all of humanity required nothing less.

In the world of pure science, in Bell's world, confidence was a mathematical construct, a numeric of probability that separated fact from speculation. By the first week of January 2001, he and Dr. Kirby were ninety-five-percent certain that a disintegration of global defense systems was imminent, a cascade of incremental failures leading inexorably to Armageddon—an all-out nuclear missile exchange between the United States and the Soviet Union. Their elaborate and ingenious computer models had revealed the near future, and it was a dead end. But their warnings had fallen on deaf ears.

Things might have been different if they'd had some kind of quick, cheap fix to offer the directors of the ultrasecret Operation Chronos, which was responsible for the first successful experiments in time travel. Kirby and Bell's research on the structure of supra-time/space had started out as theoretical and abstract, but had soon become vital to the black budget program's main thrust. Time-trawling had mindbending military and economic potential. It opened the possibility of effective social engineering on a global scale, the permanent rewriting of history in favor of those who controlled the technology. For any number of practical reasons it was easy to dismiss Kirby and Bell's conclusions out of hand. The idea that Operation Chronos had already accidentally triggered a chain reaction at the most fundamental level of reality was nothing short of heresy.

As Bell struggled numb fingers to log on to the redoubt's computer, logic told him that what he and Kirby feared most had come to pass. Otherwise they would have been discovered and reanimated by their Chronos colleagues a century ago.

With faint hope, he enabled the encrypted redoubt-to-redoubt com links. The global network was offline; he could not call up the date, time or text of the last coded transmission. Communication satellites had either fallen out of orbit or been fried by a colossal EM burst. The redoubt's conventional radio mast pulled in a hiss of static across all bands, all frequencies. Sensor indicators showed high radioactivity levels topside, and superelevated air temperatures that suggested radical local climate change.

There was no way around the evidence: buried deep in a mountainside in a nuke-hardened site, he had survived Armageddon. There was no satisfaction in having been proved right. Bell sagged back in the chair, overwhelmed by grief and guilt.

He and Dr. Kirby were at least partially responsible for the destruction of civilization, and for millions, perhaps billions of deaths, including those of his own children. In the beginning their interest had been as selfish and blind as the would-be landgrabbers and slave masters. Supra-time/space was a mathematical perspective *outside* the biologically hard-wired, human experience of time. Kirby and Bell wanted to be the first scientists to map this new, overarching dimension, and the only way to do that was to evaluate and interpret the results of successful time-trawling experiments. Had their ongoing research, code-named Project Undo, not been critical to the directors' goal of controlled manipulation of the time stream, it would never have been so lavishly funded. Analyses of the handful of Operation Chronos triumphs had revealed few facts about the boundaries of s-t/s, and even less about its apparent congruencies and paradoxes, but had convinced Kirby and Bell that time-trawling, in and of itself, could disrupt present reality in unforeseen and ultimately catastrophic ways.

With no support from their superiors, the researchers faced the most difficult of moral and professional choices. They could either sit back and watch the inevitable, dying alongside their family and friends, or they could attempt to do something to change the outcome, which meant abandoning the still-intact present to its terrible fate. In the end, they'd decided they had to act. No one alive knew more about the implications of temporal alteration than they did; for that reason, they had used cryogenics instead of time-trawling to reach the future.

The colonel rested his forehead on the desktop. He would have wept had he been able to produce tears. It felt like fibers of steel wool were embedded in his throat, his tongue was stuck to the roof of his mouth, cramps gripped his bowels. Reanimation and the subsequent vomiting had caused severe dehydration. After unlocking the wheels of the ergochair, he slowly rolled himself a yard or so to the left, to the vacuum-sealed intravenous bags suspended from a stainless-steel pole. Finding an injection site was easy—the veins stood out like soda straws on his emaciated forearms. He connected driplines of saline and nutrients, and adjusted the flow rates.

Graydon Bell was a physicist, not a medical doctor, but he understood as well as anyone the physiological aftermath of cryogenesis. Over time, despite all the precautions, minerals leached from bone and tissue, and neurochemicals in the brain degraded. He had anticipated some cell loss upon reanimation, some memory loss, maybe even the temporary loss of sanity. There was no way to anticipate the impact of a temporal disruption on the subatomics of a frozen human body.

He and his still-thawing research partner had taken the fateful leap forward fully aware of their ignorance and vulnerabilities.

At six-foot-three, Antoine Kirby had been an All-America defensive end for the University of California at Berkeley football team. Cat-quick. NFL-quick. But way too smart for pro sports. The mathematical genius had dropped football after he'd completed his athletic contract; it was a means to an end—a free undergradu-

ate education. The money he saved helped finance a
Ph.D. from Princeton. When Operation Chronos had recruited him, he was back in the Bay Area, working at
Lawrence Livermore Laboratory. Always smiling, always happy, thrilled by the potential of his research,
Kirby was unmarried, with many close friends, but no
living family.

While Kirby was away at Princeton, Bell was serving in Colombia, a U.S. Army–financed doctorate in
physics from Cal Tech under his belt. His mission had
been to lead a covert combat field test of a new genera-
tion of shoulder-fired, laser-burst weapons on FARC
narcoterrorists. Of the two, only Bell had taken human
life. Success in Colombia had brought him quick ad-
vancement to the Army's most theoretical and problem-
atic programs, and ultimately a dream assignment.
Operation Chronos's directors had paired a world-class
physicist with a world-class mathematician and turned
them loose to explore the fringes of the known and the
possible.

Racked along one wall of the lab, in hermetically sealed
plastic cases, coated with protective grease, were a variety
of conventional, combustion-fired weapons: M-16 assault
rifles, some equipped with over-under grenade launchers,
12-gauge SPAS assault shotguns, 9 mm Beretta semiau-
tomatic pistols, extra magazines, ammo canisters. Body
armor and night-vision goggles had their own cases, as did
the M-60, .308-caliber machine guns, and the heavy-bar-
reled, bolt-action, night-scoped Remington sniper rifles.

Purely rational, scientific exploration had devolved
to this.

Bell, far better than most, understood that leaping before looking was fundamental to human nature, and to discovery. It was both his species finest feature and its tragic flaw.

He switched screens to monitor the LED countdown to heart restart. As the final seconds ticked away, he prayed for Kirby's successful reanimation. He prayed that he would not have to face the coming trials alone. Then the cryotank lid popped up, compressed air valves opened, and from inside the cylinder came a terrible frantic thudding.

Antoine Kirby awoke with a thundering bellow. Bell had never heard him angry before, not in the five years they had worked together. Adrenaline jolt mixed with a wave of profound relief. Bell wasn't in the hunt by himself, after all.

He and Kirby believed they could undo the nuclear holocaust. They believed they could reverse the erasure of human history. Whether they had sacrificed themselves for nothing, only time would tell. Earth was vast, and remade primeval by the fires of hell. To locate, capture and retrieve one man could take decades. The one man who was the locus of Armageddon. The seed of destruction. The dropped stitch.

For the world to right itself, Dr. Theophilus Algernon Tanner had to die when and where he was supposed to die.

# Chapter One

"What gaudy you sluts from?"

The man standing in line behind Dr. Mildred Wyeth smelled like pan-fried shit—the cologne of a mass grave robber or a mutie skinner. He was leaning so close to her that she could feel his breath between the beaded plaits of her hair, on the base of her neck. Mildred didn't turn. She had already sized him up.

A large sheath knife rode in a scabbard on his hip. A Remington 12-gauge autoloader hung from a worn leather shoulder sling. Both barrel and buttstock had been crudely sawn off; the former at the end of the tubular magazine, the latter behind the black tape-wrapped pistol grip. He was tall and lean, between twenty and thirty years of age, with a weather-seamed, dirt-encrusted face. His pupils were dilated, his sandy-brown mustache and whiskers blackened by a tarry substance, which she recognized as the residue from smoking powdered mindburst mushroom. According to its devotees, it made live skinning and grave robbing even more fun.

Krysty Wroth faced Mildred, but she was looking beyond her, over her shoulder at the skinner. Although Krysty's eyes were emotionless pools of emerald-green, her forehead smooth as glass, her red mutant hair had coiled into tight ringlets of alarm. A chill, steady mist fell from the low-hanging fog bank. Tiny sparkling droplets clung to the tips of Krysty's prehensile curls and the shaggy black fur of her bearskin coat, which hung open from collar to hem.

"Didn't we take turns banging you two over in Byrumville?" said another hoarse male voice from behind.

Mildred ignored that question, too. The second man was shorter, bare-chested, stump-legged, just as filthy as his running buddy, and wearing the same black sticky ring in the whiskers around his mouth. Tucked into the front of his trouser waistband was a battered 9 mm Astra semiauto blaster. A violent confrontation with these triple-stupe bastards was the last thing Mildred and Krysty wanted. The idea was to blend in with the rest of the ragged queue on the predark pier.

A light onshore breeze riffled the surface of Morro Bay. The massive, 570-foot-tall rock that marked the entrance from the Pacific Ocean played peek-a-boo in the gray swirls of fog. Heavy surf broke over the bay's three-mile arch of sandspit. The rise in sea level after the nuclear holocaust put the spit under water at high tide and submerged the walkway and side railings of the concrete pier. The tide was out, now, and the pier, much foreshortened by wave damage to its seaward end, was high and dry.

Here and there along the mucky crescent of Morro Bay's exposed shoreline, amid the tangled metal and plastic refuse, lay stripped human skeletons and lumps of mud and wet cloth in human shape. In the bay, some 150 yards to the north, a three-masted white ship swung at anchor. It couldn't tie up to what was left of the pier, the water was too shallow. Prospective passengers and cargo waited on the dock to be ferried to the frigate. At the ruined end of the pier, a makeshift crane lowered crates and boxes onto rowboats; beside the crane a rickety stairway led down to a floating platform and a tethered boat. The entrance to the stairs was guarded by four thickly built crewmen with assault rifles. Before passengers were allowed to descend, they were interrogated by a man seated behind a plank-and-sawhorse table who entered information into a logbook.

The line moved forward very slowly.

Mildred remembered the last time she'd passed through Morro Bay, more than a century earlier—and a year and a half before the end of the world. In the terminology of Deathlands, Dr. Wyeth was a freezie. On December 28, 2000, an idiosyncratic reaction to anesthetic during abdominal surgery had put her into a coma. In a last-ditch effort to save her life, the operating team had placed her in cryogenic stasis, where she remained until revived by Ryan Cawdor, Krysty Wroth and their companions. Mildred and her liberators had been inseparable ever since.

If the picturesque, central California coastal town was far enough away from San Francisco and Los Angeles to avoid a stray missile hit on hell day, it hadn't escaped the nuclear shock and tidal waves produced by saturation hydrogen and earth-shaker warhead strikes both north and south. Most of Morro Bay's existing structures had been obliterated in the furious aftermath of Armageddon, yet it had hung on and survived as a human outpost, as the southernmost seaport on Deathlands' Pacific coast.

What was left of the Los Angeles/San Diego megalopolis was anybody's guess. It was widely rumored that the lower half of California had vanished into the Cific Ocean, vaporized by overlaid nuclear hits or submerged by cataclysmic slippage along the full length of the San Andreas Fault. Reports about what remained were both sketchy and farfetched. Mildred had never met anybody who claimed to have seen it with their own eyes, only those who had heard about it, third or fourth hand. It was not the kind of place visitors returned from.

Most Deathlanders she'd met believed that normal life couldn't exist there, that the air and water were poisoned by high radiation levels and reawakened volcanic processes. Moreover, they were convinced that it was the fountainhead of every manifest evil, the spawning ground of new species of predatory mutants, monsters that spread forth across the ravaged continent like carnivorous weeds.

As a twentieth century scientist, Mildred was dubious of all this speculation. For one thing, the concepts of "norm" and "mutie" were relative, not either/or. Every living thing in Deathlands had been impacted at a genetic level by the holocaust. Some of these changes were manifested externally; most were not. That a particularly heavily nuked area could generate a high rate of successful mutations did not jibe with pre-Apocalypse genetic research, which showed that the higher the rad dose, the more negative the mutations: the effected embryos rarely made it past the early stages of development. If Southern California was indeed the source of the plague of unheard-of, hostile species, Mildred suspected that something much more complicated, much more directed, had to be going on. One way or another, she and Krysty and the others waiting on the pier were about to discover the truth.

Post-nukecaust Morro Bay had been rebuilt using recycled materials from the former marina, and from the fleet of commercial fishing boats and private yachts scattered high onto the hillsides by tidal waves and hurricane-force winds. Single-story, ramshackle shacks shared walls and predark concrete block-and-slab foundations—there was not a single right angle in the entire ville. Nor was there much in the way of ground cover, save for the clumps of tiny wild daisies sprouting along the open-trench latrines. It reminded Mildred of movies she'd seen of Calcutta, India: a seething, mounded garbage dump shrouded by acrid wood smoke.

Ville folk furtively watched the line of newcomers from window holes punched in their cardboard walls; concealed in shadow, they huddled in doorless doorways. Though Morro Bay serviced the small ship trade to coastal outposts in the north, it had no gaudy, as such; that sort of business was conducted in the earthen ditches alongside the road. There were no frantic sluts pandering along the crowded pier this day. No begging children, either. Murder for profit was a growth industry here, yet the inhabitants were taking pains to hide themselves.

With good reason.

The folk who lined the dock were the foulest, most dangerous scum in all of Deathlands. Maniac mercies. Double-crossing ex-sec men. Slavers. Jolt traders. Mutie hunters. Blackheart robbers and chillers. The line of human refuse stretched past the end of the pier and wound back up the hill. Most of the cargo crates in the queue held living creatures that squealed and shrieked, but some pleaded in English for water, food or a quick and merciful death. The air holes were too small and too widely spaced for Mildred to see what or who was trapped inside.

"Hey, slut, I'm asking you a question," the skinner said. He punctuated his remark by giving her a hard poke in the kidney with a stiffened finger.

Mildred turned and looked up into his eyes. She saw animal lust, greed and seamless ignorance. "Back off," she warned him.

It was a waste of breath.

The skinner smiled. "Maybe you do so much business on your backs you can't remember faces," he said. He drew out eight inches of predark Buck knife and waved its cruel gut hook in her face. "Bet you remember this…"

"Let's bang 'em again, right here," the shorter man growled, moving closer, his hand on the butt of his remade pistol.

Krysty and Mildred were on their own. To avoid being recognized, the six companions had split up at the ville's city limits. Ryan Cawdor was far ahead of them in line and the others, Doc Tanner, Jak Lauren, and J. B., were spread out some distance behind. Although it was vital to draw no extra attention to themselves, there was another, equally important consideration: the voyage south was going to be long and in tight quarters. Unless Krysty and Mildred made a statement that could not be misconstrued, they were going to be subject to the unwanted, nonstop, belowdecks attentions of a hundred-odd, semihuman shitballs.

In a blur Mildred drew her Czech ZKR 551 revolver and jammed the muzzle under the much taller man's chin. For a fraction of an instant he stood there flat-footed, long knife in hand. Under the circumstances, there was no moral lap dance, no question of Mildred holding her fire, of just disarming him.

That option simply did not exist.

The pistol's bark was partially muffled by flesh and bone. The skinner grimaced as the .38-caliber slug rocketed out the top of his head and brains jetted skyward in glistening puff of pink. He toppled backward, bright arterial blood spurting from the ragged hole in his crown.

His running buddy tried to clear the Astra from his waistband, but Krysty beat him to the punch. Snatching her Smith & Wesson 640 out from under her coat, she lunged forward and shot him once in the heart. The close-range muzzle-flash set his matted carpet of chest hair on fire. The .38-caliber bullet zipped through his torso and out his back, skipping off the pier railing before blipping into the bay. Clutching the smoking entrance wound, he staggered sideways, his eyes bulging. His mouth opened and closed, but no sound came out. Dead on his feet, he twisted and fell onto his face.

The two women turned back to back and scanned the nearby crowd over the sights of their handblasters. Everyone had turned to look at the closely spaced shots. Some drew their pistols or unslung long guns, but when they realized there was no threat and the show was over, they all stood down. No one seemed concerned about the sudden chillings; for this scabrous crew it was business as usual.

Having made their point, Mildred and Krysty booted the still-twitching bodies off the side of the pier. Other corpses bobbed down there—bloated, slack-jawed whoppers drifting among the pilings. Overfed seagulls rode on pale chests, either dozing or pecking halfheartedly at empty eye sockets and the roots of shredded tongues.

As Mildred stepped away from the railing she glanced down the line to the ruined end of the pier. Ryan Cawdor was now three back from the interrogation table.

FROM A DISTANCE of fifteen feet, Ryan observed the frigate's captain, a mountain of brown skin and black tattoos seated behind a makeshift desk. Naked to the waist, his torso and arms were decorated with intertwined thorny vines; his front teeth, top and bottom, were filed to triangular, sharklike points. But most striking was the gruesome facial branding. Four parallel ridges of pink scar tissue ran over the bridge of his wide nose and down his broad cheeks. The corners of his mouth had been likewise disfigured, they twisted upward in a perpetual, manic grin.

Ryan recognized the islander blood, what more than a century ago would have been called Maori or Fijian. The captain's black hair hung in a braid down past the middle of his back. He had gold rings on every thick finger and both thumbs. A Government Model 1911 Colt pistol with an extended, high-capacity magazine lay on the tabletop. The .45's hammer was locked back, the grip safety permanently held down with tight wraps of waxed cord. Next to his hand, it looked like a child's toy. The armed, half-naked men at the stairway were islanders, too. They held their AK-47s casually aimed at the next man in line. Safeties off. Firing lanes clear. Index fingers braced against the outside of trigger guards.

The three mercies standing in front of Ryan wore grease-stained canvas dusters and scarred lace-up boots. They carried blueless but well-oiled 9 mm Heckler & Koch machine pistols on shoulder slings. The weapons looked to be in excellent condition. They kept their hands in view and well away from their blasters. The first guy in line, presumably the trio's boss, sported a broad-brimmed leather hat pulled down low over his eyes.

The captain waved them forward. "Where are you boys from?" he said, pencil point poised against the open logbook.

"We come from Siana country, over near Fayette," the mercie leader replied in a gravelly voice. "A bastard long walk."

"Who did you crew for?"

"Crewed for ourselves. We've been wolf-packin' for the last six, eight months."

"Wolf pack" was Deathlandese for a band of roaming, freelance robber-chillers. And wolf-packing would not appear distasteful to the captain, under the circumstances.

He didn't ask for any of their names. He didn't start writing in the logbook, either. At his elbow was a pile of tarnished metal disks with neck thongs. Every disk had a different stamped number. Those he handed a tag got a berth on the white ship and free passage south, to promised mayhem, glory and riches.

"I heard there's lots of cannies roaming the bayous these days," the captain said.

Cannies were cannibals, arguably Deathlands' most degraded and depraved human subculture. They operated in small, highly mobile clans, joining forces to hunt, to chill, to feed on the weak and the unwary.

"No more than any place else," the mercie said.

"We had a few maneaters slip aboard the last trip," the captain said. "Guess they thought it was gonna be a floating picnic. It wasn't. Bystanders got caught in the cross fire. Hell of a mess." The captain put a yellow plastic bucket on the table. "You mind spitting in this?"

The mercie leader didn't look back at his pals; he didn't take his eyes off the four AK-47s pointed at the center of his chest. He shrugged. "You want some spit, I'll give you spit." Holding the rim of the bucket close to his lips, he hawked resonantly and expelled a stringy gob, mopping the blowback off his chin stubble with his duster sleeve.

The captain reached under the table for a quart Mason jar three-quarters-full of liquid. The fluid was the color of burgundy wine, but when he poured a little into the bucket, it dripped thick and slow. Holding the bucket at arm's length, the captain sluiced around the contents, then dumped a foaming mess out onto the deck. The liquid was no longer ruby-red. It wasn't even pale pink. It was the color of predark concrete. "Gray means oozies," he told the mercie leader as he set aside the bucket. "But you already know that."

Ryan took a quick, careful step to one side. Oozies was the cannie plague. Spread by the eating of human flesh, it produced weeping lesions inside the victim's brain. In its final stage, a thick, gray pus leaked from ears and nostrils. As Ryan planted his feet, his fingers an inch from the butt of his holstered SIG-Sauer P-226, from under the table came a shotgun's deafening roar.

The table's front legs hopped from the ground and the mercie vaulted backward, arms spread wide, enveloped in a billowing white cloud that twinkled with tiny comets of burning black-powder. He landed flat on his back, a smoldering, gory crater blown from hip to hip. The awful swathe of destruction was the product of not one, but two simultaneously discharging 12-gauge barrels, the product of a muzzle loader packed with metal scrap and bent nails.

The other two mercies jumped through the smoke for the railing. Before the islander crew could open fire, they dived headfirst over it.

Their splashdowns were punctuated by the clatter of Kalashnikovs. The islanders fired over the rail, full-auto. The passenger wannabes rushed to that side of the pier, shouting and potshotting at the pale shapes swimming toward shore four feet under the surface. Ryan drew his handblaster, but didn't join the fray. There was no need. Concentrated bullet impacts churned the water to a fine froth. First one, then the other body popped up, no longer moving, leaking red from dozens of wounds. At which point, the shooting stopped abruptly.

Behind them on the deck, the mortally wounded cannie jittered—heels drumming, back arching, teeth snapping, gray mucous bubbling from his nostrils and ears. The double scattergun blast had gutted him, but missed his heart and lungs. Ryan crouched upwind, just beyond the cannie's reach, raised his blaster and fired once, putting a 9 mm round in front of the cannie's left ear, blowing infected brains out the far side of his head.

As he reholstered the SIG, the crewmen rolled the corpse off the pier.

The background racket resumed at once. Along the queue, sec men and slavers pushed and threatened one another, jockeying for dominance. Brief fist and blade fights broke out. Caged anomalies shrieked and moaned in mortal terror. The looming mass of fog, the drifting gun and wood smoke and the overwhelming reek of death from beneath the pier added to the atmosphere.

Hell's circus.

Only one creature in all of Deathlands could have recruited and assembled such a gathering.

The ringmaster.

Magus. Steel Eyes. The thing that wouldn't die.

Once he had been one-hundred-percent, flesh-and-blood human. How long ago that was, or where he had come from was not known. As his organic parts—limbs, organs, sensory arrays—failed due to age or damage, he had used inorganics such as nanotech circuit boards, memory chips, servos, pumps and titanium struts, to make the necessary repairs to himself. The melding of mechanical and biomechanical subsystems had prolonged Magus's life, but the result was not a pretty sight. Blood, machine oil and pus seeped from the joins of angry flesh to gleaming metal, erratic clicking sounds, like a box of cheap wind-up clocks, came from inside his torso, and he was enveloped in the rank odor of his own putrefaction.

Over the years Ryan and his companions had crossed the creature's path more than once, witnessing the unspeakable cruelties he wrought on the innocent and unwary. Ever the puppetmaster, Magus relied on norm and mutie minions to do his wet work, and to cover his retreat into the shadows. Steel Eyes had long ago cut out his own humanity; if he still had a heart, that organ was made of plastic and Kevlar. Animated by a seemingly bottomless evil, this reeking, lurching contraption terrified and awed even Deathlands' most degenerate human trash. He attracted lesser villains like moths to a black flame.

In the past, Magus had toyed with randomly selected, living game pieces, amusing himself by sowing localized horror, apparently on a whim. Attacks on remote, poorly defended villes required relatively small hit crews, which could be assembled from the front porch of almost any gaudy in the hellscape. His slavery/natural resource extraction operations used the same breed of enforcers. Magus was never out of pocket for any of his criminal enterprises. Slave laborers worked for free and mass murderers were paid in the spoils of carnage.

Something new and infinitely more menacing had drawn Ryan and the others halfway across Deathlands to the pier on Morro Bay. In the last month or so, groups of drifters, traders and refugees had passed the word along the network of eroded predark interstates, through roadside and dry river bottom campsites, shanty villes, skeletonized major cities, from gaudy to gaudy all the way to the eastern baronies. Steel Eyes was recruiting an army of blackhearts. The call had been sent across the whole of the hellscape. Those who signed on were guaranteed jack, jolt and joy juice in unlimited quantities, and the opportunity to indulge in savagery unheard-of since nuke day.

Magus had never shown any ambition for conquest before. He had been content to play on the margins of Deathlands' disjointed feudal system, squabbling baronies separated by vast, lawless territories. He seemed as interested in concealing his whereabouts, his motives and the true extent of his power as he was in wreaking havoc on the defenseless. Until now the location of his home base was anybody's guess—that it would be in the West Coast's most nuked-out zone, in a place no one would dare look, made perfect sense.

The captain gestured for Ryan to approach the interview table. Wide-set, heavy-lidded brown eyes took in his battle-worn face.

A face impossible to disguise.

A knife slash from his brother had cost Ryan his left

eye and had marked his eyebrow and cheek with a jagged scar. A black eye patch covered the empty socket. Losing an eye was a common enough injury in Deathlands, where fighting was often hand-to-hand with edged weapons. Other men were as tall, with similar rangy builds and long dark hair. Few had an eye so blue. Fewer still carried an eighteen-inch panga in a leg sheath and a scoped Steyr SSG-70 longblaster. But there was no sign of recognition from the islander captain. Which was just as well because diving off the pier was not going to save life and limb. Either the captain had never heard of the one-eyed man's exploits, or he failed to identify Ryan without his constant companions at his side.

Ryan stared at the man's heavily scarred forearms. This was no decorative disfigurement. The oval-shaped, long-healed wounds were three and a half inches across. He had lost great divots of flesh, clear down to the bone.

Bite marks.

"Why'd you waste a good centerfire bullet on that cannie?" the captain asked. "He was gonna be dead meat in five minutes, tops."

Ryan would've shot a rabid stickie in that condition, but Magus wasn't in the market for mercy chillers. "Had a clear shot on the rad bastard," Ryan told him. "Wanted to get in my licks while I could."

"You solo?"

"Always."

"Mercie?"

"Sec man. Came up under Baron Zepp."

"Down Florida way."

Ryan nodded. "Greenglades."

"Old Zepp got himself chilled."

"He was still breathing when I moved west."

"Why'd you leave?"

"Needed a change of climate."

The captain didn't ask for his name—names had a tendency to change, before and after wet work—but he looked hard at the bolt-action Steyr slung over Ryan's shoulder. "You any good with that longblaster?"

"Good enough to keep it."

It was the kind of rare, high-end weapon that most folks would chill for, given the opportunity.

The mountain of brown stared up at Ryan's face. "But not good enough to keep your eye?"

Ryan smiled. "One's all I need."

"Here," the captain said, shoving the yellow bucket across the table at him. "Spit."

Ryan obliged. When the mixed sputum and blood poured out red, the crewmen let the aimpoints of their AKs drift away from his chest.

"Call me Captain, or Captain Eng," said the seated man. He picked a token from the pile, wrote down the number in his log, then tossed Ryan the disk. "From now on you are called 46. Wear that tag around your neck at all times. Don't lose it. Without it, you won't be fed or paid. Go down the gangway and wait on the dock. You'll be told what to do. Make no trouble, and you'll have no trouble."

Ryan nodded, although trouble was exactly what he

had in mind. He and his friends had missed the chance to chill Magus before.

If they missed this time, all of Deathlands would pay the price.

# Chapter Two

Doc Tanner leaned hard against his oar, putting every ounce of his skinny, six-foot-three-inch frame into the effort. He sat on the right half of the eighteen-foot boat's middle thwart, facing the stern and the hulking, brown-skinned man at the tiller, a man with heavy brows and squinty, slitted eyes. A wispy black chin-beard hung down his chest, between pendulous bare breasts. Intricate blue-black tattooing, like a filigreed cape, shadowed sloping shoulders.

"Pull!" the tillerman ordered his conscripted crew as he steered into the steady breeze. A remade AK-47 with a steel skeleton stock lay across the tops of his thighs. An extra 30-round magazine was taped upside down to the weapon's clip. In the edge of the wooden seat beside him, he had stuck a machete, blade-first, its handle within easy reach. A plastic bailing can floated in the bilge water between his bare feet.

After some initial clumsiness and disorganization, the ten passengers had their oars moving more or less in sync, and the boat made smooth, gliding progress toward the anchored frigate.

As Doc dipped his oar, he recalled a more pleasant sea voyage, roughly two centuries ago. It, too, had been a journey via sailing ship. There had been no rowing required. He had been returning home to the United States from Oxford University in England, where he had earned a PhD degree in science. Shortly after his repatriation, he had met and married the lovely Emily Chandler. Their union had been blessed with two children, a girl Rachel, born in 1893, and a son Jolyon, born in 1895. The Tanners began a happy domestic life in Omaha, Nebraska. Their joy was cut short by an unimaginable turn of events. A world stood on its head in a single, terrible instant. One afternoon in November of 1896, blind fate had torn Dr. Theophilus Tanner from the bosom of his young family.

Blind fate and human cruelty.

Out for a stroll with his wife and children, he had been time-trawled against his will by the whitecoats of Operation Chronos, vacuumed up and drawn forward to the year 1998. After almost two years of close confinement, constant interrogation, physical and psychological testing, of torture in the name of a twisted, morally bankrupt science, he had been hurled forward in time again, farther still from those he had loved.

In a strange and terrible world, he had been adopted by a new family. No wife had he. No offspring. But rather, brothers and sisters of battle, fighters bound together by a common thread: survival.

As the boat drew away from the pier, Doc thought he saw Jak Lauren's shoulder-length white hair gleaming among the milling crowd. Jak was a red-eyed albino, a wild child of Deathlands, skilled with leaf-bladed throwing knives and his Colt Python handblaster, a young man of few words and great, selfless bravery. The Armorer, also known as John Barrymore Dix, was farther back in the throng, his fedora hat lost behind much taller heads. J.B. brought up the companions' rear with a 12-gauge Smith & Wesson M-4000 pump shotgun. The rest of Doc's extended family—Ryan, Krysty and Mildred—were already onboard the white ship.

Doc took in the other rowers around him. A motley crew, to be sure. Some had used strips of black plastic bags and winds of duct tape to repair tears in their boots, jackets and trousers. Their centerfire and black-powder weapons were mostly well-worn, missing handblaster grips replaced with layers of silver tape. Their knuckles were scarred, and their faces grimy and gap-toothed. Even the steady head wind couldn't blow away the smell of unwashed funk, spilled joy juice and the stink of intense fear. None could predict what they might encounter on the road to promised riches. Or if, in fact, any riches lay ahead. They kept rowing, though, heads down, backs bent. These were men accustomed to big risk and small rewards.

Only a certain kind of Deathlander would consider signing on with the likes of Magus—someone stuck at the bottom of the socioeconomic heap. Someone with a taste for chilling and the desire to claw his way upward, over the bodies of others, to the light and air. It required a willingness, indeed an eagerness, to do anything, at any time, to anyone, an amoral mentality that in Tanner's Victorian Era had been ascribed to "primitive" peoples in distant lands, and to the criminally insane.

Alone in a small boat in such company, Doc felt

considerable unease, himself. His ebony sword stick leaned against the thwart, its silver lion's-head handle pressing into the side of one of his tall, cracked leather boots. Under his black frock coat hung a massive, holstered black-powder pistol. The LeMat represented a high point in Civil War weapons technology—two sidearms in one. A .63-caliber, single-shot scattergun barrel was married to a 9-shot .44-caliber revolver. Properly angled from the rowboat's bow, the LeMat's "blue whistler" barrel could incapacitate the entire crew and tillerman in one horrendous, stem to stern blast.

Despite the undeniable appeal of that course of action, Doc put it out of his mind. When it came to evil, these were minnows.

The man rowing on the thwart in front of him had four sections of black PVC pipe strapped to his back. Connected in a crude rope frame, the pipes were two feet long, four inches in diameter, and securely capped at both ends. Air holes had been drilled along the sides every few inches. Leaning over the gunwhale a little, Doc managed to catch sight of the side of his face. It was painted a flat white from forehead to neck, ear to ear. A grizzled short beard stuck through the crusted pigment. Where the paint had flaked off, Tanner could see tiny, scattered whorls of red. It appeared the man had taken a load of birdshot full in the face.

Looking more closely at the plastic pipes, Doc saw clustered yellowish feet sticking through the air holes.

Crisp, hairy, insect feet.

"For lack of a proper name, we call them scagworms," said the black man rowing beside him. He was the same height as Doc, but the dreadlocks gathered on top of his head, sprouting up like the jutting leaves of a great pineapple, gave him another eighteen inches. He had a hugely muscled back and corded neck. He, too, wore a rack of PVC pipes.

"With a plethora of appendages, it would seem," Doc remarked. "Pray tell, precisely how many creatures am I looking at?"

"One organism per tube," the black man said.

"I am unfamiliar with the species," Doc admitted.

The face-painted man chimed in over his shoulder, "So is everyone else. That's why they're worth large jack."

"All we know about scagworms we learned the hard way," the black man said. "They're armored, bullet-headed, venomous, ill-tempered, oversize mutie milli-pedes. When we keep them head down and in the dark, it puts them right to sleep. They don't seem to need food or water. Just air."

"Inversion and light deprivation induces a state of hibernation," Doc speculated.

"Logic would so indicate."

The old man turned to stare at his seatmate. Logic—or even a pretense to same—rarely showed its face among the gaudy porch crowd. The black wild man wore a big, friendly smile, which also seemed a bit odd.

"That isn't the only reason we carry them butt-up," said the painted man. "Ugly mothers shit all over the place when they're the other way around."

Doc reached over and tapped one of the tubes.

And was rewarded by a shrill hiss and the rasp of a thousand clawed feet.

"That's not a good idea," the black man said. "They get testy when you wake them up."

"Are they fully grown?" Doc said.

"We're pretty sure these are just babies," the black man said. "We found an untended nest in an arroyo south of Phoenix. Snatched up a few before mama worm got back."

"How large do they get?"

"We didn't stick around to find out. The entrance to the nest was nearly three feet in diameter."

Tanner noted that both men wore desert camou BDU pants rimed with dirt and patched at the knees with duct tape. Their weapons—M-16 1-A rifles and military-issue Beretta handblasters—were of the same vintage and fine condition, which was unusual. In Deathlands, armament was almost always catch as catch can, a jumble of calibers and blaster types. They had either stumbled onto a well-stocked redoubt or they had traded away something very valuable.

"You two are mutie hunters," Doc said, dipping in his oar.

The black man nodded.

Of all the blackheart professions in the hellscape, mutie hunter was one of the most profitable, and the most loathesome. It involved supplying freaks to fill barons' mutie zoos and Deathlands' traveling carnies. Seeing and ridiculing something obviously mutated made the "norms" feel more "normal," more secure in the purity of their own genetic makeup. The collection process required kidnapping not just the clearly inhuman, like scagworm larvae, but the nearly human. The

two-legged. The one-headed. The scaled. The dwarfed.
The misshapen. Beings that could think and talk. And
love. If the unlucky parents objected to losing their children, they were beaten senseless or chilled. Generally
speaking, mutie hunters targeted the very young because they were more easily controlled and transported.
That meant the victims would spend their entire lives
behind bars.

"We were in the middle of selling our worms to a zoo
master when we heard about the bounty being paid for
extra-freaky freaks," the black man said.

"To what end?"

"Don't know. We changed our plans in a hurry,
though."

"For all we care, Magus can roast them over a char-
coal grill," said the man sitting in front. "Long as we
get our jack."

"You didn't have to leave shore to do that," Doc said.
"You could have sold the worms on the dock."

"For less than half of what they're worth," the black
man said. "Besides, we want to find out what Steel
Eyes has got going on down south. Figure it could be a
gold mine for enterprising types like us. What about
you? You got a specialty?"

"I'm just a mercie," Doc said. "In search of some
new scenery and paying work."

"Better keep your eyes open, mercie, and your
blaster in reach," the black man said.

The rowboat slowly approached the moored ship.
The frigate was more than 150 feet long. It had three
masts, and the main mast was at least eighty feet tall.

Its riveted iron hull had been painted and repainted in thick layers of white. Rust streaks ran from the scuppers, down the sides, like bloodstains. As they rounded the ship, they could read the name emblazoned on its battered stern: *Taniwha tea*.

"What kind of tea is that?" one of the few literate rowers asked.

"Not tea," the tillerman growled back at him. "Teeahh. *Taniwha tee-ahh.*" He put his palm on the machete handle, daring someone to crack wise. "She is my mother."

The black man leaned over to Doc and whispered, "It's in the Maori language. It means white monster."

# Chapter Three

As J. B. Dix climbed the rope ladder to the ship's gang-way, the yelling across the water crescendoed. He was one of the last of the prospective passengers to get a boarding token. The people left behind on the pier were making a loud fuss, jeering and booing, shouting pro-fanities, but they kept their weapons holstered and slung. Before the captain had taken his leave, he had warned the crowd that if anyone opened fire on the de-parting rowboats, the ship's four-inch guns would broadside them with grapeshot. If the left-behinds still wanted passage south, they were going to have to wait for the ship's return, a round trip of seven days or more, depending on sea conditions.

J.B. grimaced, thinking about the already cowering citizens of Morro Bay. They had an unpleasant week ahead.

Like the ship's hull, its main deck was made of riv-eted iron plates, canted on either side of the midline, this to speed seawater runoff into the scuppers. A gauntlet of islander crewmen funneled the passengers along the starboard rail, toward the bow. Block-and-tackled lat-tices of heavy cable supported the steel masts, and the jib and boom on the bowsprit, providing the crew with ladders to reach the high cross members. Dented sheet-steel awnings along the yard arms shielded the sails. These same crude, battered roofs protected the ship's wheel and the fore and aft companionways.

A crane had been set up amidships to shift the boxes from a cluster of waiting rowboats to a large, open booby hatch. As J.B. walked past, he peered down into the shrieking, stinking chaos of the hold. Its living cargo was scared shitless.

From the bits of conversation J.B. had overheard on the pier, he had learned that the predark frigate had been built as a naval cadet training vessel, designed to navigate near coastal waters and run up into the deeper river mouths. A recent addition was the battery of black-powder cannons on wheeled carriages, each braced with multiple cables strung through sets of block and tackle. Beside the blasters were crates of stacked 9-pound lead balls and canvas bags of grapeshot.

The islander gauntlet ended at the foremast. Under a wide metal awning supported by pipe struts was the forward companionway, a windowless iron box leading to the lower deck. Ahead of J.B., passengers filed one at a time through the door and down the steep stairs. The slanted roof of the companionway was rimmed with sharp spikes, and each spike was driven through the neck hole and out the top of a stripped, bleached skull. Though the skulls were of different sizes, the features were similar. All had an oval, almost human shape, enormous front-facing eye sockets, and elongated craniums. In place of nose and mouth was a small, parrot-like beak lined with tiny serrated teeth. It was a mixture of avian and humanoid characteristics that J.B. had never seen before.

Trophies of previous voyages, he reckoned.

He descended the stairs to the ship's galley. The walls were riveted sheet metal, the ceilings low. There were rows of small, circular portholes on either side of the room, but most of the illumination came from the soft glow of oil lamps, which smoke-stained the walls and ceiling. Looking at the built-in benches and tables, J.B. realized there wasn't enough seating for the hundred or so passengers and maybe twenty crew. They were going to have to be fed in three or four shifts. Though he was hungry, having waited on the pier since daybreak with nothing to eat but a few strips of venison jerky, the reek of scorched cooking oil and fried fish tied his guts in a knot.

He followed the man in front of him between the stationary tables, through the bulkhead door into the fo'c'stle. The bow of the ship was jammed with tiers of bunks and sweltering from all the passengers packed inside. Some smoked cigars and pipes; some passed around blue antifreeze jugs filled with joy juice. There was little air to breathe and no ventilation. The sleeping compartment was lit by oil lamps that hung on short chains bolted to the ceiling. Though not a tall man, J.B. could easily reach up and touch the I-beams overhead.

With difficulty, he pushed his way deeper into the room. There was a lot of jostling going on. Over the general din, he could hear loud bragging contests. Who had chilled whom. Who had robbed whom. Shouted bravado intended to stall or deflect imminent attack.

Having spent most of his adult life trading bullets and blade thrusts with similar adversaries, J.B. knew his fellow passengers were war gaming, coldly measuring and marking each other for slaughter. Survival in Deathlands was usually a matter of anticipation, of knowing in advance what someone else was likely to do, and getting off the first, well-aimed shot. It was too early for the long knives to come out, but come out they would, the Armorer knew. Many in the room would not live to see the end of the voyage. Fewer open palms meant bigger shares when it came time to divide the spoils of war.

While searching for a bed, J.B. passed very close to Krysty and Mildred. He didn't acknowledge them; they didn't acknowledge him. After the double chilling on the pier, the other passengers were giving the two women plenty of personal space. Somewhere in the milling throng, Ryan, Doc and Jak were laying low.

J.B. found an empty berth on the bottom of one of the three-bunk tiers. Hunkering down, he saw that the pallet lay right on the deck, a human-shaped depression in its compacted straw stuffing. There was just two and a half feet of space between the floor and the underside of the bunk above. Like everyone else, he chalked his token number on the iron frame. There was no locker to stow personal gear or weapons, which meant taking it all to bed with him, making the bunk space even smaller. He crawled in to check it out. With his head resting on the rock-hard straw, he heard sounds from the cargo hold directly below: squealing, pleading, weeping. There were smells, too, zoo smells seeping up through the riveted seams.

He had slept in worse accommodations.

As J.B. crawled back out, he noticed another passenger, maybe twenty feet away, staring at him intently. The man appeared to have large hairy ears set way too high on either side of a steeply pointed head. The bodies passing in front of the suspended oil lamps dimmed and strobed the available light and made it difficult to see. Carefully thumbing his steel-rimmed glasses back up the sweat-slick bridge of his nose, J.B. squinted. Hard.

The man was wearing a hooded cloak…with attached ears.

Even in the low light, the material glittered with thousands of tiny flecks. J.B. recognized it at once. It was the excised skin of a scalie. A skin scraped free of underlying fat, sun-dried, then worked by hand until it was glove-leather supple. Thin, light, breathable. There was a lot of shrinkage in the curing process, though. It took a mighty big scalie to make a man-size cloak like that. A 500-pounder, maybe.

A bearded face protruded from the pointy hood, lips curled, half smiling. The intermittent lamplight played over sunken brown eyes circled in deep purple. From the man's belt hung bulging black-powder and bullet bags fashioned from handsomely tanned swampie scrotums. He leaned on a big-bore, double-barreled percussion rifle, what in predark times would have been called an elephant gun. It was the kind of weapon mutie hunters used to blast through foot-thick hut mud walls, ambushing and chilling parents so their offspring could be more easily carted off.

J.B. stared back until the man broke eye contact, turned and vanished into the crowd. No name came to mind to match the face or the gear. No battlefield, either. J.B. had shot his way down a lot of dark, winding roads—chilling evildoers and defending the innocent—and in the process he had made blood enemies that he had never seen. Those who had escaped. And the relatives of those who hadn't. And that didn't take into account Deathlands' power to transform people's appearances in short order. It dried them up. Dimmed their lights. Most were guttering candles by the age of thirty, thanks to the elements and privation and constant conflict.

If Skin Hood had recognized him, or suspected something, he was keeping it to himself, at least for the time being. He either didn't know for sure, or he had some other agenda. The only thing certain was that discovery by this collection of coldhearts, in these cramped quarters, would get the companions torn limb from limb. Pronto.

The clank of the anchor chain being raised sent the passengers surging for the bulkhead door. As he allowed himself to be pushed out of the room, J.B. caught momentary sight of Ryan. The one-eyed man looked grim, determined, dangerous. J.B. moved with the crowd up the companionway to the main deck. Most of the crew was already aloft, scampering up the webs of cables, along yard arms, unfurling sails. Captain Eng stood behind the ship's wheel, bare feet spread wide, barking orders through a steel megaphone in a language J.B. couldn't understand.

As the sails filled and the ship started to tack back and forth toward the breakers, the great rock and the wall of fog outside the bay entrance, J.B. watched the passengers' arrogant bluster evaporate. They were not sailors. They were leaving terra firma for an alien, even more hostile environment. If travel in Deathlands was perilous, travel over the sea was a hundred times worse, fraught with new hazards, the most pleasant of which was drowning.

The islander crew offered their guests neither comfort nor reassurance. Sullen, humorless, they spoke only to one another in their native tongue and in sign language. They treated the passengers like so many cattle. Which was understandable as Magus no doubt paid them by the head.

Halfway down the starboard rail J.B. saw Doc conversing with a tall, topknotted black man and a shorter guy with cracked and peeling face paint who looked like a carny clown coming off a jolt binge. He didn't let his eyes linger for long. Mildred and Krysty were on the far side of the deck, standing back to back. As he scanned the rest of the crowd for Jak and Ryan, once again he locked gazes with Skin Hood.

The bearded man smiled at him. Then he very deliberately looked away, first at Doc, then at Mildred and Krysty. When he turned back to J.B., he nodded, his hand on the pommel of a sheathed dagger.

Gotcha.

J.B. measured the distance, estimated the shot spread left to right, and decided against trying to take him out then and there. At a range of seventy-five feet, a high brass buckshot round was not a precision-guided munition. No doubt about it, though, Skin Hood knew who they were. Yet he hadn't raised the alarm, and didn't appear interested in doing so. Which meant he was after something else. Because of that, and because he seemed to be working by himself, J.B. let things ride for the moment. He moved to the stern of the ship, standing beside one of two iron racks of fifty-five-gallon barrels painted red and securely strapped down.

The white ship slid around the Morro Bay rock, into the open Cific Ocean. As it cleared the California coastline, it was hit by a strong side wind from the north. The sails snapped full with a sound like cannon shots, and the vessel heeled over hard to port. A few of the passengers fell to their knees on the deck, everyone else grabbed for something solid to hang on to. Overhead, taut cables groaned and sang in the wind. The ship righted itself, accelerating through the whitecaps toward the wall of fog. In less than a minute, they were swallowed up by it. Visibility dropped to less than a hundred feet. It was wet, cold and difficult to breathe with all the moisture vapor in the air. The farther due west they sailed, the darker and wetter it got. A gently falling mist became a steady shower. To escape it, many passengers retreated belowdecks.

J.B. screwed down his fedora and stood his ground, angling his head to keep water drops off his glasses. It took about fifteen minutes to break through the far side of the fog bank. On the horizon dead ahead and to the north, darkness had fallen in the middle of the day.

Black sky.

Black roiling sea.

The rumble and crash of thunder.

Captain Eng steered south, where shafts of light speared through a dismal gray cloud ceiling. With the wind squarely behind them, the ship picked up speed, knifing through the swells, slamming into the wave troughs. Cannons bounced on their carriage wheels. Down and up, down and up, the ship plowed a shuddering track. One by one, the other passengers sought the relative safety and protection of the lower deck. Krysty and Mildred disappeared down the narrow companionway, followed shortly by Doc. Ryan and Jak waited a decent interval before separately heading for the forward stairs.

As the sea state deteriorated, J.B. watched the captain strap his legs to the helm platform—this to keep from being thrown if the wheel gave a sudden kick when heavy waves pounded the rudder. Every sail filled, Eng was trying to outrun the danger. As the ship porpoised, waves of foam surged over the bowspit and flooded the deck, knee-high.

J.B. was one of the last of the noncrewmen topside. Not because he liked the weather or the company. He was in a pissing contest with Skin Hood, who had also refused to take cover.

Staggering along the port rail into the wind, the mutie hunter joined him on the stern. Eyes streaming, he looked into the towering darkness behind them and said, "Chem storm's comin' up fast. A great big 'un. You ain't a-scared, are ya?"

J.B. didn't dignify the question with an answer. "Who the hell are you and what do you want?" he said.

Skin Hood smiled, displaying brown and yellow teeth. "Rad blast, Dix," he said, "I thought we was gonna be pals."

"Just spit it out."

"You and One-Eye Cawdor and the others got something good going."

Denying his identity seemed pointless. "Where do you know me from?" J.B. demanded.

"I don't know you from swampie shit," Skin Hood admitted. "Saw you and your crew take apart some sec men one time, though. Impressed me. Heard the stories about you since. You know, the kind of talk gets spread around the gaudies. Not that I believed even half of it."

"What do you want?" J.B. repeated.

"I want me a piece of whatever it is you're after. Only I want my piece up front…"

Skin Hood was looking for a pay-off to keep his trap shut. J.B. had no doubt that after he got what he could from the companions, he'd turn them all in for a second reward from the other side.

Miles off the stern, chain lightning flashed. The smell of ozone rode the wind. They were losing ground, fast. An armada of black clouds bore down on them.

Captain Eng picked up his megaphone and shouted for the crew to haul in all sails. The islanders raced to obey, despite the wind and the danger. In matter of minutes the job was done. Without power, the white ship bobbed, yawing and rolling between the immense seas. Eng bellowed through the megaphone again, and the crew deserted their posts, ducking into the aft companionway. The last seaman through the hatch was the captain.

Still facing off, J.B. and the mutie hunter didn't budge from the stern.

A dull whump rattled the cables and rumbled through the hull.

Behind them, fireballs lit up the ocean. Intense flares of yellow light spread sideways in the narrow seam between black cloud canopy and black water. The concussions sounded like an artillery barrage. J.B. knew exactly what was happening because he'd seen similar events on land. Pressure and temperature gradients deep in the storm had caused superdense pockets of vapor to form. Explosive vapor. The lightning strikes were setting them off like strings of two-thousand-pound firecrackers.

As the chem storm swept toward them, J.B. saw an advancing, shifting, miles-wide blue curtain, the color of robin's eggs, falling from the sky. And there was a hissing sound, so loud it drowned out the shriek of the wind through the cables. Beneath the edge of the blue curtain, the surface of the sea steamed and boiled, stippled by millions upon millions of impacts.

Methane hail.

Pissing contest forgotten, J.B. bolted for the aft companionway. When he tried to open the hatch, he found it locked from the inside. No one answered his frantic pounding, perhaps because it couldn't be heard over the building roar. Skin Hood dashed past him, heading for the bow in a full-out sprint. Up there, a light winked on and off as the forward companionway hatch banged open and shut.

J.B. raced after the mutie hunter, digging for all he

was worth. Behind him, the curtain of inch-diameter, blue iceballs hit the stern. Hail pounding iron plate sounded like machine guns, hundreds of machine guns, firing simultaneously and point-blank into a tin roof. The wall of deafening clatter made his guts, his bones, rattle. The ricocheting hail flew every which way, bouncing twenty, thirty feet in the air, zipping over J.B.'s head, skittering cross the deck in front of him.

He reached the awning over the companionway a second after Skin Hood and before the man could get through the open hatch. J.B. caught hold of the pointy hood and used it to jerk him backward, off balance, then side-kicked hard behind his weight-bearing knee. The leg crumpled and the man crashed to his back.

The mutie hunter jumped up at once, his purple-rimmed eyes wide with terror, his breath fogging in the sudden intense cold. He grabbed for his dagger and lunged at J.B., who stood between him and life.

Reacting, J.B. lunged, too, sweeping aside the blade thrust, wrist on wrist, using his forward momentum to head butt his adversary on the chin. The solid blow wobbled the man and he dropped the dagger. J.B. planted his feet and snapkicked at a center-chest bulls-eye, booting his opponent out from under the awning. The force of the kick sent Skin Hood sprawling, sliding across the icy deck.

He regained his feet just as the edge of the blue curtain reached him. The torrent of hail, like a waterfall breaking over his back and shoulders, drove him instantly to his knees. As he opened his mouth wide to scream, the cascade of ice pellets pounded him face-first into the deck, and in another second, buried him alive.

Gamble big, lose big.

J.B. backed down the companionway, pulled the hatch closed and dogged it.

Problem solved.

# Chapter Four

The long night belowdecks went from suffocatingly hot to freezing cold while passengers clung to their pallets, storm-tossed, rattled by the din of hail and the rumble of what sounded like distant carpet bombing. As dawn approached and the racket outside subsided, from his too small bunk Dr. Antoine Kirby could hear the moaning of seasick fellow passengers and the hiss of the ship streaking through the water under full sail.

He was watching when Doc Tanner rolled out of bed, stretched, then brushed the bits of straw from the lapels of his black frock coat. When Tanner moved toward the bulkhead and the galley, Kirby eased out of the middle bunk to follow. In the bed above his, Colonel Graydon Bell was sleeping, belly up. White grease paint had rubbed off onto the coarsely woven cover of the pallet. His bristling cheeks, his brow, even his ears were dappled with bright red pinpoints. His lean jaws were grinding, eyelids fluttering, a steady flow of tears streaming into his receding hairline.

As on every night when Graydon went to bed sober, he was dreaming about dead wives and dead children.

In the PVC tubes propped up at the foot of his bunk the scagworms were dreaming, too. Their millipede legs twitched in hibernation sleep, their armored, eye-less, bullet-heads full of murderous bliss.

Kirby shouldered his M-16 and headed for the gal-ley. He staggered as he hurried after the lanky man with the ebony walking stick. Kirby hadn't gotten his sea legs yet.

Having found Doc Tanner at last, over such a dis-tance of time and space, against astronomical odds, Kirby and Bell couldn't bear to let him out of their sight, and in fact were keeping tabs on him in four-hour shifts. If the ancient academic fell overboard and drowned, if some ex-sec man suddenly took it into his head to shoot him in the back, all was lost forever. In the final months of the twentieth century the physicist and the mathematician had devised a second chance for their world. It was a last chance. There would be no sub-sequent zipping back and forth in time, working the pro-blem on a trial-and-error basis, until they finally got things right. Each zip created an infinitesimal snag in present reality. When overlaid, the zips stretched the original snag into a hole, then a rip. The fabric of exis-tence was far more delicate than anyone ever imagined.

The ship's crew were the only takers for the break-fast of mixed fried small fish, squid, anchovies, herring and sardines were dropped whole by the bucketful into a wide caldron of boiling oil. After a minute or two, the floating, golden-brown clumps and clots were sieved out with a ladle and dumped in great mounds onto long enameled trays.

A one-course buffet.

Seated islanders hunkered over the tabletops, guarding their plates, eating bare-handed, warm grease running down their forearms.

The sight and the smell crushed what little appetite Kirby had. He climbed the companionway and went on deck. He stood for a moment, face into the wind, sucking down the cool, fresh air. To the northeast, turquoise sky was shot through with black wisps, the remnants of the chem storm they had endured. The orange disk of the sun was just breaking the horizon, above a thin, jagged ribbon of land. There was no way to tell how far they had come overnight; much of it had been spent without sails, bobbing in heavy waves. The sea all around was dark blue with a two-foot chop, scattered whitecaps and a blustery wind running from behind. The swell had fallen off to next to nothing.

He and Tanner weren't the only passengers on deck, but they were among the few standing upright. Most of the others knelt in front of the scuppers, heads in hands, faces corpse-white, beards matted with dried vomit. Rainfall and sixty-degree seawater had melted the blue hail and washed away its residue. Ahead of him, Doc Tanner advanced to the bowsprit, the tails of his frock coat flapping in the breeze. That wasn't all that was flapping. His long gray hair momentarily stood straight up, like one of those gee-whiz, static charge demonstrations.

Doc looked to be in his sixties, yet he was actually in his thirties. His forced jumps in time had produced intense submolecular stress. That Doc Tanner was not stark raving mad was testament to the resilience of the human spirit.

Though Dr. Antoine Kirby had arrived in the hellscape via cryotank, he faced the same stressors as the skinny Victorian—the same plus one. Doc was a blameless victim of circumstance; Kirby had helped facilitate the end of civilization. He entered cryosleep as an upper middle-class intellectual, a button-downed, closet-full-of-tailored-Italian-suits, Lexus-driving, happily-single, time-share-condo-in-Maui kind of whitecoat. A century as an ice block and four years fruitlessly roaming Deathlands had changed him beyond recognition. And not just externally.

Since his football days, Kirby had consciously repressed his own propensity for violence. He was a big, powerful, physically gifted man who hated aggression. He hated it because it was the easy way out. Because it was mindless and irrational. Because it contributed nothing to human understanding or betterment. The National Football League, which would have gleefully drafted him in the first round, sold diversion, sublimation and manipulation. That was something he wanted no part of. In his view, a life without a search for truth was a waste.

Thanks to cryogenics, the cerebral Dr. Kirby found himself thrust into a shattered and lawless world. He was suddenly forced to fight, and not just a dozen times a year on weekends, but almost daily. And not to win a game. In the process of some of these battles, he had taken human lives. Sometimes with his bare hands. To survive and further the vital mission, he had to unleash the demon within.

A case in point. Kirby and Bell hadn't found the brood of scagworms they now carried. They had shared a cookfire with the pair of mutie hunters who'd found them, men they had buried the next morning in shallow graves hacked into the desert hardpan. The mutie millipedes gave them cover, identities, a way to get close their quarry without raising his suspicion, or the suspicion of his companions.

Dr. Theophilus Tanner was a classically educated man, which meant he was trained in science, history, logic, literature, mythology and dead languages. He had suffered terrible, unthinkable losses, yet stubbornly held on to life. Kirby and Bell knew they couldn't force a man like Tanner into anything; and if they tried, their mission would fail, half completed. The action they required of him had to be performed of his own free will. There was no way around that fact. Accordingly, they had work with care and subtlety to convince him that it was the right and only thing to do. Before they could hope to do that, before they could reveal who they were and what the goal was, they had to gain his trust. They had already begun to lay the foundation.

It had come as a pleasant surprise to Doc Tanner that he and his new acquaintances had experiences in common. In their conversation the previous day, it turned out the mutie hunters had wandered the same territories, knew firsthand many of the villes, the baronies, the hazards Doc and the companions had faced. Tanner thought it was a coincidence—the small world syndrome.

It was not.

Kirby and Bell had been on the trail of the companions from the moment they were reanimated. They had picked up the scent by following tall tales, gossip and rumors from gaudy to gaudy, campfire to campfire. Then they had started tracking the carnage Tanner and the others left behind. It wasn't just the size or wildness of the country that made the task so challenging. The companions had access to the predark network of mat-trans gateways, housed in nuke-safe, subterranean redoubts. Using this still-operational, automated technology, they could jump from coast to coast in a matter of nanoseconds. Though Kirby and Bell used the mat-trans gateways, too, arriving onsite even a day late meant the trail was already cold. Just when it had begun to seem like they were never going to close the gap, they got their lucky break.

For four long years Antoine Kirby had relied almost exclusively on violence and intimidation to advance his cause. Stifling his impatience as he approached the tall, skinny man on the bowsprit was difficult.

"By the Three Kennedys!" Doc exclaimed, pointing at the sea far ahead. "What in God's name is that?"

Kirby followed the line of his arm and hand to a dark shape hanging above the distant wave tops. Long and slender, it was tapered at both ends. "It's a bird, and a hell of a big one," he said. "Wingspan has to be at least fifteen feet."

"It's flying against the wind," Doc said.

And the wind was considerable. The creature was making no headway, but the ship was rapidly bearing down on it.

From the crow's nest came the shout, "Manu tangata!"

"Manu tangata! Manu tangata!" The crew picked up the cry.

Captain Eng noted the position and turned the wheel for an intercept course.

The islanders rushed to the bowsprit, no longer taciturn and withdrawn. They laughed and spoke excitedly, slapping one another on the back and shoving one another playfully.

As the distance to intercept closed, Kirby could see the creature's head was definitely lighter in color than its body or wings. Like a bald eagle. Only five times larger. With the ship traveling about fourteen knots and the bird thing essentially standing still, a collision was imminent.

At the last instant, the creature deftly angled itself to miss the half-dozen cables supporting the bowsprit. It crashed feet-first into the lowest of the foremast's sails, momentarily tangling in the rigging. Flapping its great black wings, it dropped to the foredeck. Its yellow eyes were huge and terrified as it faced the gathered islanders. It opened its short beak and let out a piercing shriek of warning. Kirby could see small, sharp white teeth and a black tongue. It had no feathers on its face, which was uniformly pitted and pale. The head was entirely bald except for a tuft of downy-white fluff on its peak. The creature was not only exhausted from fighting the chem storm but clearly injured. It was missing flight feathers on its wings, and in places along their leading edges red bone showed through.

The crew immediately closed in and tried to test the extent of the damage. Gleefully, they lunged and feinted, trying to grab for it. The bird thing was very quick. Its snapping beak and the black talons on its long narrow feet kept the islanders at bay. It soon tired of the game and, avoiding their grasp, hopped and flapped back up into the foremast's rigging. From this perch it looked down with dismay.

"I'll get your birdy," offered one of the passengers, a man so ground-in grimy that he looked like he had been sprayed with cooking oil then rolled in coal dust. He pulled a big black-powder handblaster from his rope-cinched trouser waistband. The .44-caliber single-action revolver was a predark reproduction, probably Italian, of the Walker model Colt, first manufactured in 1847. Four-plus pounds of case-hardened steel, and that was without bullets and powder. The man thumbed back the pistol's hammer and, squinting along the barrel, took careful aim upward.

"Don't shoot!" Eng bellowed as he barged through the massed spectators.

The would-be bird hunter paused, looking warily over his shoulder. Before he could lower his weapon, a belaying pin clonked him soundly on the back of the head. Steel pipe on a ripe coconut. As his knees buckled, the big pistol discharged straight up in the air. Thanks to the tail wind, the cloud of black-powder smoke lasted only seconds longer than the yard-long muzzle-flash. The beating of the unconscious man continued until the captain shouted for the crew to stop.

At Eng's direction, islanders swarmed into the rigging, climbing above the creature, then onto the yard arms. From that vantage point, they managed to drop a heavy a net over it. Crew men waiting below caught hold of the net's lines and pulled the thing screaming to the deck. It thumped and twisted, but it couldn't get free. The islanders threw their bodies on top of it, forcing it onto its back. Then they grabbed hold of wings through the mesh, stretching them out to full length, kneeling on them to pin them to the deck.

Kirby saw curving, fingerlike extensions of bone on the ends of its wings. The index was nearly a foot long, the others much shorter. He was staring at its strange, birdman face when it threw back its head and spoke, jolting him to the core.

"Don't do this!" it cried in a high clear voice. "I mean you no harm. I only want to rest for a little while. I have young ones. Without me, they will starve." Then it made the lilting, musical sounds of the islander language, presumably repeating itself for those who didn't understand English.

The crew paid it no mind. They seemed almost possessed. Grinning, laughing, they held down the great bird with brute force. One of them yanked a feather out of its wing and stuck the bloody quill in his coil of braided black hair.

"It is speaking!" Doc said, pressing forward. "This creature is intelligent!"

"No," Eng told him. "Manu tangata is a stupid thing. It just repeats what it's heard. It has no wairua, no soul."

A conclusion the evidence seemed to contradict.

"Are you deaf, man!" Doc exclaimed. "It is sentient and it is talking to you!"

The captain glowered at him and snarled, "*Porangi.*"

Clearly not a compliment.

Doc tucked the lapel of his frock coat behind the

tooled leather holster and his LeMat. The hulking captain stiffened.

A chill crawled up Kirby's spine and into his scalp. Doc was about to intervene on behalf of the bird creature. It was something Kirby hadn't anticipated. He knew how life in the hellscape had affected him, how its unrelenting brutality had inured him, bit by bit, to the suffering of others.

But this was no bluff.

The old man was about to let it rip.

Kirby leaned close, turning his back on Eng while he rested his hand heavily on the butt of the LeMat, blocking Doc's draw. "Long odds on chilling them before they get you," he whispered. "And if you do manage it, there'll be no one to sail the ship. We'll all die. This is a battle that can't be won, mercie."

Tanner looked at him for a long moment, then said, "It would seem a concession to barbarism and blind ignorance is in order."

"Not the first," Kirby said.

"Nor by any means the last," Doc said, sweeping the large black hand off his gun butt.

From a bucket under a bench, a crewman produced a two-pound hammer and a fistful of four-inch, steel nails. From under a tarp, three other islanders hauled out a large, chipped and dented wooden cross. At the foot of its vertical member was a steel eyebolt. While the rest of the crew lifted, the trio of crossbearers slid it in place under the supine and helpless bird thing.

"Please, please," it begged. "Don't do this…"

The islanders ignored the desperate pleading. They

continued to celebrate the capture, some danced around exuberantly, waving their black-tattooed arms in the air and thrusting their wide hips.

Kneeling on the deck, a crewman pounded spikes through the fattest part of the creature's wing bones and deep into the wood. The creature squawked in agony at every blow. It squawked even louder when its feet were nailed together at the ankle joints. A line was attached to the eyebolt, and at a signal from the captain, crewmen began to hoist the cross, upside down.

Warm rain splattered the deck around them.

Blood drops

"Why me?" the bird thing moaned as it was jerked higher and higher. "Why me?"

"Manu tangata on the mast brings fair winds," the captain explained, answering the question of a creature that could not think but only mimic.

The irony was lost on Eng.

# Chapter Five

As morning progressed, the seas calmed and the wind dropped off. The swells became gentle and widely spaced. Around noon, Krysty Wroth started feeling well enough to struggle out of her bunk.

She walked into the galley, which was full of feeding islanders. The residual ache in her cramped stomach muscles and the sour taste of vomit in her mouth made her never want to eat or smell food again. The menu for lunch and dinner on the ship was the same as breakfast: deep fried, unboned, ungutted small fish and crustaceans. She had the choice of remaining belowdecks and watching the crew wolf the chow down with their fingers, or getting some fresh air. She chose fresh air.

Most of the passengers had recovered sufficiently to come out on deck. They sat and stood in singles and small groups. Subdued. Drained. Wary after the night of storms. They squinted in the bright sunshine, clearly out of their element.

Krysty picked Jak and Doc out of the crowd, but made no eye contact with them. Until they reached their destination, the other companions were to be treated as strangers. Krysty stepped up beside Mildred who stood at the port rail, amidships.

"How far have we come?" she asked the black woman.

"Not very," Mildred replied. "Maybe a hundred miles or so. We had the sails down most of the night, going nowhere but up and down, up and down."

"Where are we?"

"If Point Conception still existed, we would be grounded on the rocks right about now."

Krysty gave Mildred a puzzled look. Like most Deathlanders, she knew little of the detailed geography of the predark West Coast.

Realizing the problem, Mildred explained. "All the tales about the southern half of California falling into the sea are true," she said. "That ragged line of purple above the haze is what's left of the Sierra Madre. They used to be fifty or sixty miles inland from the coast. The Pacific's lapping on their flanks now. So far, it looks like everything south of Morro Bay is history. The cities of San Luis Obispo, Santa Maria, Lompoc are gone. There's no sign of Santa Barbara, either. My guess is that the Soviets pounded the San Andreas Fault, well to the east of Los Angeles, with earth-shaker warheads. Deep surface detonations caused the fault to shift cataclysmically along its entire length, and the western plate sheared clean away. We're talking maybe 350 miles of coast under water."

As Krysty stared toward land, she could see scattered pillars of smoke rising from the surface of the glassy sea. In some places, it was white and opaque like steam; in others it was black and dense like oil fire smoke. The steady onshore breeze was blowing it away from them in seemingly endless low plumes to the distant mountains. Even so, the air smelled faintly of rotten eggs and brimstone. "How far did it all sink?" Krysty said.

"No telling how deep the water is between here and those mountains. Deep enough to submerge all signs of human habitation, for sure. It's like no one ever lived here."

"What's burning on the sea?"

"It's not really burning," Mildred said. "Those clouds are from volcanic vents and fumaroles. The white steamers are on the sea floor. The black smokers are on seamounts just under the surface. They must have opened up along the fault and deep fracture lines, post-cataclysm. The clouds are created when cool seawater makes contact with superheated gases and molten lava. Some of it's bound to be highly corrosive, full of concentrated sulfuric and nitric acid. Get a lungful of that stuff and presto, no more lungs."

"Good thing the wind is pushing it away from us."

Scanning the sea Krysty saw a mature tree, floating about seventy-five yards away, presumably uprooted whole and blown into the ocean by the chem storm. Branches and leaves trembling, it moved along with them. Then, apparently of its own accord, it abruptly reversed direction. A sucking, roaring sound grew louder and louder. "What in the rad blazes?" the redhead exclaimed, grabbing the cables and climbing up on the gunwhale for a better look.

Mildred scrambled up alongside her.

The oak tree glided in a foaming circle, picking up speed as it spiraled inward toward a shifting, dark core. A black hole. Krysty could see the tree wasn't alone.

Other debris was caught in the powerful current. White plastic bags. Plastic bottles. Coils of seaweed. Bits of paper. A half sheet of delaminating plywood.

The crew on the port side shouted urgently back at the helm, waving their arms for the captain to change course.

As Eng brought the rudder hard over, Krysty saw a line of similar whirlpools that stretched on for miles, paralleling the redefined coast. The floating garbage had no chance. Swirling, roaring funnels of black inexorably drew everything to their centers. Some of the vortexes were big enough to pull down house trailers.

Or sailing ships.

Captain Eng gave the whirlpools plenty of room, steering for the low island. His course set, Eng pulled a wad of white cotton batting from his pants' pocket, tore off a couple of sizable hunks, and thumbed them up his wide nostrils.

The rest of the crew was following suit, plugging their noses with cotton wads. This done, they began passing out plugs to the male passengers.

"What's that for?" Krysty asked an islander handing out cotton.

"Not for you," was all the answer she got.

"If there's danger, we want some, too," Krysty told the man, holding out her hand.

"No danger for you. You are safe. So is she." The crewman quickly moved on, ripping the batting into small tufts.

Krysty started to follow him and insist, but Mildred stopped her. "If there's some kind of poison in the air, nose plugs made of cotton aren't going to help us, anyway," she said. "Look around. Nobody's covering their mouth. It makes no sense. Breathing toxics or corrosives through your mouth will get you just as dead as breathing them in through your nose."

"If it isn't poison or acid, then what is it?"

"Your guess is as good as mine."

"What do you suggest?" Krysty asked. Up near the bow, Ryan was accepting a pair of nose plugs from a crewman.

"Wait and see how it plays out…" Mildred said.

Avoiding the suckhole obstacle course brought the ship to within a hundred yards of the island's shore. Closer in, deep blue water shoaled, changing to a light turquoise color. The island's summit was a rounded, low mound of sun-blasted rock and dirt. Below an eroded bluff a broad, shallow cove was fronted by a narrow beach. Along the base of the cliff stood four crude stone huts with no glass in the windows and no doors.

"I can't tell which island it is," Mildred said. "There's so little left of it. It has to be one of the bigger ones, though. Either Santa Cruz or Santa Rosa."

The breeze sweeping across the island carried the scent of perfume, although there was no evidence of flowering plants. Indeed no evidence of plants of any kind. The scent got stronger and stronger.

"Ooof!" Krysty exclaimed, instinctively averting her face and covering her nose with her hand.

The odor was pungent and cloyingly sweet. Like rotting fruit.

When Krysty looked back at the shore, she saw white

forms eerily rising from the beach stones. Human forms. Four beautiful, young, naked women beckoned languidly, invitingly, holding out what looked like plates heaped with food and pitchers of drink.

The male passengers along the rail were drop-jaw riveted by the sight; some were obviously sexually aroused, pitching tents in their BDUs.

"Men can be such triple stupes," was Krysty's comment.

"It's not their fault," Mildred said. "There must be something in the perfume."

"It's not doing anything for me…"

"Me, either," Mildred said. "The islanders seem unaffected, too, maybe because they know what to expect, or how to fight it. That scent must contain pheromones, chemicals that selectively stimulate the male of the species. Look around. Our fellow passengers are getting turned on, despite the nose plugs. Dammit, that island's giving off aerosolized Viagra."

The crew stepped in before things got way out of hand. They brutally shoved the dazed men to the starboard side of the ship, and forced them at blasterpoint to look the other way.

"Atarangi," a passing islander told Krysty, gesturing at the beach with a collapsible brass spyglass. "Not what they seem." He opened the telescope and offered it to her.

When she looked through the lens, she saw the lovely faces were not faces at all. Blotches of dark pigment formed seductively lashed eyes and smiling mouths. They had discernible heads, necks, breasts, waists, hips only from a distance. Up close, they were just white ob-long shapes, ingeniously shaded to look human. Their long flowing hair was made up of frantically waving filaments, like the tendrils of albino sea anemones. The plates of food held colored rocks; the jugs were empty.

"Not real wahines," the islander said. "Set foot on the beach, you find that out, quick. Looks like four, but there's only one. They are fingers on a hand that hides beneath the sand and rocks. Hand is evil. Its smell is sweet and loving but it eats men. Sucks the blood and marrow from their bones."

At that moment two of the passengers yanked out their nose plugs and jumped overboard. They swam around the stern of the ship, through the wake, strok-ing hard for the island. To forestall a further stampede into the water, the crew fired their AKs in the air.

All the passengers lined up along the stern, watch-ing the deserters grow smaller and smaller, still swim-ming with great determination toward the alien and deadly shore. Even Ryan seemed fascinated by their slow, steady progress. Krysty noted with satisfaction that her lover displayed no spectacular trouser effects from the pheromones.

The ship sailed on, turning southeast, and the cove slipped out of sight. By the time the swimmers reached the beach, they were too far away for their screams to be heard over the wind singing in the lines.

That same sea breeze blew away the last of the sirens' perfume. Some of the passengers began weep-ing into their palms, as if they had lost their true loves. Krysty was amazed to see crazy, murdering scum acting like brokenhearted teenagers—grieving, inconsolable, their humanity revealed by an illusion of biochemistry.

Gradually the bereft bastards recovered their senses. After an hour, they couldn't remember any of it. Not the island, not the sirens, not the pain of separation. Total brain fog. The less dramatically affected passengers remembered, though, and taking the public displays of sorrow for signs of weakness marked the criers for an early death.

Driven by a steady twelve-knot wind, the ship plowed on. The fore and aft rocking motion and the hiss of the hull was soothing, even stupefying after the sleepless night. Krysty dozed for hours in the warm sun. When she awoke, Mildred was by her side, watching over her.

Krysty rose from the deck and took in an even more dismal vista.

"That's where Los Angeles used to be," Mildred said, her voice gone suddenly hoarse with emotion.

It looked positively primeval. Plumes of molten lava and caustic smoke jetted from the black tips of emerging seamounts. A rain of superheated ejecta swept across the sea, hissing like fifty thousand snakes. Scattered lakes of flame danced on the surface from petrochemicals that had oozed up from the bottom.

On the land, volcanic cones thousands of feet tall spewed ash clouds, creating a low ceiling of gray that blocked out the blue sky to the east. Everything in that direction was tinged with yellow, smoke-filtered light. The bases of the Sierra Nevada in the distance were barely visible for the haze of sulphur and particulate matter.

"It's a graveyard," Mildred said after a moment, "for as far as you see. Millions of people died here on nuke day. There used to be a central core of skyscrapers and gridwork streets filling the great basin, edge to edge, stretching to the desert in the east. Whatever the fireballs and nukeblasts left behind, geologic forces have toppled and buried. Los Angeles has been scraped clean of everything human and everything made by human hands."

"What about the radiation?" Krysty asked. "Is the place poisoned?"

"Definitely," Mildred said. "See anything flying over it? Anything swimming in it?"

"What about us? Aren't we too close?"

"Moot point, I'm afraid. What few extra rads we might pick up in passing aren't going to make us ill. The eruptions are the real problem. They've been sending radioactive material aloft, into the upper atmosphere for more than a century. All that stuff has to come down somewhere. In fact, it comes down everywhere."

"Then we've been breathing it and eating it all of our lives. But none of us are sick, though."

"Short of a massive dose of gamma rays, radiation doesn't kill its victims quickly. It can take decades for the damage from lesser levels of exposure to show up as cancer. Even folks with terrible superficial burns sometimes recover—whitecoats found that out after Hiroshima, Nagasaki and Chernobyl. It's a matter of genetic luck and total rad exposure. Most people in Deathlands don't live long enough for the sickness to ever show up. They get chilled by other things first."

"Look at that!" Krysty exclaimed, pointing at a sudden commotion on the surface, about 150 yards from the ship and five miles off the hellish, uninhabitable coast. It was definitely not volcanic. A huge living creature thrashed and rolled out there. It was at least thirty feet long, and splashing fountains of water tinged with gallons of blood.

"It's a whale," the black woman said. "And it's under attack."

Only when the animal stopped thrashing could Krysty see it clearly. The barnacle-covered skin along its flanks was torn to shreds, torn through the thick white layer of blubber, gory pits gnawed into the dark purple meat. Though the whale floated quietly, gathering the last of its strength, the surface around it churned and humped.

There were things in the bright red water.

Much smaller creatures. Streaking pale, people-size shapes.

They were tearing at it from underneath. Hundreds of them.

The whale smashed the water with its tail flukes, fighting in vain to drive off the horde.

From the helm, Captain Eng bellowed through his megaphone for more sail. The deck crew leaped to the task. As the additional canvas dropped and filled, the ship surged ahead, pulling away from the carnage.

"What is it?" Krysty demanded of a passing crewman. "What is it?"

The islander did not turn, and he did not answer.

WHEN SUPPERTIME CAME, Krysty and Mildred joined the others assigned to the second feeding shift. The galley's tabletops were covered with slick film of fried fish oil, and littered with discarded squid beaks and shrimp shells. Krysty had to take off her coat to keep from getting the mess on the long fur. After a day to recover, she found her appetite had returned with a vengeance. Ignoring the gut bomb sensation that came from swallowing cupfuls of grease, she chewed the golden crispy bits. She paused to spit out the larger bones and scales, then reached in the trough for another handful.

Krysty was using her back molars to tackle a particularly tough and rubbery hunk of squid, when from the deck above came shouting, then the ship's bell began ringing. First crew, then passengers abandoned their dinners and rushed for the stairs. Krysty and Mildred joined the throng.

Above deck, the wind was dying down; the sea was a polished mirror.

Off the bow, framed by a sunset of orange and salmon-pink reflecting off the smooth water, of bloodred underlighting the tiers of volcanic clouds to the east, lay a ship slightly smaller than their own, painted black and brown. Instead of three masts, it had two, each rigged for four sets of sails.

It was adrift, riding low as if overloaded or in the process of sinking. Its canvas was torn and hanging in strips, its cables broken, trailing in the water. Nothing moved on deck. A few oil lamps glowed weakly; all the others were extinguished. It looked like they had been burning since the night before.

Captain Eng cut a wide, cautious circle around the vessel, then began to spiral closer. Every time he turned downwind, an awful stench engulfed them. The stench of death. Facing the foul, carrion breeze, the crew began to mutter and moan.

When they got a little closer, Krysty could see the wreck was a wooden ship. A coastal cargo trader, like theirs. Overlapping planks formed the hull; there were holes in it above the water line. Dozens of them. They didn't look like damage from cannon shot. Their edges were ripped out, not blown in. The holes were big enough for a person to crawl through.

Behind them, the captain of the *Taniwha tea* turned his face to the sky and screamed like a wounded animal.

# Chapter Six

Eng barked orders through his steel megaphone.

Ryan didn't understand the islander language, but the meaning became obvious as the crew scurried to pull in the sails. The white ship glided to a stop, upwind of the derelict vessel and its pall of death.

Eng barked again, and Ryan was forced back from the rail as islanders rushed to open a blaster and prepare the cannon for firing. They unblocked the wheels, removed muzzle plug and fuse hole cap and rolled the weapon forward on its tracks.

Likewise, every cannon on the starboard rail was readied to broadside the brigantine that foundered just forty yards away.

Because the two-master was so much lower in the water, Ryan could look down on its main deck, which was a wreck. Cables, ropes and chains lay in tangled heaps; tool chests and worktables were overturned. Some of top-deck cargo had come loose from its safety netting: huge bags of grain had broken and spilled.

The chem storm could have done all that, easily, Ryan thought. It was less likely, though still possible, that the storm had tossed every living soul overboard.

But no way could it have torn those holes in the hull.

Up close, Ryan could see marks where the black paint had been pulled off, masses of overlapping, tiny circles that exposed the bare wood beneath. The marks led directly from the water line to the ragged hull breaches. Paths of popped paint. They weren't made by bullet impacts or grappling hooks or ballpeen hammers. Something had climbed up from the sea, up the side of the ship in great numbers, and once there, had gnawed and ripped through the inches-thick hull planks.

All the bullet holes were on the main deck; the gunwhales, the superstructure and the masts were absolutely riddled. The scuppers gleamed with a litter of spent brass. Certainly thousands, maybe tens of thousands of rounds had been fired. Apparently to no avail. In broad swatches, congealed blood glazed the deck like purple varnish.

Along the *Taniwha tea*'s rail, between the cannons, other crewmen took positions with their Kalashnikovs and rocket-propelled grenades, ready to put up covering fire for the longboat that had already been lowered into the water on the port side.

Sunset, like a second Armageddon, lit the ruined ship and the rapidly moving longboat. As six rowers pulled hard, a seventh islander stood braced in the bow, his AK shouldered and aimed.

No targets appeared.

Nothing stirred on the opposite deck.

Shipping their oars, the rowers tethered the longboat to the side of the brigantine. Captain Eng ordered his cannoneers and riflemen to hold their fire as the boarding party deftly scrambled up the broken lines and cables onto the main deck. Once there, they fanned out with assault rifles, sweeping the area, kicking over anything that could hide an attacker, quickly confirming there were no signs of life—or death.

The boarders then split up, entering the fore and aft companionways in a simultaneous rush. After a few minutes belowdecks, the crewmen spilled back into view and immediately lurched to the rail, coughing and gasping for air.

Eng raised the megaphone and shouted an unintelligible question across the gap.

One of the boarders raised his head and drew a forefinger across the front of his throat.

All dead.

A quiver of shock ran through the white frigate's crew. They were stunned speechless.

Ryan turned to look at the captain. Under the man's heavy brow ridge, glistening stripes, tear tracks ran down his scarified cheeks. Blood trickled over and off his broad chin, dripping upon his chest. He had sunk his sharpened teeth into his lip.

A moment later the groaning and lamentations began.

Passengers watched uneasily, hands on weapons, as the islanders wept openly, as they beat their chests and pulled at their own hair. Ryan figured that they not only knew the dead crew, but were probably related. Only ties of blood could wring forth such grief.

Meanwhile, the boarders hastily departed the death ship. They didn't pause to rifle the cargo on the main deck, which seemed strange to Ryan, as it was there for the taking, and in great quantities. They climbed back onto the *Taniwha tea*, seven hard men shaken to the core by what they had seen.

The bowrider stepped up to the captain, reached out a trembling hand and carefully placed a half-dozen gold rings on his palm. Rings of great weight, fashioned to fit huge fingers, like his.

Eng clutched them in a white-knuckled fist. Raising the megaphone to his bloody mouth, he bellowed another urgent command. The crew scrambled to reset the sails.

The islanders were abandoning their dead.

Only now there was barely enough wind to put the iron ship in motion. It crept slowly south for about twenty minutes, then the wind died off altogether. They hadn't sailed far. Ryan could still see the silhouette of the derelict on the horizon, backlit in crimson.

When the wind went slack, it got very quiet. Quiet enough to hear a faint croaking noise from high above them.

At the captain's signal, the crew began lowering the upside-down crucifix from just below the crow's nest.

The bird creature nailed to it was still alive. Still talking, albeit in a weak, rasping voice.

"See?" the flying mutie said to Eng as the cross came to rest on the deck. "The wind is gone. I can't bring it back. I can't bring it back because I have no power over it. Never had. Never will. It's superstition that makes you think my kind has any control over the wind. Blind superstition. We ride it, that's all. We ride it in the air just like you ride it on the water. Please, let me go, now. Please, I'm begging. My suffering is worth nothing to you."

Eng gripped the handle of a machete proffered by one of the crew. Using the cross beneath as a chopping block, he swung the blade down in a blur, and in one swipe hacked off the bird man's head at the neck. While crewmen pried the nails from twitching feet and wings, the captain planted the severed, startled head on a vacant roof spike.

Suffering had decorative value.

Deathlands kitsch.

*"Porangi!"* the captain shouted at the passengers, spraying blood and spit out the big end of his megaphone, and waving impatiently for them to step forward. "Death swims these waters," he howled. "It is closer than you can imagine. It will find us long before dawn. Without wind, we cannot sail away to safety. Without wind, we must stand and fight."

"Fight what?" a familiar voice demanded.

Ryan turned and saw Jak Lauren, arms folded, a defiant scowl on his white face, his ruby-red eyes glittering with menace.

"The *taua*," Eng said. "That is our name for them. Things that swim and crawl. Things that climb and leap. Broad-tailed, slime-covered things. The *taua* roam the southern sea shelf in great schools, killing and eating every creature they find. These are no triple-stupe, pea-brained fishes. They are organized, like a war party. Some among us believe they were once human. Now they breathe the air like porpoises, through the tops of their heads. They talk to each other under water. They swim faster than the fastest sailing ship. They chill with their razor teeth and the suckers on their hands and feet. They eat only flesh, the fresher the better. Last night, the *taua* slaughtered and ate my cousin Karetu and his crew. They pulled his ship apart to get at him. For islanders, revenge is a duty, and a pleasure. The creatures who have stolen our blood, shall give their blood. In buckets…"

The crew standing behind the passengers sent up a howl, shaking their AKs in the air.

"This ship is not as easy to break into as Karetu's," Eng continued. "When the *taua* come to chill us, we will face them and take their lives. You *porangi* are welcome to stand and fight at our side. Those who are too afraid to fight the *taua* should go belowdecks. Don't block the stairways. Get in your bunks. Hide under your mattresses, and pray for dawn."

"And if things get inside ship?" Jak said.

"*Taua* can't rip through iron, little *korako*," Eng told him. "But they will wear out their teeth and sucker hands trying. We will take our bloody vengeance on them, then pull back from battle. Below the metal decks, we are safe. They can't sink this ship. They must eat to live. They will move on by daybreak, in search of easier meals."

Only a couple of passengers decided to go below and wait out the conflict. To the rest, it sounded like big fun. Like shooting fish in a barrel, despite the fact that Eng had said these foes were nothing like fish. The assembled scum of Deathlands began checking their weapons.

Ryan carefully set the Steyr butt-first in a lidless plastic drum, leaning the forestock against the rim. This wasn't going to be a long-range battle; it was going to be nose-to-nose. Or perhaps nose-to-blowhole. He unholstered his SIG-Sauer and racked the slide back a half inch, making sure the chamber held a live round. After checking his front pockets for spare full magazines, he tested the release of his eighteen-inch panga knife from its leg sheath. It came out of the scabbard like it was spring-loaded.

When he looked up, the sky had changed from red to lavender. Out on the placid sea, in the distance, Ryan saw scattered disturbances. Boils. Rings. Bubbles. Signifying movements just beneath the surface. He couldn't tell what was making them. Only that whatever it was, it was big—and plentiful.

The captain ordered all the fixed deck lamps lit. From covered storage bins along the rails, islanders hauled out dozens more of the oil lamps, which they fired up and hung from the ends of long metal poles. At intervals around the perimeter they extended the poles over the gunwhales and lashed them in place, illuminating a broad stretch of the surrounding water as darkness closed on the drifting ship.

Ryan moved to a corner of the stern, beside one of the racks of red, fifty-five-gallon barrels. The *taua* were coming, no doubt about that. Even without the boils and splashes, he could feel them, like a pressure, building on all sides, and from beneath. Without the wind, the night was very warm. Humid. He wiped the sweat from his gun hand on to his pant leg.

Faint kissing sounds came from the blackness beyond the ring of lamplight.

The familiar kiss of death.

Ryan visualized a thousand bobbing pale heads, lipless mouths pursed, dead eyes closed tight. It was impossible.

Stickies didn't swim.

He leaned over the stern rail, straining to see deeper into the dark. In the water directly below him, blood and air suddenly upwelled, a great undersea belch. The coppery stench it gave off made his throat slam shut.

Then he saw them, about fifteen feet down. Squirming pale bodies, bodies thick in cross-section. So many of them it looked like the sea floor had risen up. Though individuals were difficult to make out, the general body shape reminded Ryan of mud puppies or salamanders, only grown to full human size. They had short, muscular arms and legs folded and tucked tight to their torsos, and wide, powerful tails close to half of their overall length.

The shoal of *taua* was visible, churning to the very edge of the light. And presumably well beyond. There was no telling how deep or how far it went.

Too many, Ryan thought, adjusting his grip on the SIG. More than they had bullets for.

Passengers around him started yelling, some in panic, others in frustration and fury because there was nothing yet to shoot at. The enemy that surrounded them was hanging too deep for blasterfire to reach.

Ryan checked the positions of his battlemates. Krysty and Mildred stood amidships on the port side,

Jak and J.B. along the opposite rail. Doc was near the forward companionway, just short of the bow. All had weapons drawn. Their fighting circle was stretched as far as it could get. If the battle went badly, if the *taua* broke through the human ranks, they would contract the ring, drawing in until they were fighting back to back.

A slick pale head surfaced twenty feet off the stern. It blinked dead black eyes at Ryan. Like a stickie, it was hairless, earless and lipless. Stickies had no noses, just nostril holes in their flat faces; this creature had a snout, but no nostrils. Over the snout and splayed across the cheeks were four parallel folds of excess skin, permanent deep wrinkles. Row upon row of needle teeth lined its gaping jaws. Jaws that twisted up at the corners in an exuberant, expectant grin. Its blowhole opened, making that wet kissing sound, then it sent forth a spray of exhaled mist.

A hand puppet from hell.

Ryan realized with a jolt that he recognized the face. It was the same one Captain Eng wore. Sharpened teeth. Corrugated brandings. Insane, red-hot, poker-sculpted smile. A crude replica mask of the sea beast, executed in human flesh and bone.

Autofire roared to Ryan's left.

The *taua* ducked as 7.62 mm rounds hammered the water to a fine froth.

"Hold your fire!" the captain shouted.

The islander stopped shooting on command. He looked back at his skipper, then sheepishly kicked the blistering hot, spent shells out from around his bare feet.

Seeing what they were up against, a few more passengers decided to return to their bunks. Most of the rest looked torn between following their suddenly sleepy comrades and fighting the *taua,* but a few of the more lunatic mercies leaned over the gunwhales, aiming their weapons at the water, hoping that another slick head would pop up.

From the edge of the light, Ryan saw a V-wake shooting toward the middle of the hull, beneath it a streaking oblong shape. It looked like a beige torpedo homing in for the kill.

"Get back!" Eng ordered the overeager mercies.

As the captain spoke, the charging *taua* exploded from the water. Using the power of its tail and its surging forward momentum, it leaped high in the air. At the peak of its arc, it was five feet above the gunwhale.

For an instant it looked like it was trying to jump onto the deck, then it dropped, crashing its full weight onto the back of an outstretched—and momentarily frozen—mercie. It landed with its five-fingered sucker hands latched on to the seat of its victim's pants and the base of its tail draped over the man's head. The tail's tip had transverse lobes, like the flukes of a porpoise or whale. A ridge of hard knobs rose up under the skin along the middle of its back, like cornrows of tumors, the result of a head-to-tail muscular contraction. From its blowhole came an awful, piping hiss.

Before anyone could get off a clear shot, or otherwise come to the mercie's aid, he was pulled headfirst over the side. He and the *taua* hit the water together and sank out of sight beneath the living shoal.

The mercie never came up for air, but almost immediately bits of him began to surface. Blood billowed and bubbled from the depths; swirling in it were tiny shreds of flesh and sinew.

"Back!" Captain Eng screamed into the megaphone, urgently waving with his Government Colt blaster. "They're coming!"

And come they did, as the passengers and crew jumped away from the perimeter. Instead of launching themselves over the rails and onto the deck, something the *taua* were clearly capable of doing, they threw their bodies against the sides of the ship. Hundreds of booming impacts set the cables humming, decks vibrating and loose objects rolling about. The chorus of blowhole kisses grew louder as more and more of the creatures jumped from the water to the hull, clinging there with sucker hands and feet.

The *taua* couldn't tear through the riveted iron plate, but their shifting, rapidly building weight made the vessel sway alarmingly from side to side.

Steadying themselves on whatever came to hand, the passengers and crew pulled back farther, to the middle of the sloping deck, and closed ranks. Some knelt, some stood as they faced the gunwhales with raised, cocked blasters.

Wave after wave of the creatures struck the ship, then the sound of the impacts changed. No longer flesh on metal.

Flesh on flesh.

Having covered every square inch of the hull above waterline, they were slamming onto each other.

Then the *Taniwha tea* began to groan and creak from deep in its iron bowels. Here and there, rivets in the deck plating started popping loose.

Ryan realized what was happening. The *taua*'s main force was crawling from the water, crawling over the backs and heads of those that had attached themselves to the hull. Combined weight of this oncoming, living mass quickly pulled the ship lower, bringing the main deck four or five feet closer to the sea. The sheer number of bodies required was mind-boggling.

The one-eyed man wasn't alone in the sudden realization. A handful of passengers bolted for the companionway and the relative safety of their bunks. Everyone else seemed frozen in place, unable or unwilling to turn their backs on what was about to happen.

Only when the *taua*'s 360-degree launch platform was complete did they attack en masse. Upon some silent signal, from all sides at once, they leaped from the shoulders and backs of their hull-stuck fellows, bounding over the gunwhales.

Which tripped the switch of battle.

In the first seconds it was possible to see, if not to hear.

Basterfire reports sledge hammered the sides of Ryan's head. Autofire, single shots, centerfires, muzzle-loaders, all cut loose at once, blowing apart the initial wave of *taua*, sending a slurry of blood, flesh and guts flying in all directions. Multiple gunshot impacts hurled decapitated bodies and whip-sawn torsos backward and overboard.

Ryan keyholed his focus dead ahead, over the SIG's

sights. Finding targets was no problem. He ripped off
head shots one after another, as fast as he could pull the
trigger—instantaneous skull-shattering kills. In less
than fifteen seconds of rapid fire, the SIG's slide locked
back, ejection port smoking.

As he dumped the spent mag and dug in his pocket
for a fresh one, another rush of *taua* leaped onto the
deck, stumbling over their fallen, soaking up autofire.
Even the mortally wounded, the blinded, the gut shot
somehow found the strength to press forward into the
teeth of the withering fusillade and certain destruction.
In five seconds a hundred died, their blow holes spout-
ing blood, then another hundred, and another.

Ryan grimaced as he slapped the full mag home. He
knew the reason for their ardor.

There was a blood feast on offer.

Already their spilled gore flowed like syrup into the
scuppers; ravening, repeated bullet impacts aerosolized
their flesh into a pink mist that incited the creatures that
jumped through it to an even greater frenzy.

Stickies were like that, too, Ryan knew. Because
there was something horribly wrong with the wiring of
their mutie brains, they got high on death.

Even their own.

Ryan raised the SIG and snapfired into the gaping,
teeth-lined black maw of an oncoming *taua*. He stepped
aside, letting the suddenly brain-free body hurtle past
him, fountaining red from its blowhole. The creature
following right on its heels dropped like a stone at
Ryan's feet. The single slug had zipped through the
mutie, slapping into the second *taua*'s head, cutting an

irregular, slotlike hole between its eyes. As it lay on its back dying, its legs kicked wildly. They were much longer and larger at the thigh than they appeared under water. When folded for swimming, they tucked into a kind of depression, a bone-plated wheelwell, that reduced drag.

This mutie species relied on overwhelming numbers, not individual defenses, for its survival. Their relatively soft skulls were easily cored by Parabellum full-metal-jacket rounds, so Ryan concentrated on his shot placement, going for two-fers whenever the opportunity arose.

As other shooters dropped out of the fray to reload, the steady roar of basterfire became ragged. These lapses created gaps, cracks in the perimeter that allowed some *taua* to leap to the cables and up into the rigging. At the upper limit of the deck lamps' light, through the haze of gunsmoke, they jumped back and forth from mast to mast like crazed flying squirrels.

Ryan ignored them, methodically taking out the closest targets to hand, clearing the deck in front of him. Long before the task was done, his SIG locked back again.

There seemed no end to them.

And there was no obvious organization to the attack. No field commanders led the suicide charges. Just ground pounders. Droves and droves of ground pounders. All of them working solo. All of them trying to get in their licks. Or bites. Looking for a taste of the red.

He quickly reloaded and resumed the close range wet work.

With no wind to drive it away, the gunsmoke around the knot of human fighters grew thicker and thicker. It became hard to breathe, and hard to pick out fresh targets as they cleared the rails, which meant the *taua* were dying at arm's length. Blood mist coated Ryan's hands, face and hair. He backhanded it from his one good eye.

As he did so, he glanced up and saw a mutie poised to leap from a yard arm into their midst. Ryan ripped off five shots, stitching them up its exposed belly. The *taua* slammed back against the canvas, and its stomach popped open like a dropped suitcase. Its underside was soft and thin-skinned, like a frog or a newt. A staggering wad of guts flopped from the gaping wound, and as the creature bounced off the sail and fell from its perch, the loops tangled and snagged on the yard's cables. It slammed headfirst into the deck, trailing a forty-foot streamer of pink bowel.

Ryan dumped yet another empty mag—he was already four down. The passengers and crew who were shooting full-auto had gone through way more than that in the same space of time. Empty brass rolled everywhere underfoot. Some of the select-fire weapons had gotten so hot that chambered rounds were cooking off at six hundred per minute.

Uncontrolled, maximum cyclic rate autofire.

Just before it actually fell apart, Ryan sensed it was about to happen. The number of piled enemy dead. The gore stink, like molten copper. The unrelenting onslaught. The arm's-length chilling range. It all combined to take a toll on the defenders' confidence. As the endless minutes passed, their chill lust became fury, fury became desperation, and desperation became doubt.

A kneeling passenger to Ryan's right had had enough and stood. Too quickly. The man right behind him was already tightening down on his scattergun's trigger. The 10-gauge's point-blank muzzle-blast took off the top of his head from the ears up, and hammered him face-first and flop-armed into the iron plate.

The plume of brains and skull fragments splattered across an oncoming *taua*'s chest. In the midst of battle, unable to stifle the urge, it paused to lick.

And was meat-grindered by crisscrossing AK fire.

The scattergunner broke his single-shot weapon and tried to thumb another high brass shell into the chamber. Before he could snap the breech closed, he was set upon. The *taua* had soft bellies but they were rad-blasted strong. The mutie clamped sucker hands on his face, then ripped it off like a tea towel.

The man just stood there, flat-footed, eyes bugging out through a white mask of shock, a white mask oozing pinpoints of red, watching as the *taua* fisted the face into its mouth.

The creature juked suddenly sideways, blown off its feet and onto the deck by half a dozen blasters. It was still chewing the face as it died.

Another *taua* darted in a blur left to right, grabbing the mutilated man around the waist and jumping, carrying him like a mannequin into the smoke and over the side.

If Ryan sensed impending disaster, the sea beasts

sensed looming victory. They threw themselves even harder into the fray, and arm's-length battle became hand-to-hand. Men were being pulled screaming out of the firing line and into the cloud of burned cordite and black-powder. Not just passengers, either. An islander mate, easily three hundred pounds of him, was hauled backward by the braided ponytail, into the pall. For a horrible instant he reappeared from the smoke. It looked like he'd been run over by a ten-ton wag. His right was arm torn off at the shoulder, and divots of flesh were missing from his face and bare chest. Sucker hands yanked him off his feet and he was gone.

With the tide clearly turning, Captain Eng cried, "Enough! That's enough! Pull back!"

Ryan did a quick head check, making sure his friends had closed ranks. They had. Like him, they were misted with blood and peppered with the grit of gunshot residue. He stood his ground at the entrance to the for'c'ste companionway, putting up covering fire for the mass retreat until an islander shouldered him through the doorway, then shoved him ahead, down the steep stairs to the crowded, low-ceilinged galley.

Behind them on the steps, the last man through the companionway slammed and bolted the hatch.

The *taua* hurled their bodies against it, trying to batter it down.

Not a chance.

The surviving crew and passengers started yelling, laughing and backslapping, congratulating one another on the slaughter of slaughters and their nimble, timely escape.

Their celebration was short-lived, silenced by the groan and shriek of metal directly above them.

The *taua* were pulling up the deck plates.

# Chapter Seven

Creatures of nightmare cleared the gunwhales in prodigious, whistling bounds, their pale bellies underlit by the oil lamps' glow.

Though Doc was accustomed to facing hellish nightmares come to life, this one was in a league all its own—a combination of the frenzied, chaotic attack, the volume of randomly hurtling bodies, and the proximity of sudden, violent death. Though sometimes Theophilus Algernon Tanner wished with all his soul that he was dead, wished he was one with his wife and children in the numbness of Eternity, oddly enough such thoughts never popped into his head in the heat of battle.

In combat, a much deeper, much more primitive urge took control of his lanky frame. Like a malarial fever, it raged in his brain. The man of science and philosophy, the man of reason, of history, of sentiment, seized the opportunity to flat-out retaliate. Every wrong done him by a cruel fate, he repaid in kind, and a hundredfold. He did this with his remarkably perfect teeth bared, his haggard face set in stone.

Left foot back, bracing himself with his ebony swordstick, he fired the LeMat one-handed, duelist style, adding its sonorous booms, blinding flash and jetting plumes of smoke to the melee. As the pistol design was single action, he had to recock it for each shot. The recoil wave lifted the muzzle of the heavy handblaster skyward, and as it dropped to horizontal he used the momentum of the fall to thumb back the hammer. Out of necessity, the melding of man and his device, the rhythm of his shooting was fluid, easy and relaxed. Unlike the mutie hunters on either side of him—the black man and his white-painted partner—who fired their M-16s full-auto, sweeping the gunwhales with 5.56 mm tumblers, Doc had an extra second or two to choose his next target.

The LeMat's .44-caliber lead balls caught *taua* in midair, caught them as they landed, caught them square in head, throat and center chest. Though the weapon he fired was as old as he was, its knockdown power had not diminished over the years. His targets dropped to the deck, some from heights of fifteen feet or more, legs quivering in the throes of death. Only when he had emptied the nine chambers in the cylinder did he cock the .63-caliber undergun.

The LeMat's shotgun barrel was designed for close-range, last-resort mayhem. Short in length, with an unchoked bore, its shot load fanned out as soon as it exited the muzzle. In this case, what fanned out were the small bits and pieces of metal Doc had scrounged up in his hellscape travels. There was nothing blue about these "whistlers." They were the kind of stuff you might find in the bottom of a machine shop trash can. He had packed steel, brass and copper nuggets and shards into the muzzle-loader's single chamber, along with a hefty dose of Deathlands' best homegrown black-powder and enough cotton wadding to hold the charge in place.

Doc let a pair of *taua*s get within five yards of him, one slightly behind and to the right of the other, before he cut loose with the stubby scattergun barrel. He didn't aim for one or the other, but between them. Three feet of flame belched forth, and the weapon bucked wildly against the tightest grip he could muster. The shot spread at a fifteen-foot range, shoulder to shoulder, across both bodies. The impact knocked the *taua* backward, hard onto their haunches. Blood sheeted down their chests from gaping throat wounds, but they died attacking each other, either confused by the terrible pain or excited by the spilled gore.

Even though Doc had a pair of spare .44-caliber cylinders in the pockets of his frock coat, the LeMat was a clumsy, time-consuming and dangerous weapon to reload in pitched, near-hand-to-hand combat. Attending to the scattergun barrel was out of the question. Accordingly, Doc was one of the first fighters on the deck to holster his sidearm and draw cold steel.

With a flourish, he pulled the rapier blade from its ebony sheath. Holding the swordstick's scabbard in his left hand for balance, he lunged, meeting an onrushing *taua*'s charge. His perfectly timed thrust slid over the creature's blocking wrist and the double-edged point probed six inches into the middle of its chest, just below its breastbone. In his trained hand, the blade had a tension, a presence, a life that was in part due to its external shape, to the blows that had forged it, in part to the alignment of its very molecules. The rapier yearned to penetrate flesh, and to penetrate it to the hilt.

Not this time.

As Doc drew back the flexible sword, with lightning back-and-forth twists of the wrist, he made the steel serpent's tongue cut a figure eight through heart and lungs.

Or at least where he assumed were the creature's heart and lungs. The purpose of breastbone being universal, the same for every species, norm or mutie: to protect the vitals at the body's core. His figure eight had the desired effect, instantly reducing a live enemy to a heap of shuddering flesh.

He dealt with a half-dozen attackers in a similar manner, and in short order, sending them stumbling backward, their innards severed, over the growing pile of corpses.

As the *taua* pressed harder and harder, throwing themselves at their intended victims, Doc had to abandon his customary finesse with the long blade. He simply met the creatures as they launched themselves at him, letting their body weight fall on his upraised swordpoint, burying it. It was like spearing a cooked jacket potato with a steak knife. Doc pivoted on his back foot, dropping the swordpoint as the body swept past, and the blade slipped out. All in a single motion.

And back for more.

The Victorian swordsman remained clear-headed, fully aware of his surroundings, even while staring into the teeth of hell. It was as if he was looking down on himself from one of the yardarms, a spectator in his own fight for life. It didn't escape his notice that the mutie hunters kneeling beside him were taking care of his business as well as their own. The kill zones of their assault rifles overlapped at the rail, and, in so doing, took out about half of the *taua* he otherwise would have faced, leaving him to do battle with onesies and twosies, as opposed to threesies and foursies.

Why they were looking after his well-being, he had no inkling. Elsewhere along the firing line it was every man for himself. Some were doing better than others. As Doc fought on, he saw passenger after passenger yanked over the side by the attackers, to certain death.

After the first islander was torn apart by the *taua*, the captain called for a retreat.

Doc felt strong hands gripping his elbows and biceps. Human hands, as luck would have it. Before he could shrug them off, the mutie hunters had turned him by main force and were driving him, stiff-legged, toward the for'c'sle's entrance.

"Wait!" he protested, unwilling to leave the battlefield without his companions. "By the three Kennedys, wait!"

"No time," the black man told him. Without another word, they bum-rushed him down the narrow flight of steps and into the galley.

Doc shook off their grip, his dignity ruffled. Bloody sword in hand, he watched the stairs, making sure that Ryan, Krysty, Mildred, Jak and J.B. made it safely down.

Only when they had did he turn to register a complaint about the rough handling, but the surviving

passengers and crew started cheering their victory and
he couldn't make himself heard over the noise.

The shriek of deck rivets coming loose put an end to
the hooting and yeehawing. The rows of fasteners were
all that secured the iron plates overhead. Many of the
flush-mounted rivets had been jarred and vibrated up
from their sockets by the *taua*'s initial, hull-pounding
onslaught. Which gave the attackers sucker-purchase
along the edges of the tight-fitting plates.

A hundred blasters aimed point-blank at widening
gaps in the creaking ceiling.

"No!" the islander captain howled at the passengers.
"Put your blasters away! I don't want any blasterfire
from you belowdecks! You'll end up chilling all of us
with the ricochets and misses. Leave the shooting to my
crew. They know what they're doing. If the *taua* get in
here, use your blades on them!"

Doc would have substituted "when" for the captain's
conditional "if." The old man had little doubt that given
their vast numbers, their physical strength and determination, and the ship's weakened armor, the creatures
were going to be among them shortly.

When they broke through, there were five or six simultaneous breaches and not in the obvious places,
where the plates were visibly being rocked up and
down. The *taua* were devilishly clever. Using the pry
bars, chisels, shovel blades they had found on the deck,
they had carefully levered loose entire rows of rivets,
freeing some of the plates on all sides, plates that came
away cleanly and suddenly. Without warning, pale
bodies dropped through the ceiling, landing heavily on

the tables and floor, effectively dividing the human fighters.

Despite the captain's order, blasterfire exploded from all sides, with disastrous consequences to both *taua* and the ship's defenders. Wild shots and through-and-throughs hit the galley's iron walls, sparking, then zipping through the crowd. Men and *taua* dropped as if their strings had been cut.

The black mutie hunter hurled his full weight onto Doc's back, driving him to his knees and out of the line of fire.

The islander crew turned on the frantic shooters with the steel-shod butts of their AKs, battering them into submission.

"Pull back!" Eng shouted, waving for everyone to retreat behind the for'c'sle's bulkhead door.

It was easier said than done because more *taua* kept pouring through the gaps in the plating. The galley's low ceiling restricted their jumping, otherwise the battle belowdecks would have been one-sided and short.

The black mutie hunter and his comrade stepped between Doc and three pairs of grasping sucker hands. The old man couldn't bring his sword into play—there wasn't room overhead to swing it or space between the two big men to drive home a thrust.

His tall topknot mashing against the ceiling, the black man whipped a knife back and forth. Not just any knife. It was a SOG Desert Dagger. Its six-and-a-quarter-inch, 440A stainless, double-edged blade had a blood gutter, a steel pommel and Kraton grips. The white-painted man had an even bigger knife from the same manufacturer, a Tigershark model. Its heavy, nine-inch blade was designed for chopping and hacking. As with the pair's mint-condition long and handblasters, Doc knew it was not run-of-the-mill mutie hunter armament. In the shortlist of the most lusted after predark edged treasures, their stabbers were right up there.

As quick as the *taua* were, the mutie hunters were quicker. To Doc it seemed the black man no more than twitched his right arm, and the belly of the beast before him suddenly came unzipped from crotch to breastbone. His partner had a much heavier touch. As guts flopped steaming to the floor, he lopped off first one, then the other sucker hand reaching for his chest. The third strike across the front of the throat all but decapitated the attacking creature, and slung its thick blood across the tabletops.

The black man turned and pushed Doc along the wall, toward the passenger cabin. "Move!" he said. As he spoke, another *taua* darted in and seized hold of the back of his huge bare arm.

Doc was almost nose to nose with him at that instant. He could see the astonished pain in the big man's eyes.

With a single, chopping blow, the white mutie hunter severed the offending hand at the wrist, leaving it hanging by its suckers from his friend's bicep. His second blow was to the heart, driving the long blade all the way through the creature's torso.

Ripping the knife free, he shoved both his partner and Doc, hurrying them around the galley's walls. Ahead of them, the crew wielded boat hooks like spears, jabbing to hold the *taua* back while the passengers slipped through the for'c'sle door.

Inside the cabin, among the other survivors, Doc was relieved to see his companions alive and unhurt. When the last islander stepped inside the doorway, the crew slammed shut the iron hatch and dogged it.

Doc could hear the thump, thump, thump of *taua* throwing themselves at the far side of the barrier. And the even heavier thuds as more of the creatures dropped feet-first into the galley.

"Don't worry, they can't get into this cabin," the captain assured everyone. "The deck above us is protected by the bow's superstructure, and that bulkhead is three inches thick."

"What do we do now?" one of mercies said.

"We sit and wait until they decide to move on," Eng told him. "See to your wounds and try to get some rest."

The black mutie hunter stared at the *taua* hand still affixed to the back of his arm. He took hold of the stump and pulled. His ebony skin came with it, stretching from the ends of the sucker fingers. "Oh, shit…" he said.

"Perhaps I can be of assistance?" Doc said. "I have had some rudimentary medical training."

"Be my guest," the man said.

As best he could, Doc examined the join of fingertips to human flesh, then he drew back. "I'm going to have to cut the hand away to see how the fingers are attached to you," he said. "May I borrow your knife?"

The mutie hunter handed Doc his Desert Dagger. With great care, the old man filleted flesh from bone, removing all but the skin of the *taua*'s fingertips. With the clammy hand out of the way, he could see the edges of the small, circular wounds more closely.

"It appears the suckers are lined with teeth," he said. "Like the suckers of a squid or an octopus. I'm going to have to remove them from your flesh or the wounds will become infected."

"So do it," the black man said.

Doc sterilized the knife point in an oil lamp flame, then proceeded to work with the tip of the blade, prying out the teeth one by one. They were embedded so deep that if simply torn free, they would have left craters in the muscle. The mutie hunter endured the procedure in stoic silence. After Doc popped out the last fang he said, "Let the wounds bleed a little, then wash them with joy juice. The alcohol will sterilize them."

The man looked up and thanked him.

As Doc passed back the knife, handle first, he said, "For some reason, you two gentlemen seem to have taken responsibility for my safety. Concern for the welfare of strangers is rare in the hellscape. And as such it is always suspect. I do not require your protection. I can defend myself, I assure you. I am neither enfeebled nor addle-witted."

"No one said you were," the black man responded.

"Wouldn't you have done the same for one of us, if the situation were reversed?" the white-painted mutie hunter asked.

"No," was Doc's succinct reply.

"Forget ulterior motives," the black man said. "We don't have any. This is straight business. We're looking for another fighter, an ally to help us deal with what lies ahead, at the end of the voyage. Three blackhearts always make out better than two…"

"Thank you very much, but I prefer to fight alone."

"We have more in common than you can even imagine," the other mutie hunter said.

"Somehow I very much doubt that," Doc said, amused at the thought. "Now if you will excuse me, I think I will take a bit of a nap. I did not sleep well last night."

Doc located his bunk, climbed into it and turned his back to the cabin. He regretted there was no water to wash up with. He had to let the *taua* blood dry to a powdery crust on his hands, face and hair before he could brush it off.

As it dried, it itched like blazes.

Lying there on the hard pallet, Doc considered how far the mutie hunters had gone to win his allegiance— if that's what they were really up to. Twice they had dragged him out of danger like a pair of overprotective mother hens. Anyone with eyes could see he was not a man of substance, even by Deathlands' miserable standards. Doc had nothing of value for the mutie hunters to steal, certainly nothing to compare with the weapons they already owned. Nor were the men cannies in disguise, looking for a bit of well-aged long pork. They'd obviously passed their sputum tests with flying colors.

In truth, Doc was more concerned about the downside to personal entanglement with strangers than any physical threat from his new acquaintances. His goal, and that of the other companions, was to make no ripples on the southerly voyage, to arouse no interest or suspicion. So when it came time to vanish from the passenger ranks altogether, no one would notice. Until it was too late to do anything about it.

Doc closed his eyes and in familiar stages, mental stepping-stones, withdrew into himself, to a dark, warm place he had created in his imagination. A refuge of memory where his dead wife and children still lived, where he could see their sweet faces, hear their voices and the sounds of their laughter. After a few minutes of slow, deep breathing, he dozed off.

Sometime later, though how much later he couldn't tell, he was nudged from a dreamless, exhausted sleep by the black mutie hunter.

"We're under way again, mercie," the man told him.

Sure enough, Doc could hear the hiss of the hull slicing through the water, and the wind singing in the rigging. Sails that had been left unfurled and slack were now filled with a freshening breeze.

There were no sounds coming from the galley next door.

Captain Eng let the ship sail on without a helmsman for a long time before he finally ordered the bulkhead door opened a crack.

The galley beyond, though free of invaders, was a ruin. Everything not bolted down had been cast aside and smashed. The *taua* had overturned the food trays, it appeared without eating any; they had mashed and smeared most of the fried fish into the ceiling and walls. Scattered over the tables and floor were peaked, circular mounds of what looked like gray-green softy-serve.

"Dude!" the white-painted mutic hunter groaned, bolting for the steps.

The meaning of the odd exclamation was lost on Tanner—until he inhaled through his nose.

Dude, indeed!

Doc raced for the stairs, carefully skirting the mine-field of squish. He passed within a yard of the ship's cook, who howled in outrage as he attacked the piles of *taua* shit with his spatula, flopping them into a garbage pail.

On the main deck Doc gulped fresh air with the other passengers. He and J.B. caught each other's eye for a second. The Armorer gave him a quick wink before thumbing his smeared spectacles back up the bridge of his nose and looking away. The sun had already broken over the eastern horizon, but it was a sickly thing, filtered, diminished by dense sulphurous clouds that tainted the entire sky.

The light of day, however dim, made shockingly evident the carnage they had wrought the night before. Because so many of the *taua* bodies had been torn limb from limb, it was difficult to put a number on the enemy dead. Certainly hundreds of corpses littered the deck. It was difficult to walk without kicking a dismembered part or stepping in a blood puddle.

After Eng took control of the helm, returning the ship to its original course, he used his megaphone to bark a new set of orders to the crew. At once the islanders started examining the *taua* bodies, making sure they were dead, then flinging them overboard. They worked methodically, clearing one area at a time. After the corpses and their severed parts were disposed of, three crewmen moved in with buckets of seawater and hand brushes, and began scrubbing away the residual purple goo.

Among the tangled bodies the islanders discovered three *taua* that were still alive, if barely. Gleefully the crew dragged these wounded creatures out of the piles by their tails, pinning them to the deck by kneeling on their backs and legs. The *taua* twisted their necks and snapped their jaws, but they couldn't reach their tormentors.

After the captives' wrists and legs were hobbled with wraps of gray tape, and their muzzles likewise sealed shut, heavy rope harnesses were slipped over their backs and secured.

Doc followed with the rest of the passengers as the three *taua* were dragged thrashing to the stern. When he saw the crew attaching the ends of heavy ropes to the iron rings in the harnesses, he thought the *taua* were about to be keel-hauled, a sadistic punishment that involved pulling a roped person under the length of the ship, to either drown or be torn to shreds by the sharp barnacles on the hull.

The three bound and helpless creatures were tossed off the stern, just as he expected. But instead of hauling, the islanders continued to pay out rope, hundreds of feet of it hissed from the deck, uncoiling in the ship's foaming wake.

# Chapter Eight

Ryan leaned against one of the twin racks of steel drums, squinting into the steady tailwind. About 150 feet off the stern, well beyond the ship's wake, three objects popped in and out of the gray wave tops, leaving streams of bubbles in the sea. As they popped out of the water the heavy lines that tethered them to the stern cleats snapped taut, then went slack as they sank back. The rhythm of this constant jerking in and out, in and out was erratic, dictated by the jumbled seas and porpoising ship. Dragged along at a fine clip, the trio of harnessed *taua* twisted and spun.

The islanders were trolling them.

Ryan figured the splashes and scent trail left by the wounded creatures would draw hungry predators from a wide area and up from great depths, much the same way a staked-out live bait on land would attract lions and wolves. He guessed the islanders were trying to restock their destroyed food stores.

Exactly which predators they were after wasn't clear, though they had to be big to attack a 150-pound lure. The crew ignored Ryan when he asked them about it, pretending they didn't have a clue what he was talking about. But he noticed that every few minutes they would look to the wake in anticipation of something exciting happening. When nothing did, they returned to their assigned work, scrubbing and polishing the deck, recoiling lines, and reorganizing and cleaning the spilled contents of various tool chests and lockers. As the day wore on, the time between aftward glances grew longer and longer, until the islanders stopped looking altogether.

Ryan had to stop looking, too. Staring so fixedly at the troll lines was doing strange things to his vision. It made the ship's deck swim with the same churning motion as the water.

As they continued to sail south, he concentrated on the eastern horizon, comparing what lay before him with the predark maps of Southern California he'd seen.

The landscape bore no resemblance to the maps.

There was no landscape.

Millions upon millions of square miles of the southwestern corner of the former United States were simply gone, swallowed up by a turbid gray sea. The 4500-foot mountains that had separated San Diego and its sprawling suburbs from the sea level desert to the east had vanished. The Cific Ocean stretched unbroken to the far horizon, and there was no telling how deeply the ocean had invaded the land. The reshaped coastline was somewhere beyond the curvature of the earth, under an ceiling of colossal thunderheads. Those midnight-black clouds bulged, not with a burden of torrential rain, but with particulate matter, mineral spew and toxic ash from awakened and emerging volcanoes. The stench of burning sulfur rode the humid wind.

This was the same caustic sea that drowned the nuke-craters of Los Angeles. Its flats and reefs boiled and steamed, dotted by the dark tips of emerging volcanic cones and the black vortexes of whirlpools. The danger that surrounded them was palpable.

Few times in Ryan's life had he ever been so acutely aware of his own helplessness; few times in his life had he felt more like an ant than a man. This peril was nothing like face-to-face combat with norms, or muties or savage beasts. Nonliving physical processes dwarfed the ship and everyone on it, forces of awesome power capable of wiping them out in an instant, and without warning. Death was everywhere. A superheated steam cloud bursting from a subsurface vent could cook them in their skins like sausages. A barrage of molten ejecta could set all the sails ablaze, then overwhelm and sink the stranded ship with its sheer weight. An eruption-spawned tidal wave could sweep them to their doom. These disasters were all possible, maybe even likely. And there was no safe place to land for hundreds of miles.

Trapped on the too small ship, on the too-vast ocean, Ryan and his companions stood witness to the savage last throes of their world, a sight humans were never meant to look upon…and survive the looking. The risks of the mission at hand were terrible, and the chances of success were remote. Ryan and the others were going in blind, on the basis of gaudy house rumor and the exodus of Deathlands's worst. There was no guarantee they would even find Steel Eyes at the journey's end. Yet there had been no arguments over the course of action. And no second thoughts once they had begun.

Magus was a plague on all their houses.

It was said that his artificially prolonged life had allowed him to master everything there was to master. That he knew everything there was to know. That this mastery and knowledge had elevated him to a higher level of existence. To a kind of junkyard godhood. He had become his own creation, a malevolent deity whose dark schemes and willing soldiers victimized and degraded a desperate world.

The companions had taken on the mission because they all knew some things were worth dying for, even when the odds were slim.

And ridding the Deathlands of Magus was one of those things.

A crewman shouted alarm, breaking Ryan's somber train of thought. He looked off the stern and saw a fountain of foam erupt behind one of the trolled baits. Then another fountain, and another, water spraying in all directions. It looked like artillery shells falling into the sea, but shells that missed their targets, the hip-hopping lures. Fifty yards behind the row of baits, V-wakes by the hundreds slashed through the wave tops, swimming much faster than the ship could sail.

*Taua*. Homing in on their own.

Ryan couldn't believe his eye. If the crew had wanted to eat deep-fried *taua*, they had had plenty on the deck earlier in the morning. What kind of triple stupes would purposely recreate the same situation they had barely survived the night before?

Captain Eng, alerted by the crew, turned the helm over to a mate and rushed to the stern. He took a position beside Ryan, watching without apparent alarm the growing number of creatures surfacing in their wake. Every *taua* within fifty miles was chasing the skipping baits. Eng gave an order and crewmen set to work on the twin racks and the red drums closest to the stern. They unlocked the racks' rear gates, and using box wrenches, removed a small hex plug from each of the first four barrels.

Meanwhile, the *taua* fell upon their half-dead but enticingly jerked brethren. The troll lines snapped taut again and again, creaking from the strain and throwing off sprays of water as the baits were struck by heavy bodies and slashing needle teeth. With their school surrounding the hapless victims, individual *taua* were competing against each other, darting in and out, trying to chomp away the biggest chunk.

"First barrel gets a twenty-five-second fuse. Give the rest fifteen seconds," Eng told his waiting men.

The crew quickly measured and trimmed the waterproof fuse cord to the correct lengths, fitted the fuses through special caps and then screwed the caps into the drums.

*"Aianei!"* the captain shouted.

At his signal the longer fuses were lit, and a moment later the levers dropped on both racks. The first of pair red barrels lumbered down the rails and plummeted off the stern. Ryan watched them slowly sink as the ship rapidly pulled away.

*"Aianei!"* Eng cried again.

At once two more fuses were torched, the rack levers dropped and red drums rolled off the stern.

Ryan had heard stories about depth charges, of course, but he had never seen them in action.

The pair of drums with shorter fuses exploded with a rumble and hard crack, one hundred fifty feet upwind. The sea domed in two rapidly expanding circles of froth, twenty then forty feet across; towering geysers of water, foam and smoke erupted from their centers. These plumes tossed dark chunks over a wide radius.

Seconds later, having sunk deeper, the other barrels detonated with a more subdued rumble and crack, and a less dramatic set of geysers.

Ryan could appreciate the captain's strategy. Eng had figured that the *taua* who hadn't been injured by the first explosions would instinctively drop back from the troll lines, diving away from the shock waves, directly into the other charges.

And he was right.

As the tailwind whipped the smoke from burned high explosive past Ryan, he saw pale bodies and parts of same popping to the surface like corks in a broad swathe. Blood spread in a greasy film across the gray sea.

But Eng was not done, not by a long shot. Anticipating his enemies' next move, he cried, *"Ano! Ano!"*

By the time four more cans rolled over the side, the *taua* outside the initial killzone were drawn into the wake by the smell of gore in the water, which sent them into a chilling frenzy. They greedily attacked their own struggling wounded, the large, floating pieces of flesh and each other.

Eng's last volley of depth charges put an end to their

sport. The tightly overlapping explosions blew surface-feeding *taua* and their prey high into the air. Through the clouds of white smoke, sundered parts pelted the sea.

As the ship sailed away from the carnage, crewmen quickly hauled in the three trolling lines, their frayed and broken ends dancing through the bloody wake.

Ryan studied the captain's scarred face. Despite what Eng had said about revenge being an islander's pleasure, the one-eyed man saw no joy, no triumph, in his eyes. No tears, either. Only grim satisfaction.

A score repaid in full.

Ryan turned away, looking to the south and immediately picked up something on the far horizon, something that hadn't been there fifteen minutes earlier. The tiny smudge of dark purple stood alone, between the gray sea and black clouds.

It was the Baja.

As bad a pounding as Southern California had taken on nuke day, Mexico's Baja peninsula had suffered even harder punishment. Not from direct nuke strikes or errant MIRVs, but from the massive geologic shifts that followed the all-out assault to the north. The Sea of Cortez no longer existed, it had been taken over by the Cific. Of Baja's thousand-mile length and one-hundred-fifty-mile width, all that was left were its high points.

For the rest of the morning, the ship rushed headlong toward the speck of land. By late afternoon, it had become a broad purple shadow on the horizon.

Ryan had already guessed that it was Picacho del Diablo, Devil's Peak, the highest summit on the Baja peninsula, ten thousand feet above sea level before nuke day. There was no telling how tall it was now—its peak was hidden somewhere in the cloud bank.

Because of the cloud cover, evening turned to starless, moonless night in a matter of minutes. The ship was within three miles of the island as darkness fell. Campfires danced along the facing shore, and rows of torches illuminated a rickety pier. Heat waves rising from vents beneath the sea filtered the light, making it shimmer and blur. A volley of autofire rattled along the hidden beach, answered by a flurry of single shots. And scattered screams.

The campers were restless.

# Chapter Nine

Silam stood at the end of the pier, raptly watching the white ship's approach. Against the backdrop of black clouds and sea, its sails underlit by the deck lamps, it glided like a ghost into the wide, protected cove. The night wind stirred his past-shoulder-length cascade of blond curls, his pride and joy, which served to conceal a head far too high at the crown to be considered entirely normal—it looked like he was wearing a crash helmet under a wig hat. Silam's pale, fine features were compressed in the center of his face, and seemed too small for the width of his head. Though fairly tall, he was cursed with a narrow chest and shoulders. To counter the less than manly impression this produced, he favored slightly oversize garments and broad shoulder pads. And to make doubly sure that no one got the wrong idea, he walked with a rolling, exaggeratedly masculine gait.

By his own account, and the accounts of the two sycophants who stood beside him on the pier, Silam was a certified genius—a poet, showman, illusionist, choreographer, scholar, spell caster. Fantasist extraordinaire.

If he had lived his life before the Apocalypse, those

talents would have most certainly gone unrecognized. The horror show of January 21, 2001 and its cruel, century-long aftermath had elevated Silam, as it had other unworthies, by eliminating 99.99 percent of the competition. By the grace of nothing less than global annihilation, he had become Deathlands's Homer, Shakespeare, Tennyson and Patricia Cornwell.

Chief among his mental gifts was the ability to invent and widely circulate a great volume, if not a virtual library, of terrifying and misleading rumors. A close second was his knack for dreaming up truly horrible experiences for other people to endure. In Deathlands there were no limits of taste or decorum, nor codes of law when it came to psychological operations.

And the nightmares Silam dreamed up, Magus made real.

"This is your best work, by far," remarked the shorter of the two hangers-on. Rish had a big, bony head and droopy-lidded, sunken, dark-circled eyes. He wore a perpetual, hang-dog look on his long face. From a distance he could have almost passed for a swampie; up close his soft, hairless—and rather petite for an adult male—hands and feet were proof of his pure norm blood. Rish had long ago appointed himself Silam's biographer-historian, and the official keeper of the minutiae of Psy Ops continuity.

Silam considered the compliment in lofty silence. It was difficult to decide on a crowning feat in a career so studded with successes. As Magus's personal myth-maker for sometime, he had come up with some doozies. In a dark land of ignorance and fear, a land ruled by deceit, Silam was head liar...

Magus traveling back and forth in time, that had been his idea.

Magus creating the Adam and Eve of the stickie race; that had been his, too.

The list of memorable falsehoods went on and on.

Magus was a fugitive from another dimension. He paid top jack for the rare muties he used in his genetic experiments. Magus was immortal. His steel fingers were everywhere at once, invisibly controlling the course of human events. He had manufactured countless doubles of himself, using spare parts from his victims. He was a thousand years old. He had originally been the 43rd and last President of the United States of America. He had engineered skydark.

He was gathering an army of human scum to conquer all of Deathlands.

Even by Silam's high standards, that one had been inspired.

"Rish, you may well be right," the propaganda master conceded. "It's certainly way up there on the list."

"Where would Magus be without you, Silam?" gushed Jaswinder. As the balding, stubble-bearded, round-bellied man spoke, he leaned closer to his hero and wrung his hands nervously.

The remark fell like a unexploded bomb in their midst.

Silam stared into the man's dark, doting eyes. The longer he stared, the faster the grimy hands twisted. Jaswinder was always over the top with his fawning, although he sometimes had a point.

"I am the humble servant of Magus," Silam said. "I only follow his lead. His glory is my delight."

"What a team you make!" Rish exclaimed.

"Silam, your wisdom and art define our existence," Jaswinder continued, merrily wringing away. "You draw the lines even Magus must follow."

Rish gave Jaswinder a hard jab in the ribs with his elbow. The unexpected blow made the man say, "Ooooof!"

Punished for speaking dangerous truth.

That Magus had the power to bring Silam's horror shows to life didn't change the fact that they were *his* horror shows. The products of *his* imagination. Imagination was a mental facility Magus appeared to lack; if he had one, it was unrecognizable as such. Perhaps because he was no longer technically speaking a human he had somehow lost touch with human fears. He relied on his hireling, his head liar to choreograph the worst that people could do to each other. In a way the hireling commanded the master. In a way, he had created Magus's world. Yet Silam's accomplishments were unsigned, his genius shadowed, obscured by the legend he had so carefully constructed.

There were other, more pressing realities than public acclaim.

Silam restrained a powerful urge to look over his shoulder. One did not display hubris before Magus—nor dread, nor disgust, nor an excess of curiosity about his physical-mechanical attributes—and survive. One never knew where Magus lurked, or when he was eavesdropping. Silam couldn't see anything beyond the range of the pier's torches and the beach fires. The rock wall that abutted the cove's shoreline faded out of sight about forty feet above the rude camps. Actually, the sheer bluff rose ten times that height before vanishing into the perpetual cloud bank. Higher still, lost in the clouds atop the granite mountain was Magus's lair. He only descended to sea level to savor the island's regularly scheduled entertainments.

In Silam's darkest moments, even he was unable to spin-doctor his position. His blowhard's mantra, the hidden genius, the poet, the fantasist extraordinaire, rang hollow. He was a jester to an audience of one, to a criminally insane, demonically unpredictable lord. His task was to top himself, constantly. And by succeeding in topping himself, he only made the future more difficult. If his work ever disappointed Steel Eyes, it would mean a horrible death. Magus wouldn't have to invent something for the occasion. He could use any one of the ten thousand grisly fates Silam had devised for others.

Constant creativity was the propagandist's lifeline. If the sweet juices ever stopped flowing, Magus would remove his heart and make it beat in some other chest.

As the white ship docked alongside the pier and crewmen hopped off to make fast the mooring lines, Silam hurried over to intercept the group of heavily armed, uniformed men marching onto the dock, pulled aside the platoon leader, and spoke into his large, hair-fringed ear.

"Tell the ship's captain not a soul is to leave the vessel tonight," he said. "All hands must stay on board until tomorrow morning so a proper accounting can be made. Heads and cargo must be tallied in broad daylight or he will not be paid for his services. There will be no discussion on the matter. Do you understand?"

The platoon leader nodded, barked an order to his men and set off to do Silam's bidding.

# Chapter Ten

Locked overnight in the for'c'sle cabin with the other passengers, Mildred slept hard and woke up thick-headed and little woozy. The fight against the *taua* had taken its toll on her. She had fired so many rounds in such a short time that her shooting hand felt like it had been pounded with a hot rock. In the face of the suicidal mass attack, handicapped by the six-shot capacity of their revolvers, she and Krysty had worked as a team to control their section of deck. While one fired, the other dumped empties and reloaded. It went on like that until the retreat was called.

Mildred cleared her throat and she could still taste burned cordite. She could still smell *taua* blood. The gunpowder residue didn't bother her, she was plenty used to that. But she'd been drenched in the bodily fluids of a top-of-the-food-chain predator. She knew top-dog predators were where all the circulating chemical, biological and radiological contaminants of an ecosystem ended up. There was no way of telling what infectious and parasitical agents had been floating around in that rank red mist. To fully protect herself, she would have needed a biohazard suit with self-contained air supply. In Deathlands no one could be that fussy and stay alive, short term.

"Looks like they're finally going to let us out of here," Krysty said, leaning into the bunk. "You'd better get up."

As Mildred swung off the pallet and stood, her stomach started rumbling and churning. Part of her dizziness was due to the fact that they'd had no food since the night before last, only water. At that moment even a plate of the greasy, bony little fish sounded delicious.

Along with the other passengers, she and Krysty were herded by the crew up the stairs and onto the main deck. The view off the ship's stern was of an empty sea, as placid as a pond this morning. Smooth gray water blended seamlessly into a threatening gray sky, a vista without boundaries that Mildred found disorientating.

The view in the other direction was little better.

The island before them was all mountain, a looming pillar of granite a half-mile wide that seemed to be holding up the horizon-to-horizon cloud bank. The rock glistened in the weak, filtered light. Water trickled steadily down its steep walls, through its cracks and fissures, oozing from a source somewhere above the cloud line. Despite the plentiful fresh water, the only thing green was the moss on the beach rocks where tiny waves lapped and hissed.

On a wide ledge above the tide line were two single-story buildings made of native rock and the sea's bounty: scrap lumber, plastic sheeting, chunks of foam, hand-trimmed logs and branches. The larger building was long, but shallow, with many doorways, like a pre-dark motel. There were no doors in the doorways, no glass in the windows.

To Mildred, it screamed "barracks."

The smaller, even more slap-dash structure had a prominent rock chimney from which black smoke plumed. It looked like a cook shack, with cooking in progress. The very thought made Mildred's stomach rumble anew.

On the strip of beach below the ledge were firepits and crude lean-tos made of piled driftwood and plastic sheeting. All were deserted.

From the fires and the shooting of the night before, she had gotten the impression that the place was well-populated. It was clear now that was wrong. Or maybe the situation had changed while they were locked in the ship. As she scanned the bluff, she caught sight of a rope handrail fixed to the rock. It marked a narrow path cut into the side of sheer cliff. It switchbacked up four hundred feet or more, into clouds.

The islander crew began shoving the passengers toward the gangway and then down it, onto the pier. Mildred and Krysty were met at the foot of the ribbed plank by a firing squad of full-auto longblasters. AKs, Galils, M-16s, H&Ks. The weapons were held by thirty men in olive-drab uniforms and jungle boots. At first glance they looked like they were from a predark recruiting poster. On closer inspection Mildred saw that most of the uniforms were threadbare. Some were stained with blood and pocked with bullet holes—the clothes of the dead inherited by the living. These "armies of one" had faces and hands rimed with dirt and were missing most of their teeth.

When the passengers started to shuffle toward land,

Mildred and Krysty shuffled along with them. They moved a short distance, then everything stopped. Because of all the people milling in front of them, Mildred and Krysty couldn't see the end of the line. The redhead leaned out over the pier railing to get a peek at what lay ahead. After a moment, she stepped back.

"What is it?" Mildred said. Even as the black woman spoke, she had the answer to her question. Before her eyes her friend's prehensile hair was drawing up, corkscrewing into a mass of tight coils.

"Look for yourself," Krysty said.

Leaning out, Mildred saw that a temporary barrier had been set up across the pier, this to facilitate the all-important head count. She had expected to see Captain Eng stationed at the barricade, along with the leader of the men in uniform. Eng was there with his logbook, all right. By his side was a tall, long-haired man with shoulder-length fall of blond curls, unarmed and obviously not a soldier with that baggy shirt and those excessively wide shoulder pads. At his elbow were two much shorter men, who gazed up at him like spellbound schoolgirls.

What drew and riveted Mildred's attention was the creature standing farther along the barricade. It stood upright, but it wasn't a man.

And it was naked.

Mildred had lived and fought in the hellscape for quite some time. She knew it was a Pandora's box of horrors. Every nightmare humanity had ever dreamed took physical form in this place, like a self-fulfilling prophesy.

The end of the world.

The fall of civilization.

Nature run amok.

Even so, shock sent a rush of adrenaline coursing through her veins and set her fingers and toes tingling.

The two-legged animal was unlike anything she had ever seen or heard tell of. It had a thick, knobby, faintly greenish skin, a huge mouth, small sharp teeth and wide-set yellowish eyes. And it was stout, with massive thighs and buttocks. A five-foot-eight-inch, 300-pound cannon ball. Mildred estimated that nearly five percent of that weight was concentrated in its wedding tackle. But for the coloration and knobby topography, the withdrawn apparatus looked mammalian, and very much bull-like. The creature had three-fingered hands, with cruel amber talons on both thumbs, and wide feet with webbed toes.

It was sweating.

Copiously.

Rivulets of perspiration peeled down its warty arms, over the bony, protective plates on its belly, down its legs and off its pot-roast-size testicles, pooling at its feet.

Mildred moved back into line.

"Some new kind of mutie, huh?" Krysty said.

The doctor frowned. In Deathlands, all questions about biology could be answered with "the nukecaust" or "mutie." According to popular and long-held belief, all muties, or genetic mutations, were a direct consequence of the Apocalypse. The term was used to describe a broad spectrum of bizarre humanoid species, like stickies and scalies, the less obvious mutations such as the precognitive "doomies," as well as gigantism and other extreme variations among lower forms of animal and plant life. Most people thought muties of all stripes popped up out of nowhere, like mushrooms.

Like magic.

In her former existence Mildred had been a medical doctor and a researcher. She understood the mechanisms of inheritance. She knew what mutations were, and how evolution worked upon them. Quite simply, the variety and strangeness of Deathlands's biology fit neither the established facts nor the prevailing theories of twentieth-century science.

Producing mutations with overdoses of radiation was like playing horseshoes with hand grenades. The resulting chromosomal damage was not confined to one or two specific locations; it was widespread and totally random. Vital genes were as likely to be destroyed as nonvital ones. Most mutations, whether caused by radiation, chemicals in the environment or spontaneously malfunctioning DNA/RNA, were not adaptive, which meant the organisms that inherited them usually didn't live long enough to breed and pass them on. They were almost always evolutionary dead ends.

Although some of the living horrors that prowled Deathlands were the result of radiation and other random, low probability effects, that they all were was inconceivable.

Mildred knew that in nature new species evolved only under certain conditions. First of all, the variant-mutant genes had to exist in the population, and they couldn't be harmful. Members of the population possessing these genes had to be physically separated from the majority for an extended period of time. The longer the groups were separated, the more different they became. In Mildred's opinion, the differences between predark and mutie species were too great for the time that had elapsed. As a result, they couldn't be explained by Darwin's twin theories—natural selection and descent with modification.

An alternative hypothesis, nonrandom and nonradiological, had only recently surfaced. Deep in the belly of the desert southwest, the companions had found living evidence that before the Apocalypse a program of ultrasecret transgenic experiments had been under way. In a hidden, high-security underground facility, whitecoats had spliced together specific genes from plants and animals and produced a new and viable organism—a distinct species not in ten thousand years, but in a matter of months. These designer life-forms were assembled with particular attributes and functions in mind. They were supersurvivors, living weapons systems. This black-budget military program had been underwritten to the tune of billions of dollars, despite the fact that the administration in power had branded such experimentation "immoral" and "against God's laws," and had banned it in the public sector.

Though the research program had been derailed by the events of January 21, 2001, there was no way to gauge the postnukecaust impact of the "trannie" experiments because their number, their precise methodology and their scope was unknown. But it was possible that Deathlands had been poisoned by more than just radiation.

"Whatever it is," Mildred said, "it should be wearing pants."

"Or at least a five-gallon bucket," Krysty said.

As the line slowly advanced toward the barrier, the crew began offloading the cargo of crated muties from the hold. The creatures howled and screeched as they were transferred by crane to a fleet of small boats on the far side of the ship. The overloaded dories were then rowed not toward land, but in the opposite direction, out of the cove.

When shouts and curses rang out from the head of the line, Mildred and Krysty rushed to the rail to see what was going on. At first it looked like Doc Tanner might be involved in the fracas. The lanky time traveler was standing behind two big men at the barricade, one white, the other black. The white man was arguing heatedly with the ship's captain, apparently over the PVC tubes they carried strapped to their backs. At a signal from the guy with the bond hair, the hulking creature started toward them. Its approach abruptly ended the discussion. The men surrendered their tubes, were given a chit for payment and allowed to pass beyond the barrier. Their weapons weren't confiscated, which was a relief to see.

When Doc passed through the barricade without incident, the women slipped back into line. It took the better part of half an hour for them to reach the checkpoint.

"Your tag numbers," Eng said without looking up from his log. As they rattled them off, he located and marked them with his pencil.

The blond-haired man, not Eng, was clearly in charge. His pasty face wore a constant smirk. Mildred couldn't help but notice his misshapen skull, which bordered on the hydrocephalic. The way he carried himself, as if posing for a full-length oil portrait, reminded her of a nineteenth-century fop—Percy Bysshe Shelley in a too big bowling shirt.

The captain wasn't the only person with a notebook. One of the blond man's adoring fans, the dour-faced, sunken-eyed lackey, quickly jotted down some notes, which he then offered up for his hero's approval.

Mildred glanced along the barricade, at the silent, staring, 300-pound guardian. It stood in a shallow puddle of its own sweat. It opened its mouth and thrust out its tongue at her, a human-looking tongue, only much longer and broader. It wasn't a gesture of contempt. She realized after a moment the thing was tasting the air, tasting whatever aroma she and Krysty gave off. Its own scent was chemical, a mixture of ammonia, ether and acetone. As it waggled its tongue, it began to perspire even more profusely.

From twenty-five feet away, Mildred could sense its murderous volatility. The gut-twisting fear she felt at that moment was instinctive, hard-wired into her nervous system. She wanted to shoot it through the eye, then and there, but couldn't make her hand move to the ZKR's butt. Some creatures by their very appearance had the power to intimidate, to disarm, to induce rabbit-in-the-headlights paralysis. This was one of those creatures.

Even the ferocious Captain Eng would not look it in the face.

"What the hell is that?" Mildred said, managing to point a finger at the thing.

"He's a trainer," the blond man replied.

"For combat?" Krysty said.

"All recruits receive instruction upon arrival."

"It can talk?" Mildred said.

"There are many other ways to communicate."

"Who are you?" Krysty said.

"I am Silam," the man with the blond hair said. "We have noted your tag numbers. You two are cleared. Pass under the barricade. Pick a campsite on the beach. You'll be fed in a little while. You'll find out about the trainers later in the day."

Mildred wasn't about to leave, yet. "What happened to all the people who were here last night?" she said.

"They shipped out," Silam snapped back, suddenly impatient. "Now move along."

The two women ducked under the barrier and walked toward the island. Mildred's initial question hadn't been answered to her satisfaction. Silam had told her what the creature's job was, not what it was.

The transgenic weapons the companions had fought in Pueblo Canyon were simple killing automatons, following a preset biological program. If this new creature could interact on a human level, maybe it wasn't a trannie. Whatever it was, it wasn't alone. Mildred could see a few other trainers, all of them prodigiously male, standing on the ledge in front of the barracks. They were directing the recruits away from the ramshackle building and onto the rocky beach.

"Guess we don't rate first-class accommodations,"

Mildred said. "They must be reserved for the boys in uniform."

She and Krysty climbed down onto the stony beach. All the campsites were in the same condition: mucky, yucky, with exposed pit toilets. Under the low, drift-wood eaves of the crude lean-tos, the beds were tattered sheets of plastic laid over the rocks.

They chose a site as far up from the water line as they could get. When they crawled inside, the women saw the graffiti their predecessors had carved into the under-side of the roof.

Kep yr blaztur.

All lyes.

Aynt no r mee.

"No army?" Krysty repeated, translating from the Deathlands-ese. "What kind of hellhole is this?"

# Chapter Eleven

"We want gold in exchange for our muties," Graydon Bell told Captain Eng. "Precious metal, not a stinking slip of paper."

"We don't have any gold here," Eng said.

"Then we'll keep our muties."

"You two signed on to train and fight along with the others. Sorry, no pets allowed."

"Well, consider us unsigned."

Graydon Bell didn't give two hoots in hell about the baby scagworms, or how they got paid for them. What he and Kirby were looking for was a quick handle on the island's personnel and their pecking order. Intel they could convert to their advantage.

The blond man stepped forward and with authority said, "Now that you're here, you can't back out."

Before his cryogenesis, Colonel Bell had played in the Big Show, the Pentagon-DOD league, the byzantine corridors of power, intrigue and one-upmanship. A world-champion button pusher, he knew how to read people and their weaknesses. He read the guy as a total fruit loop, his psyche a squirming pile of contradictions, of desires and fears working at cross purposes. From the top of his too tall head to his size thirteen feet, the guy radiated arrogance, vanity, insecurity and, oh, yes, self-loathing.

"Surrender the muties and take your chit," Silam ordered. "I guarantee you'll be paid in gold later."

"Who the fuck are you?" Bell shouted in his face. "This is Magus's op. We want to see Magus. We want to talk to Magus."

Button pushed. Ding-ding. He was not in charge.

Silam's pale face and high-rise forehead rapidly took on an unhealthy ruddy glow.

Bell had to give the guy credit, though. He didn't respond by shouting back or reaching for a hidden weapon. He didn't do anything stupid. Instead he signaled for backup, which was smart.

The colonel took one look at the 300-pound enforcer and started shrugging out of his tube frame's back straps. As he passed over the scagworms to Eng, he saw the self-satisfied expression on the blond man's face. The guy actually thought he'd won. But he'd lost. Bell had neatly established the island's chain of command. And if necessary, the top-to-bottom chill sequence he and Kirby would follow.

Before that moment, Bell's greatest concern was that the one in charge might be the naked ugly thing, whose desires and intent he couldn't read. Unlike four-star generals, chairmen of congressional subcommittees, captains of the military-industrial complex or his white-coat research competitors, it was a closed box. Inscrutable. Alien. There was no exposed button to push, no obvious weakness to exploit, no way to manipulate it to his advantage.

For a reason that had nothing whatsoever to do with outward appearance, it reminded Bell of a Kodiak bear, a creature capable of almost unthinkable violence whose trigger was internal, accessible only to itself. Looking into the enforcer's slitted yellow eyes, he had no clue as to what flipped its switch, just the feeling that it was either on or off.

Kill now or kill later.

After Kirby handed over his rack of tubes to Eng, he snatched the payment chit and stuffed it in his pants' pocket. Like the people in line in front of them, they weren't asked to give up their weapons before they hopped the barrier.

Well short of the end of the pier, Bell caught his partner by the arm and said, "Let's wait for the geezer."

"We need to start breaking the news to him," Kirby said. "Get an idea of how he's going to react before he goes off and rejoins his pals."

Bell nodded in agreement. The inevitable reunion of Doc Tanner and his companions presented a problem. They didn't know exactly when or how Doc and friends were going to make their move, but had no doubt that a move of some kind was upcoming. From the gaudy house stories they'd heard about the crew's past exploits, they were certain that signing on with Magus's free-booters to pillage the hellscape was not the real agenda. From the companions' reputation, it was more likely some kind of preemptive strike against the recruitment operation. Or a rip-off. Or an assassination attempt. Or even a bit of all three. Once Doc linked up with his running buddies and their plan was put in motion, the main chance for winning him over peacefully was lost. Taking him by force was a last resort.

"How do you want to work this?" Kirby asked. "Two on one, or one on one?"

"We'd better make it one on one. Tanner will be less likely to get his panties in a twist that way. Find us a campsite, and I'll lay it out for him, as gently as I can."

Bell leaned on the pier's rail, watching Doc amble toward him. All their effort, their suffering, their sacrifice had come down to this. For an instant, desperation fluttered like a big fat moth in the back of his throat. Powdery wings beating. Beating. He wanted his kids to grow up, even if he wasn't around to see it. He wanted his wives to grow old. He wanted his world to endure. Bell swallowed hard, crushing the imaginary bug to pulp. The skinny man in the frock coat was the key to undo, to resurrection. He could return life to those it had been stolen from. At least in theory, he could do it by taking a single step forward at the right moment. The question was, would he take that step if given the chance? Would he do it if he knew the likely consequences to his companions?

Doc stopped beside him and gestured at the rocky beach and rude dwellings with his ebony stick. "It was on tiny, remote, lifeless islands like this that Roman emperors exiled their political enemies and troublesome relatives. Suetonius writes that the Lady Agrippina endured exile in such a place, the victim of Tiberius Caesar's treachery."

"Gaius Suetonius Tranquillis," Bell said. "Sex and violence, circa second century A.D."

Doc gave him a stunned look. "You know his work?"

"Through a series of filters. I saw some television films based on the books of the poet Robert Graves, which were based on the histories of Suetonius."

"You saw these films recently?"

"Only you and I would call a hundred years ago recently, Dr. Tanner."

Doc pulled back to a proper fighting distance, switching the swordstick to his weak hand and tucking the tail of his long coat behind the walnut grips of his LeMat. "You have the advantage of me, sir," he said. "I know you by a number around your neck, not a name. Who are you? And more to the point, what do you want from me?"

Bell licked the ball of his thumb and used it to draw a clean stripe down his right cheek. Under the cracked white paint were many small red dots. In clusters. They weren't from birdshot. "I'm a freezie," he said. "I went into cryosleep days before the nukecaust."

"You and your large friend?"

"Yes. We went under at the same time, in the same place. My name's Bell. His is Kirby."

"If I may ask, what prompted you to consign yourselves to deep cold prior to Armageddon?"

"I suppose you could say it was a premonition of doom."

"Any charlatan psychic could make that prediction, but few, if any, could act upon it in the manner you describe. How did you come by this 'premonition' and how did you get access to the machinery of cryogenesis?"

"You already know the answer."

"You're whitecoats," Doc said, practically spitting the words.

"Not just any whitecoats," Bell corrected him. "Dr. Kirby and I were theoreticians, pure researchers. Although we were funded by Operation Chronos."

"Chronos!" Doc exclaimed, his hand dropping to the LeMat's grip, murder flashing in his eyes. "By the fires of hell—"

Bell held up a palm, begging for patience. "We worked independent of that bureaucracy," he said, "without close supervision, in areas of our particular professional interest. In the course of our investigations into some unusual electromagnetic phenomena, we got a glimpse of the near future. Our computer models predicted doomsday."

"And so you decided to desert the ship you helped scuttle."

"That is an oversimplification based on insufficient facts, as you well know."

"If you and Dr. Kirby were able to anticipate the nukecaust based on a computer model," Doc said, "the primary cause must have been evident. It had to be part of the calculations. So tell me, what precipitated the world blowing apart?"

Graydon Bell had read Tanner's Chronos files a hundred times. He and Kirby had discussed their implications endlessly, both before and after their cryosleep. Theophilus Algernon Tanner was obsessed with guilt over leaving his young family to an unknown fate. Tanner's suffering was a mirror image of Bell's. A button in common.

He looked Doc straight in the eye and said, "It was you, Dr. Tanner. You caused the end of the world."

Before he could get another word in, Doc had the big black-powder blaster out of its hand-tooled holster, his thumb on the hammer spur.

"The second time jump you made, from 1998 to Deathlands, was the pivotal event," Bell told him.

"If you know about that, then you know it was not of my choosing. Nor was the initial jump. I was taken against my will."

"Yes, you were. But the hard fact is this—when your physical form was transported from the twentieth century to the near future, damage was done to the fundamental structure of existence, to what Dr. Kirby and I choose to call supra-time/space."

"You can call it anything you want. What proof do you have of any of this?"

"In the beginning all our proofs were mathematical. Rational, not empirical. But they led us to suspect that a vantage point outside our own existence might exist. After you were trawled from November 1896 by Dr. Herman Welles, Kirby and I began monitoring subtle changes at the submolecular level. That damage was the first indirect evidence we had of s-t/s. We tried to persuade Dr. Welles and others in power to call off further Chronos experiments until our data could be analyzed elsewhere and the results independently confirmed. Despite our warnings, you were sent on to the future."

"The consequences being?"

"Almost imperceptible electromagnetic shifts, which at first caused only minor, isolated problems in the world's most sensitive and sophisticated computer systems. The problems were kept out of the news for national security reasons, and because their impact on performance was negligible. The troubles were blamed on viruses and on faulty software and hardware. In less than a month, the random charge shifts suddenly cascaded, disabling the nuclear failsafes and triggering an immediate, all-out global exchange."

"I was the instrument that destroyed your world."

"Yes."

"Apropos, as you destroyed mine."

"What if I told you it wasn't destroyed."

"I'd say you were stark raving mad. My world is dust. Yours is ashes. I repeat my original question, what do you want from me, sir?"

"I want your help in undoing what has been done."

"As if such a thing were possible!"

"I assure you it is. Dr. Kirby and I didn't freeze ourselves to escape the nukecaust. We did it so we could come to Deathlands and find you. Gaining access to files to discover how far into the future you were sent was very difficult. We took a calculated risk that we would actually thaw on the preset dates."

"I am flattered to be sure, but I fail to see where all this is leading."

"There is a way back to your Emily, to Rachel and little Jolyon. It already exists. It is within reach. We can show it to you."

Doc drew back the hammer to full cock. "I should destroy you now, like a rabid dog."

"If you do, you'll never know if I'm telling the truth.

You'll never know if you could have seen their faces again, if you could have lived the life that was stolen."

The old man let the sights of the LeMat drop from the man's crotch to the planking at his feet.

"There is only one stipulation to the deal," Bell said, "and it is nonnegotiable."

"Why doesn't that not surprise me?"

"You can't mention any of this to your companions. Not a word about what I have offered."

Doc was incredulous. "Assuming your offer is bona-fide, you expect me to take my leave of Ryan and the others without saying goodbye? These are my dearest friends, my battlemates."

"Goodbyes are overrated. It's the hellos that count. Especially to a long lost family."

"I don't understand...."

"When you leave with us for the past, your existence in Deathlands will be completely erased. If you were never trawled from Nebraska in 1896, you could never have arrived here. What's the point of saying goodbye to people who won't remember you a nanosecond after you go?"

Doc seemed to wobble on his feet, as if from a physical blow. The possibility had finally sunk in that this might be the answer to all his prayers. He reholstered the pistol with difficulty, then leaned hard on his swordstick. "I need time to think," he said.

"Go ahead and think, but remember, if you say anything to Cawdor or the others, the offer is withdrawn. You will remain in Deathlands forever. Your family will be forever dead to you."

Doc nodded, still dazed.

Bell hadn't told him everything that he and Kirby knew. The truth didn't depend on obscure mathematics; it was simple Aristotelian logic. Caught up in the resurgence of lost hope, Doc wasn't thinking in an organized way. He hadn't asked the most pertinent question.

Perhaps the truth would dawn on him someday, a eureka moment after he returned to his own time.

For everything there is a price.

*Caveat emptor.*

# Chapter Twelve

From his position at the end of the long line leading up to the barricade, Jak Lauren watched the exchange between Doc and the mutie hunter. He was too far away to hear any of what was being said, but whatever it was, Doc took serious offense. His antique handblaster cleared leather in a blur, and for a second it looked like he was going to cut loose on the empty-handed, rapidly talking man.

Jak knew he had seen the guy before, him and his black partner. And he knew just where: in a rowdy, trailerhouse gaudy beside a fallen Interstate 15 overpass southwest of the ruins of Vegas, the companions' last stop before making the jump to California.

Forget about that eighteen-inch-high dreadlocked topknot, the white paint had struck a deep and sensitive nerve. When Jak had glimpsed that pale, gaunt face across the crowded, smoky saloon, his heart jumped and he dropped his spoon into the plate of hot chicken pie he was gobbling. For an instant he actually thought he'd found another albino. Without a word he left his friends at the low, corner table. When he moved closer to the man, he saw the troweled-on pigment and brown eyes.

Not an albino.

A seedy clown.

Embarrassed and angry at himself, Jak had turned away before the man noticed him. Or so he'd thought.

When he'd seen the pair again, belowdecks on the white ship talking with Doc Tanner, his hackles had gone up, bigtime. Jak could only think of one way the mutie hunters could have gotten to Morro Bay so fast. Unless they had sprouted—and subsequently lost— wings, they, too, had used a mat-trans gateway. And it had to have been the same one the companions used. The mutie hunters had either followed Jak and the others to the desert mountain redoubt, or they had known it was there all along. And they knew enough about gateway operation to follow the companions.

What the pair was after wasn't clear. Jak realized it might not have anything to do with the companions. The mat-trans jump could have been the easiest way for them to reach the Morro Bay rendezvous point. Or it could have been something more sinister. The agreed- upon mission rules left Jak in a bind. Until they were in position to make their assault, the companions were supposed to keep strict distance, and not intervene on each other's behalf. It was every man for himself, with the exception of Mildred and Krysty, who were teamed up.

Not wanting to endanger his friends or the mission, Jak had kept a discreet eye on the situation. There was no doubt Doc could handle whatever the mutie hunters dished out. And it was always possible that he already knew about their mat-trans jump, that the men had volunteered the information. It was also possible that Doc remembered them from the gaudy's pie parlor, so a warning was unnecessary.

When the *taua* broke into the galley and the mutie hunters saved Doc's life, Jak figured he had made the right decision. Now that things had taken a sudden 180, he was having second thoughts.

Doc cocked the LeMat and aimed it at the man's painted forehead. The range was no more than five feet. Jak could see the tension in the old man's arm and raised hand, and knew the trigger was drawn right up to break point. Life and death were separated by an ounce or two of finger pressure. The mutie hunter stood his ground, looked down the .44-caliber bore and kept talking. After a bit, Doc's aim wavered, then dropped. When he slid the LeMat back into its holster, his shoulders slumped and he seemed to stagger on his feet. Only his swordstick kept him upright.

Whatever the mutie hunter had said to Doc, it devastated him. As the old man moved down the pier toward the island, he dragged himself along stiff-legged and slow. Jak could only watch and worry. Doc's brain had a tendency to overload, to vaporlock, a product of the damage done to him by the Operation Chronos whitecoats. It was hard to know what would set it off, or how long the problem would last. Sometimes it was over in a matter of seconds. Under the circumstances, all Jak could do was hope for the best.

It took quite a while for him to reach the barricade, which gave him plenty of time to size up the mutie enforcer. It was big and solid, but it looked quick on its feet, too. It had that slumbering horror feel—like it could go from cat nap to blood bath in the blink of a yellow eye. Taking in the thick, armored plates on its belly, Jak had to wonder if they could they deflect lead or absorb a few thousand-foot pounds of point-blank .357 magnum.

He had never seen a mutie—or anything else—sweat like that. Perspiration peeled off the knobby skin in a steady drip, drip, drip into the shallow puddle at its feet. It occurred to Jak that the sweat might be poison, or some kind of weak acid. In a face-to-face fight, it would fly off, blinding an opponent. What he liked least of all were the twin talons, like amber gut hooks. In Jak's experience, a mutie didn't come equipped with something like that for no good reason. Aside from size and physical strength, the talons seemed to be its main offensive weapon.

This beast belly-slashed for a living.

And it didn't work alone, which was odd. Mutie-norm collaborations were rare in Deathlands. As a rule, muties were either hunted for sport or worked as slaves by their pure-gene betters. A creature as large as the enforcer was something you might see caged and chained in a mutie zoo or a carny show. It was too big and too powerful to control with threats of physical pain or deprivation.

Too big to control with voice commands. Or hand gestures.

Although the guy with the double-stack forehead was doing just that.

As Jak stepped up to the barrier, the enforcer showed

him its tongue. It licked at the air, eyes narrowed, like it was concentrating real hard, memorizing the molecular signature of his scent.

Ever since Jak was little, butt-ignorant people had treated him like a mutie. The white skin and hair, and the ruby-red eyes made them jump to the wrong, the easy, conclusion. Even though Jak was purebred albino, people saw what they wanted to see, and as a result he'd spent some time in a baron's mutie zoo as a featured attraction. He had that same sense of being penned in now, with the sea at his back and a looming pile of rock in front of him. Jak Lauren was born to live in the wide, boundless spaces. His worst fear was being caged, trapped, a fear he forced himself to face down and crush for the sake of the mission.

Magus was worse than the worst of Deathlands' murdering, raping, robbing barons. Even the vilest baron had a spark of humanity. Magus was a black hole that trapped all light. Jak wanted to take him apart, bolt by bolt, strut by strut, wire by wire, and quick-lime the debris.

The tongue lashing stopped, the sweating continued at a steady rate. The enforcer stayed put.

After Jak showed Eng his tag number, he was let through the barrier. As he passed, the captain said, "Good luck, little *korako*."

Jak didn't know what a *korako* was, but he gathered it was not an insult. He instinctively liked the man. Both were free wild spirits, fighters, Jak on land, Eng on sea.

"That's the lot?" the guy with the blond hair said.

There was a kind of mocking, superior laugh in his voice. It made Jak stiffen, then pause and turn.

"Yeah, that's the last one," Eng said.

"In that case, I want you and all your crew on the beach, as well."

"What?"

"Your presence is required on the beach."

"Why?"

"You didn't bring me enough recruits this time. You're at least twenty bodies short."

Eng carefully tucked the logbook into the back of his trouser waistband, freeing up both hands. The shoulder-holstered Government Colt was practically lost in the fleshy folds of his left armpit. "Look, Silam," he said, "a lot of people got chilled on the trip down. Way more than usual. I do my best to keep them all alive, but I can't control everything that happens between here and Morro Bay. I'll make up the difference next time. You know I'm good for it."

The man he called Silam smiled a little smile with his too little mouth. "You have to make up the difference now," he said.

Jak watched Eng's facial scars suffuse with angry blood, like crimson tiger stripes. "I am an islander," he growled, showing every one of his filed teeth. "I am captain of my own ship. I will sail on the next tide with all my crew. Whether you pay us for this trip or not."

"You will sail when I tell you to," Silam replied. "Until then you will do as I say. Or I will have your precious ship scuttled while you and your crew watch."

Eng's right hand crept toward the butt of his .45-caliber Colt.

Silam raised a single finger and the enforcer responded. As Jak suspected, it was quick. Before the captain could yank the blaster from its holster, the enforcer stood between him and Silam, blocking his shot. The islander and the mutie were roughly the same height and weight. There the resemblance ended. The enforcer leaned forward and extended its tongue, waving it in Eng's furious face. The captain did not retreat, but he did not draw his weapon, either. Behind him, uniformed soldiers raised their assault rifles and took beads on his crew. The other enforcers left the beach and ran onto the pier.

"Make another move, Captain," Silam said, "and that ship will be your coffin, and the coffin of all your crew."

Jak expected Eng to fight to his last breath. After all, he hadn't shied away from battle with the *taua*. But the captain hesitated. He looked at the exposed razor-sharp crescents of amber horn, carefully weighing the odds that he could clear leather and get a shot off before his insides were flopped down around his bare feet.

Meanwhile the enforcer's sweat drip-drip-dripped onto the ground, starting a brand-new puddle.

How fast was the thing really? Jak wondered. How accurately could it strike with those talons?

Too fast for the captain, apparently. Eng let his right hand fall from the gun butt and shouted to his crew, waving them off the ship and onto the pier.

As Silam and his two-man entourage led the procession of uniforms and crew toward the island, the captain stepped up beside Jak.

"There's an important lesson here, little *korako*," he said bitterly. "A lesson I already knew, but chose to ignore for the sake of a nice profit. It's the same lesson everyone in Deathlands is taught at their mother's knee."

"Lay down with devil, wake up fucked."

"Bright boy," Eng said.

# Chapter Thirteen

Ryan stuck his head under the plywood-and-sheet-plastic roof of the cook shack and held out his bowl. The bare-chested, hairy-shouldered cook wore sagging, stained longjohn bottoms with makeshift, twine suspenders that kept the overstretched elastic waistband from falling down around his knees. His oily face and salt-and-pepper chin stubble were dusted with soot from the roaring driftwood fire. He stopped stirring the contents of a tall, blackened metal caldron, and carelessly slopped a portion of lumpy, brownish soup into Ryan's dish.

The one-eyed man carried his steaming dinner to a nearby flat rock. After taking a seat, he gingerly held the bowl up to his nose. It didn't smell that bad, he decided. Kind of like stewed mushrooms with a hint of prune. Anything hazardous lurking in it had been boiled to death, which was comforting as the soup looked like a bad case of Montezuma's revenge: dark flecks of seaweed and nameless chunks of gray flesh floated in a watery mocha gruel. And as he investigated deeper, he found other stuff in it, too, rubbery stuff that wasn't animal flesh. Not abalone, either. Or clam. Or even squid. Ryan picked a piece out with his fingers and examined it.

A translucent, pebbly gristle strip.

He tried chewing it. It was like trying to eat a wag head gasket. The gristle maintained its shape, refusing to be torn or pulverized, even when he attacked it with his back teeth. He had a choice, spit it out or swallow it whole. He chose to spit.

Lower down on the beach, the islander captain and his crew were huddled together in a circle, speaking in low voices and eating their soup. All of it, Ryan noted. He hadn't expected them to sign up for Magus's new army. From their expressions, they hadn't, either. If the islanders appeared standoffish and arrogant on the ship, on land they looked downright hostile, ready to lash out at anyone or anything.

The conscription of the captain and crew was not Ryan's first clue that something was very wrong with the setup. So far, nothing fit with his own military experience. On close inspection, the story about Magus recruiting an army to take over Deathlands had more holes than the seat of the cook's longjohns.

The naked, sweating "trainers" apparently couldn't talk, but looked strong enough to rip off a person's head off. They acted more like prison camp guards than drill instructors, ready to slap down—or chill—anyone who even thought about stepping out of line. They, not the armed uniforms, kept order on the beach, with hard looks and unspoken threats. Ryan figured the trainers would go into action, soon enough. When things started getting tough, examples would be made of the stragglers.

Ryan couldn't decide whether the trainers were

human, reptile or bear, but they didn't need blasters or blades. They came equipped with thumb talons that looked like amber scythes. With a couple of swipes, those hooks could clear out a body cavity all the way to the backbone. There was something unclean about them, too, and it wasn't just the buckets of sweat they oozed, or the knobby skin, or those slitted yellow eyes. They reminded him of the trannies the companions had battled at Pueblo Dam: beneath the trainers' surface calm Ryan sensed a frenzied jumble of competing, mismatched instincts.

Maybe a case of too many gene donors spoiling the stew?

The trainers kept a good distance from the cook shack, standing upwind as they watched the recruits wolf down their dinners. Ryan counted six of them on the beach. He wondered if the army's officer corps was made up of similar creatures. Which raised the question, how could they lead norm troops into battle if they couldn't talk?

There were other glaring questions, too. Where was the weaponry needed to break into the barons' fortified villes? The cannon? The armored wag fleets? The heavy MGs? Aside from the uniforms' assault rifles, the only weapons on the beach were the ones the recruits had brought with them. Likewise they carried the only ammo.

The island was like no boot camp Ryan had ever seen or heard tell of. There was no training facility. No exercise or endurance course. No target range. No contingent of recruits in residence who were further along in the training. Shipping small groups of fighters to some other staging point made no sense. Why start here and then move the troops to another location?

Another thing, Magus couldn't successfully tackle the eastern baronies with less than three thousand men. And four thousand would be more like it. There was room for maybe seventy in the rat holes dug on the beach, with another thirty uniforms in the barracks. Looking around, Ryan saw a little more than forty recruits had survived the trip south.

A hell of a long way from the magic number.

He fished around in the soup with the point of his panga, flicking away the clear strips of gristle. Then he picked out the gray meat and ate it. It had the texture of overripe banana, and went all to mush in his mouth. He washed the mush down with the brown liquid, all but the dregs of it. The dregs had sand in them. He wiped his tongue on his sleeve to get rid of the grit.

While Ryan sat there, listening to his belly grumble over what he had just poured into it, the long-haired guy left the pier in a small rowboat with his two pals. The smaller pair struggled with the oars while Silam lay stretched out in the bow, his ankles crossed, his forearms cradling his oversize head, like the queen of Sheba.

Ryan watched them disappear around the point, heading in the same direction that the mutie cargo had been taken. He had Silam pegged as a talker, a bullshit artist. Definitely not a fighter. If he had a weapon under that baggy shirt, he kept it hidden. But it was obvious he controlled the trainers, and that put him squarely in charge of the whole beach show.

In Ryan's experience, Magus always put people like Silam—weak-willed, foolish, internally twisted—into positions of authority. They were living buffers between Steel Eyes and his victims, and easily sacrificed if the natives got restless and wanted some payback. Not that Magus was adverse to getting his own hands bloody, but he considered large-scale wet work to be manual labor, and therefore beneath his virtuoso talents. If the chilling had nothing to do with him directly, with his secret experiments, or with personal revenge, he kept his distance. Distance was required to soak in the full effect of a mass slaughter.

Magus hadn't put in an appearance, yet, and the companions couldn't make their move until they had a visual on him, or at least some better idea of where he was. Ryan had no doubt that Steel Eyes lurked somewhere close by; it was in his nature to spectate. And this operation had all the trappings of a made-for-Magus extravaganza. There was psychological as well as physical suffering on the program. Magus enjoyed nothing more than wringing the emotions of his intended victims, playing with their hopes, and force-feeding them nothing but horror.

All Ryan knew about the vast block of granite to his back was that it was highest point on the Baja before the nukecaust, and at that time there was an astronomical observatory sited on the peak. He suspected there had to be a mat-trans unit, as well. It was a likely spot for a redoubt. It was extremely isolated. It was made of impervious rock. Prior to Armageddon, it was ten thousand feet above sea level, and it had a whitecoat installation already in place.

No way would Magus undertake a dangerous and unpredictable sea voyage to get here. That wasn't his style. A mat-trans unit would provide him with personal transportation, and a quick exit if need be. Ryan guessed he either was on the other side of island or somewhere in the dense, dark clouds above.

Magus would reserve the ordeal and hazard of sea travel for his intended victims, to soften them up prior to their arrival.

Even though everyone on the beach was armed, even though everyone probably already suspected the worst, there was no uprising. It wasn't just due to the intimidating presence of the trainers. The recruits—and the sailors—were still clinging to the hope that they'd get something out of the deal. The hardships of the voyage had etched away some of their bluster, but having swallowed the bait whole, and though it sat like a leaking sack of poison in their guts, they were reluctant to puke it back up. Besides, it was evident that they were trapped, stuck on a lifeless piece of rock in the middle of a hostile sea. If the ex-mercies, sec men, and mutie hunters knew they'd been righteously had, they couldn't fully admit it to themselves.

On the other hand, Ryan and the companions were fully aware of their predicament. They were awaiting their window of opportunity. Counterpunching, thinking and fighting on their feet was what they did best. The only way they could get close enough to Magus to chill him was to let themselves fall into his clutches, to step into the jaws of his closing trap. He was too quick, too elusive to be caught in someone else's snare. He could only snare himself. Magus would be there to watch the jaws snap shut, to enjoy the final throes of his victims. That was guaranteed. All this effort, this orchestration, this expense would be wasted if he wasn't here to see it.

Once again Ryan checked the position of each of the companions on the beach. Everyone looked okay except for Doc.

The old man was definitely not okay.

Alone on his knees on the wet rocks, Doc faced the empty sea. He was talking a blue streak, gesturing animatedly to no one and nothing. Ryan gritted his teeth and looked away. Doc's mind, wrecked by unthinkable grief and loss, ripped from its own Victorian element, dragged through the hell of Deathlands, always teetered just on the edge of madness. It only took a nudge to send it toppling over.

Ryan stifled the powerful urge to go to his friend's side.

There was nothing he could do for him. No comfort. No repair.

Not now. Not ever.

DOC WASN'T TALKING to himself. He was praying for guidance from a God he once adored, but now by turns doubted and despised. It was measure of his internal turmoil that he had reverted to that basic core of belief. Dr. Theophilus Tanner was caught in a moral tug-of-war, a battle of mutually exclusive responsibilities and desires, one of the most difficult choices he had ever faced.

On one hand, there was the promise of seeing his beloved Jolyon and Rachel again, of watching them grow up and bloom; the promise of once more sharing a bed with his dearest Emily; of stepping back into a safer, cleaner, simpler, saner, more hopeful world; of undoing the nukecaust, the greatest tragedy in human history, and thereby saving the lives of billions upon billions of people.

On the other hand, he would be abandoning his treasured friends moments before a terrible battle, betraying them like Judas Iscariot after a vile last supper. Not for thirty pieces of silver, but for the return of his stolen life and most precious lost loves. Doc knew Ryan and the others could and would survive without him. They were arguably the best fighters in all of the hellscape. It was a question of his turning tail in a crisis, of deserting them like a coward, that stuck deep in his craw.

Doc did not doubt Bell's bonafides. The man had to be a freezie, and he had to be in the predark ultrasecret loop, otherwise he couldn't have known about Emily or the children, or any of the details of Operation Chronos. Bell even knew the name of the whitecoat bastard who supervised his abduction and torture—Dr. Herman Welles.

While Doc, Bell and Kirby sat on the beach, waiting for their supper, the freezies had carefully explained the crucial elements of their theory of supra-time/space, which defined existence as an infinite number of simultaneously unfolding, parallel chronologies or time lines, untold possibilities and permutations existing side by side, but hidden from one another.

According to the hypotheses of s-t/s, if Doc returned to his original time line at the precise moment of his departure, it would start a new unfolding, with its own, self-driven, evolving consequences. The Deathlands experience would remain in his memory, but Death-lands itself would cease to exist because Doc was no longer part of it—such was the prison of human perception. We each see ourselves as the center of the universe.

"Will the Deathlands time line move on without me?" he had asked the whitecoats-turned-mutie-hunt-ers. "What will happen to my companions?"

Kirby had said, "Does a tree falling in a deep forest make a sound if no one's there to hear it? The problem as stated is circular and unsolvable. There is simply no way to know."

"What if I meet myself when I return to my time? What are the consequences of such a paradox?"

"Nothing will happen because the paradox is an il-lusion of perspective," Bell had replied. "You can run into the other Tanner but you can't meet 'yourself.' You aren't the same man who was trawled against his will in November 1896—you've lived several years longer than he has. Your body consists of different molecules, arranged in a different order. You don't occupy the same space. Your perceptions are not identical. His destiny is not yours."

"I could kill him, then? With no harm to myself?"

"Perhaps you could," Kirby had said. "The theory of s-t/s also predicts that individual time lines are similar to living organisms in that they are constantly repair-ing themselves within finite limits."

When Doc had expressed concern that his friends would grieve his sudden disappearance, Kirby said that was just another tree falling with no one to hear it. In Doc's new time line the companions would never know him because he would never be trawled. He would be dust long before they were ever born. If as the result of his return, the nukecaust never happened, Deathlands would not exist. Ryan and the others would live out their lives in a lush green world, a world of relative peace and stability, thanks to him.

Doc took some comfort from that, even though he knew that the consequences of a jump back in time couldn't be predicted with any certainty. Though his mind was reeling, his scientific training had not deserted him. The vantage point of s-t/s was mathematical, imaginary, the product of time-imprisoned human brains, and, by the theory's own definition, suspect.

Infinite lines of parallel time, like guitar strings vibrating at the touch of an invisible hand.

Entire universes completely oblivious to one another, yet closer than the atoms that made up his own skin.

If Doc Tanner hadn't already seen evidence of the existence of parallel worlds with his own eyes, he never would have bought into Bell and Kirby's story. But what they proposed seemed entirely possible. A while back, he and the companions had broken bread, rattlesnake actually, with black-suited warriors from an overpopulated, doomed shadow Earth—something he chose not to mention to the freezies.

As Doc weighed his options, his lips moved and he whispered to himself. If he did nothing at all, his future was clear. He would spend the rest of his life in torment, wandering the hellscape in mourning, raging at the unfairness of his fate. No drug, no liquor existed here that could ease his pain. No frenzy of chilling or orgy of sex could still his terrible anger. He either remained in this strange, brutal world or risked all, abandoned all, to return to the peace and civility of Nebraska. To home. To his real life.

He weighed the sweat and blood he and his companions had shed over the years, the shared danger, the constant battle and hardship. He owed them everything, a debt so large it could never be repaid.

Ryan, Krysty, Mildred, Jak, and John Barrymore had kept him alive long enough to see and seize this final opportunity.

# Chapter Fourteen

"Kill it!" The thready voice of doom echoed along the narrow corridor.

As the enforcer-trainer rushed into the dank stone cell, Silam backed deeper into the hallway to avoid the possibility of being hit by flying gore.

It was culling time in the menagerie.

They already had more than enough scalies for the afternoon performance. Even though this one was exceptionally big, about six hundred pounds in its crusty stocking feet, it had to go.

In captivity, scalies ate like hell-spawned demons, and complained with equal ferocity if so much as a shovelful of food was withheld. In unscripted mortal combat they provided little in the way of action or suspense. By nature, they were pouncers. In the wild, scalies sat still for long periods of time behind cover, waiting for prey even dumber than they were to stumble past. The biggest specimens were capable of quick movement only in very short bursts, and over very short distances. In an arena where they did not have the advantage of cover or surprise, they were largely a set dressing that could be relied on to bleed profusely and die on Magus's command.

As the six-hundred-pounder did now.

With a blindingly quick upward slash of its razor sharp thumb talon, the enforcer unzipped the scalie's torso from hip point to opposite armpit. As the mutie shrieked and staggered backward, the enforcer plunged its arm deep inside the diagonal wound, clutching then crushing the still-beating heart in its fist like a ripe grapefruit. The scalie's bowels explosively released. Dead on its feet, its eyes bugging out, the slack-jawed mutie slid down the wall.

Magus turned down the corridor, leaving the enforcer to clean up the considerable mess. Overhead, in the volcanic rock ceiling, a series of rebar-grated openings let much-needed sunlight and fresh air into the subterranean maze of mutie coops.

Silam walked five strides behind his lord and master. Twelve feet away was his minimum comfort zone. Any closer and Steel Eyes's aura seemed to invade the very marrow of his bones, sucking away his energy, making it difficult for him to breathe.

Magus had a shambling, lurching gait because his right leg was a good deal shorter than his left. Muscle and bone had been more heavily trimmed on that side to remove gangrenous bits. The remnants of living flesh could only be stretched so far between the titanium struts. To keep his balance while walking, Magus had a habit of throwing his left arm in the air on every right-footed stride. He looked like a ghastly, life-size marionette animated by an unseen, spastic puppetmaster.

The island's saltwater environment had worsened Magus's range of motion problems, stiffening his artificial knee and hip joints. The corrosive atmosphere attacked even the hardest steels, and the high humidity promoted bacterial growth and sepsis. The joins of meat to metal were particularly vulnerable to weeping sores. As a result, a lengthy and thorough cleaning was part of Magus's daily toilette.

Magus was very secretive about his bodily functions, even his eating and drinking. Silam knew he used various machines, remote robots and video cams, set up in his "play room" to perform hygienic tasks and make repairs and modifications to himself.

Silam disliked visiting any part of the island's redoubt, and had never been invited into its upper reaches. He had seen the play room, though. It was the abbatoir-cum-machine shop where Steel Eyes relentlessly searched for self-perfection. A more efficient mechanical heart. More sensitive internal gyros. A better fit between his various human and cybernetic components. All this required constant experimentation upon living subjects.

It was getting harder and harder for Silam to tell where the Magus the mechanism ended and Magus the living being began. Harder to say what, if anything, of the original creature remained.

Whether Magus was improving himself with his incessant tinkering was difficult to decide, as well. Silam was neither whitecoat nor physician; he was an artiste, a visionary. He could only judge success by the pungency of the aroma his lord and master gave off. Magus lacked the faculties to measure his own stink—his olfactory sense had been destroyed during the implantation of his chromed steel replacement eyes.

Of late Magus had been smelling particularly sickly sweet and funky, a very disturbing sign. The reek reminded Silam of his Uncle Lester on his deathbed, a man who had started out triple smart and finished up triple stupe, with shit running down the backs of his legs. It wasn't rad cancer that did him in. He had poisoned himself by accident, while working the Hammurabi grift.

Uncle Lester had made up Hammurabi years before Silam was born, on Day Seven of an eight-day jolt binge. By the time he started augering in—but before he took to plucking every hair from the left side of his head—he had drawn a highly detailed sketch of the graven idol he named Hammurabi. It had seven skull heads on long, snakey necks, heads representing Fire, Plague, Pestilence, Radiation, Mutation, Flood and Chem Rain.

It was more of a commercial than a religious revelation.

Silam's uncle took to traveling the hellscape by oxcart, showing off a homemade statue of his hideous god with its seven, bobbling skull heads, and spreading the new gospel according to Lester. To all who would listen, he made predictions of impending disaster and calamity. At night, before moving on to the next ville, he poisoned selected farm fields and wells. A process he called "Getting the buzz going."

When he circled back around three or four weeks later, the buzz was going strong. And the people still alive were primed for the bottom line: only by sacrificing valuable goods and services to Hammurabi through its chosen intermediary, Uncle Lester, could anyone hope to escape the god's wrath.

Abandoned at a tender age by a family that considered his skull shape a threat to their norm standing, Silam began riding in the back of the Hammurabi oxcart. On a daily basis, the boy witnessed the power of even the most mediocre fiction on a slow-witted, ignorant and laughably gullible audience. People were afraid of Uncle Lester because of Hammurabi, his jolt-binge fraud. That fear allowed him to separate the hicks from their gold, from their gear, and if possible, the virginities from their teenage daughters. It was an important life lesson for the narrow-shouldered, mutie-headed whelp.

Part of Lester's pitch included the retelling of stories about other farmers, traders and gaudy-keepers laid waste by the vengeful god because they refused to kick in tribute, or because they didn't kick in enough. As Silam matured to manhood, it became obvious that he was much more gifted at making up scary stories than Uncle Lester, whose generally weak line of bullshit constantly needed human intervention—poisonings, kidnappings and murders—to get and keep converts to the faith. For Silam, hands-on was always a last resort.

When Uncle Lester's health started to fail due to the all toxins he had sown in the service of his make-believe god, Silam inherited the oxcart and the pitch-man job. His descriptions of plagues of boils and burrowing mites kept his hayseed audiences itching until they bled. They cringed at his stories of invasions of rats and fleas carrying mutated diseases that ate the eyes and tongue from the inside out. They blanched at tales of midnight visitations by packs of hungry cannies and stickies.

Silam had quite a little operation going, and he knew how to control even the smartest of his victims.

"Why does god only do bad things to people?" a dirt farmer had asked him once.

"'Cause that's what gods are about, or haven't you noticed?" Silam had replied.

"I heard about a place called heaven?"

"I don't know anything about heaven. You're missing the point. The idea is to do something about the here and now. To make our lives less horrible. Which is why we sacrifice to Hammurabi."

Although the farmer backed down, the other stump pullers seemed to take what he'd said to heart. And the collection plate suffered.

Overnight the smart-mouth bastard swelled up so big he couldn't get out of bed. So big they couldn't carry him through the cabin door. Silam was two villes away when he heard that the man had actually exploded. He had let out a great belch and the open flame from a candle set him off, chilling him, his wife and one of their three kids.

A bit too much of Uncle Lester's tried and true recipe, that time.

Months later when Silam awoke from a sound sleep and saw those steel eyes looking down at him, lit by the embers of the dying campfire, he knew at once who it was. As a youngster, he had hung around gaudy back doors, listening to bragging, drunken stories of mayhem and revenge while Uncle Lester got his whistle wetted and his gopher petted. At the time, he had thought the tales about the steel-eyed half man-half machine were fables, primarily because the facts were so disjointed and contradictory. He didn't understand until he was much older that therein lay their strength and their terrible fascination. Magus personified unintelligible science and mindless human hubris. He was a living symbol of the hellscape.

In the flesh he was the scariest fucking thing Silam had ever seen.

While he lay trembling in his bedroll, Magus had informed him that he'd been watching the Hammurabi show from the shadows, and that he liked it very much. He set Silam at ease by talking at length about what he considered to be the best parts. Farm folks begging the pitchman's forgiveness and his intercession after he had poisoned them. It was too late for the fools to get religion, but not for the relatives and neighbors who had to watch them die in agony.

"I could use a brain like yours," Magus had said.

Words that had made Silam's sphincter seize up. He thought Steel Eyes intended a transplant. That turned out not to be the case. It was an offer of gainful employment. A grander, living god to serve. And he had served faithfully.

In the menagerie's next mutie coop, shiny-black, cylindrically shaped creatures scuttled through the deep piles of straw on the rock floor.

"Now, those definitely look promising," Magus said, peering through the cell's steel bars.

Silam could hear the shrill whine of the servos in his metal eyes as he focused on the two-foot-long muties.

"Catch one so I can examine it more closely," Magus told an enforcer.

Catching was the easy part. Holding on proved much more challenging. The segmented armor back-plates were as slick as snot, and there were all those scrabbling, rasping, bug legs underneath. As the baby scagworm squirmed to get free, it simultaneously hissed and shat, its blue-black jaws snapping like bolt cutters.

"Beautiful!" Magus exclaimed. Then he turned on Silam and said, "I trust you lined up some hardier norm stock for the afternoon's entertainment. The group this morning put on a truly pathetic performance. I'd rate it one star out of a possible five. The muties tore their opponents to shreds well before the final act, so there was no final act. It was all build-up and no crescendo. Very, very disappointing."

Silam knew better than to make excuses to his master, or to ever look him straight in the eye. Every time he stared into those chrome hen's eggs, he felt like he was being sucked into the pinpoint pupils, drawn down into spinning metal blades.

Lowering his top-heavy head, Silam accepted the negative criticism, even though he knew there had been nothing wrong with the previous group of norm fighters. The screams from this side of the island got very loud at times. And depending on the wind direction, Magus's blaring recorded music didn't always drown them out. Left waiting on the beach too long, their firearms already confiscated, the recruits had guessed their fates. The uniforms had had to use blasters and cudgels to drive them from their driftwood hovels and into the rowboats. It was understandable that they hadn't gotten into the joyous spirit of the morning's contest.

Understandable to him, if not to his lord.

"I'm getting bored with this diversion of yours, Silam," Magus said. "Frankly, it's not living up to its initial promise. It's all complication and no substance. It's wheel spinning. Directionless. Redundant. It has become a hollow mockery of itself. What else can you offer me?"

Not a question, but a command.

And one that Silam had anticipated. Knowing Magus's taste and attention span, he figured the army recruitment scam had just about run its course.

"Would you be interested in a grand finale, Magus?" he asked.

"Anything grand and final interests me."

"I've added an outlandish twist to the afternoon's performance," Silam said. "Something I hope you'll find appealing."

"Go on."

"I've conscripted our islander captain and crew. As you know, they are renowned throughout the hellscape as savage and determined fighters, a tightly knit band of brothers, cousins, fathers. They will do themselves great honor in the arena, you can be sure of that. And when the final act comes, it will be brother against brother, and father against son."

Steel Eyes's tie-rod-throwing laugh made Silam flinch. That clanking, grinding noise was something he could never get used to, no matter how many times he heard it. As his master rattled with glee, the spin doctor noticed a spreading wet spot on the floor between the metal strutted legs. Magus had sprung another pinhole leak in his tranny.

Rish and Jaswinder noticed the stain, as well, but said nothing. At the first crash of that unnerving laugh, they had both taken three giant steps backward. Rish buried his long, miserable face in his clipboard and resumed frantically scribbling. He was keeping track of the number of muties and their fighting capabilities, just as he had with the newly arrived recruits. The data was indispensable for staging the upcoming contests; and for developing the charts of victories and defeats, woundings and chillings he used to predict outcome probabilities. The oddsmaking was not for gambling purposes but to ensure Magus got the very best in live theater.

The entourage continued down the underground corridor, following the lurch and jerk of their master. Silam glanced into the cells and cages that lined both sides of the hall. Some of the races of captive muties had been given names by the people of Deathlands. Stickies. Scalies. Swampies. Wazls.

The menagerie's stickies were chained together at the ankles and necks, this to keep them under control at all times. As Silam passed their cell, the naked muties made soft kissing sounds at him, and sniffed through the holes in their faces where noses should have been. They showed him their needle teeth and drooled, playfully reaching out between the bars with sucker hands. Their idea of "play" was not his.

The cannon fodder scalies were unchained and caged

in same-sex pairs, squatting amid mounds of their own dung. As Magus walked by, they banged empty slop buckets against the bars. From every scalie cell came the same whine about how long it'd been since they'd been fed.

Scalies fought better hungry. As did all the others.

Starvation was a motivational tool.

The five Wazls seemed particularly agitated. The leather-winged, reptilian muties gnawed and clawed at bars of their wheeled cages, deeply scoring the metal with serrated teeth and curving black tri-talons, pausing only to unleash sawing cries of bloodlust. Their long, tapering wings had been clipped on arrival, so they could barely fly. Next to the cages lay the steel mesh nets and prod poles necessary to pacify them.

Much more subdued than the Wazls were the swampies, a race of sour, squat, hairy, blockheaded humanoid muties. Their beards and arms were still spattered with blood from the morning's fight. Crude clubs in hand, their dark, squinty eyes carefully measured their captors for a murderous bludgeoning.

There were other muties, too. Species specially imported by Magus. Species no one had ever seen before.

One was the size of a small dog with prominent fangs like a Tasmanian devil, bulging reddish eyes and a long, naked, ratlike tail. The pack of starving rat devils threw themselves at the bars of their cages, trying to wedge their bodies through the gaps to get at the spectators.

The next cell contained six norm-looking females, ages roughly thirteen to fifteen. Their mouths were gagged and securely taped shut. Their wrists were bound in front of them with more tape. They looked like virgin wraiths from some predark Nordic myth. They had long, pale blond hair woven into a thick single braid down their backs. Their porcelain-white skin revealed a faint tracery of bluish veins. Their eyelashes and eyebrows were the color of cornsilk. Pink tea roses tinted the centers of their cheeks. They wore long, gauzy white gowns, gathered under their budding breasts by belts of colorful woven rags. Staring up at him from the straw where they sat, knees drawn up to their chests, their piercingly blue eyes radiated lethal hate.

Silam had dubbed them screamies.

An obvious choice, as screams were their primary offensive weapon. Not normal screams that you could actually hear, screams that might make you cringe or shudder, but high-intensity screams that shot up into the ultrasonic. When riled, screamies rolled their eyes back in their sockets, opened their perfect pink lips, revealing black teeth, a black tongue and mouth, and cut loose in unison. The sound they made tore eardrums apart, it burst blood vessels in the eyes and nose, it disrupted heart rhythm. At close range it destroyed brains. In battle, they advanced in a solemn procession, two abreast, palms pressed tightly together, chilling like a scythe.

Though the six screamies sat muffled and gagged, they could still hum through their delicate, upturned noses. Silam knew they were humming because he found himself with a sudden splitting headache. It speared up through the roof of his mouth into his brain pan, like he had eaten something very cold too quickly. Rish groaned and shut his eyes as he, too, was stricken. Jaswinder suffered the worst of all, springing a copious nose bleed. The humming had no apparent effect on Magus or the enforcers. Only when they moved away, did Silam's pain diminish and Jaswinder's nose stop bleeding.

The last cage in the corridor was made of clear plastic and sat on a low table against the wall. To the uninformed its contents would have seemed an anticlimax.

It was full of flies.

Buzzing clouds of flies.

Inside the transparent cage was a sort of hive. The hive's foundation, all but obscured by the mass of black, hairy insects that crawled over it, was a decapitated human head, stripped of skin and flesh down to the crimson bone. The bugs paraded in and out of the nostrils, eye sockets, mouth, ears and neck stump.

They were not house flies, or horse flies or deer flies. They were muties, born of and shaped by the nukecaust. These insects both bit and stung their victims, savagely swarming and attacking anything warm-blooded. Their venom caused massive tissue swelling. After many stings, the accumulated toxins incapacitated the prey, bringing on a partial paralysis, which allowed the flies to bury their eggs in every square inch of the helpless body. The victim was still alive when four days later the larvae hatched out and ate their way to freedom. Once freed, they turned around and ate the nest.

According to Silam's running script, the flies were to be withheld until a pivotal moment in the combat, when their release would become a complicating factor and make things "even more interesting."

As showtime neared, the enforcers began stirring up the muties. They used prods and whips on stickies, scalies and swampies. They threw buckets of seawater on the Wazls and rat devils. The screamies they punched and kicked unmercifully. It was obvious they loved their work.

Silam didn't know where Magus had found the enforcers. They just appeared with him one day on the rocky beach. After years of service, there was so much about his master that remained a mystery. Magus was in the habit of disappearing for extended periods of time, months even, and then returning without warning or explanation. Sometimes he came back less aromatic and more energetic. Sometimes he came back with new servants, like the enforcers. It was entirely possible that the sweating muties had been on the island all along—the upper levels of the secret redoubt, Steel Eyes's private domain was a veritable cornucopia of predark treasures and unheard-of technology.

How Magus moved about, where he went and what he did was a puzzle that had no answer.

At corridor's end, beneath a huge, tightly grated roof opening, was a foyer of sorts. The menagerie's only exit, a pair of heavy steel double doors stood ajar. With Magus in the lead, the parade left the underground chamber, stepping onto the edge of a dish of mostly beige rock, a hundred yards in diameter. The islet on which they stood was roughly two acres of coarse-grained volcanic tuff. To their backs, framing the steel

# Get FREE BOOKS and a FREE GIFT when you play the...

# LAS VEGAS

## GAME

*Just scratch off the gold box with a coin. Then check below to see the gifts you get!*

**YES!** I have scratched off the gold box. Please send me my **2 FREE BOOKS** and **gift for which I qualify**. I understand that I am under no obligation to purchase any books as explained on the back of this card.

**366 ADL ENWS**

**166 ADL ENX4**
(GE-LV-08)

| | |
|---|---|
| | |
| FIRST NAME | LAST NAME |

|  |
|---|
| |
| ADDRESS |

| | |
|---|---|
| | |
| APT.# | CITY |

| | |
|---|---|
| | |
| STATE/PROV. | ZIP/POSTAL CODE |

| 7 | 7 | 7 | Worth TWO FREE BOOKS plus a BONUS Mystery Gift! |
|---|---|---|---|
| 🍒 | 🍒 | 🍒 | Worth TWO FREE BOOKS! |
| 🔔 | 🔔 | ♣ | TRY AGAIN! |

Offer limited to one per household and not valid to current subscribers of Gold Eagle® books. All orders subject to approval. Please allow 4 to 6 weeks for delivery.

**Your Privacy -** Worldwide Library is committed to protecting your privacy. Our privacy policy is available online at www.eHarlequin.com or upon request from the Gold Eagle

## BUSINESS REPLY MAIL
FIRST-CLASS MAIL    PERMIT NO. 717    BUFFALO, NY

POSTAGE WILL BE PAID BY ADDRESSEE

**GOLD EAGLE READER SERVICE**
**3010 WALDEN AVE**
**PO BOX 1867**
**BUFFALO NY 14240-9952**

NO POSTAGE
NECESSARY
IF MAILED
IN THE
UNITED STATES

doors, was a low, broad cone of solidified volcanic
ejecta.

Nothing grew in the wind-sculpted bowl. The natural
arena was surrounded by a flat, gray sea, and overlooked
by the towering mass of granite, some 150 yards away.

The islet was a sacrificial altar.

No place to run.

No place to hide.

High in the island's sheer cliff face, weak sunshine
reflected off a rectangle of glass—the window of
Magus's private sky box.

Here and there the islet's porous rock was stained
black from the blood that had soaked into it. The enforcers had already collected the edged weapons dropped
during the morning's show, but were still cleaning up
the wide scatter of body parts, gathering them up and
tossing them as far as they could toward the granite island, into the smooth sea.

By spinning, discus-thrower style, they could chuck
an arm or a leg a very long way.

The distant splashdowns were met with huge boils,
eight or ten feet across, with exposed back fins and
gaping maws. Between the volcanic cone and the island
was a reef of lava. The monstrous residents of its submerged caves and grottoes were rising up to fight over
the spoils of battle.

Magus smiled at the sight.

Silam averted his eyes—not from the gorging fish,
but from his master's face. Even from an oblique side
view, that grin of white bone and metal, of stainless guy
wires and Teflon rivet holes, of slowly dying human

flesh, was a thousand times more horrid than the grotesque spectacle that had inspired it.

As Magus limped around the perimeter of the shallow arena, the spin doctor feverishly flipped through the odds sheets, then dictated the entertainment's final details to his little lackey. Event schedule clutched in a tiny hand, Rish turned back for the underground menagerie. It was his job to see that the program was followed to the letter.

Circling the rim of the dish at a trot, Silam joined Magus at the waterline, where a row-boat waited. A pair of enforcers held it steady while Steel Eyes got in and took a seat on the stern. After Silam braced himself in the bow, the enforcers pushed off and began to stroke for the far shore, and the southerly flank of Devil's Peak.

There wasn't enough sun for Silam to make out the pale spine of the reef, bracketed by plunging depths on either side, but he could see the mass of dark purplish shapes hanging in the water just above it.

Attracted by the rhythmic splash of oars, the dark shapes rushed toward them. Mutated dog-toothed pargo, two hundred pounders, peered up at Silam through a foot or two of water, their canine fangs long, straight and pointed, like killing dirks. Dozens of broad backs rolled in front of the boat, the orange-red skin showing through the thick, hornlike plates of scale. The inshore predators began jostling the boat with their backs, bumping into it as the enforcers rowed harder. But for the scrape of scales and back fins against the hull, it was like riding through a whirling, spinning current. For the fish it wasn't a game. They were trying to tip over the craft and have at the passengers.

The giant pargo bumped them all the way to the shallows. The mass of wide purple backs only turned away when they stepped out of reach onto the narrow, rocky shore.

With Magus in the lead, they walked along the foot of the precipitous cliff. A cleft had been cut or blasted into one of the perpendicular granite buttresses. The nook was angled so it could not be seen from the water. It concealed a doorway made of dull, gray metal.

The enforcers blocked Silam's view as Magus did something to a keypad set in the door frame. Something clanked, then the predark door slid back with a whoosh.

Steel Eyes limped into the mountain. The enforcers did not follow, but stepped aside to let Silam pass.

He entered the elevator after Magus, his knees suddenly weak, his heart racing up under his chin. When the door whirred closed, a crushing sense of doom descended upon him. The car was just ten by eight. No windows. No air. No headroom. Just Magus, at arm's length. As the elevator started up with a jerk, he pressed his back hard against the wall, fighting down towering and familiar waves of panic.

Steel Eyes was not a creature he could kill, nor raise a hand to. He was afraid even thinking that thought that Magus would sense it somehow and strike him down. As the car rocketed upward, the poet laureate frantically rationalized the urge he felt to prostrate himself, to grovel facedown in the tranny drip. He didn't want to die. He didn't want Magus to vivisect him, to laugh that

awful grinding laugh while he peeled back the layers
of skin and muscle and fat, yarding out his intestines,
playing pitty-pat with his beating heart. Magus could
not be battled or bartered with, what he wanted he simply took.

In this confined setting, the ten-by-eight vanadium
steel box, with no one to see or hear, their true relationship was revealed.

Silam was in control of nothing, he understood
nothing. Ego gone. Intelligence gone. Spine gone. That
Magus had one day "discovered" him was base self-flat-
tery, and more bad fiction.

Steel Eyes had turned him out.

# Chapter Fifteen

Dr. Antoine Kirby rechecked the mag in his M-16. It was a nervous habit he'd picked up. Too many fire-fights in too many hellholes had left him with the persistent, nagging feeling that every mag was a bullet or two light, no matter what the round counter said.

Bell noted the dropped clip with a smirk. It faded as quickly as it appeared. Under other circumstances, he would have given his partner grief about the tic, asking him if he was really sure he was topped off, asking him if a round-counter would lie, and if so, why; asking if he wanted to maybe swap mags. From the colonel's dead silence, he was plenty anxious, too.

And with good reason.

Two-thirds of their escape route was exposed to up-angled fire. The rope-railed path up the cliffside was long, narrow, steep as hell, with a sheer drop-off to the beach, and had more than a dozen tight switchbacks to navigate. If Doc Tanner didn't come along under his own power, they were going to have to coldcock him and drag him by his bootheels. Either way, unless they got a big jump on their adversaries, they were in trouble.

The freezies' main advantage was surprise, no one would expect them to bolt in a vertical direction. That and the fact that they more or less knew where they were going.

Because Kirby and Bell's redoubt had not been looted and ransacked, they had access to vast amounts of predark information, both inside and outside its strategic confines. Its surviving computer banks allowed them to identify other undestroyed redoubts in the global system, and to remotely monitor their mat-trans activity and ambient power levels. Redoubt linkage and communication had been critical to the reestablishment of social and political order, postholocaust. Order that had never come.

After following Doc and his companions to Morro Bay, and learning the direction of the voyage was south, they had a good idea where they were headed. They already had confirmation that the Devil's Peak redoubt was operational and that its advanced cyber and mat-trans systems were in use. It was also the only functioning facility within range of a three- to four-day sail.

By a strange quirk of fate, Kirby had actually visited the site once before, during a visit home to California while he was on semester break from Princeton. Some mathematician colleagues of his at the University of Mexico who worked at the National Astronomic Observatory had invited him up to the summit to have a look through the installation's 2.1 meter telescope. Before the nukecaust, the remote Baja mountaintop was the second-best viewing spot in the world, after the Mauna Kea Observatory in Hawaii.

Outside the computers of their redoubt, the freezies' main source of information was gossip and rumor gathered along the hellscape's overland trade routes. There was a certain, undeniable consistency to some of the stories about Magus. Steel Eyes was reported to have appeared in a variety of places separated by long distances, distances impossible to span even by wag if the dates were even close to being correct. From this, Kirby and Bell had guessed that the companions weren't the only ones using the mat-trans system.

There was other gossip, as well, widespread rumors of Magus's time traveling, of his popping back and forth between the aeons to steal whatever material or weapons or slaves he fancied.

Kirby and Bell had dismissed this tale out of hand, based on their s-t/s models. Their computer simulations had shown the first jump, or trawl, of an individual caused a slight degradation in the time line's fundamental structure. The second jump initiated catastrophic anomalies. Because Kirby and Bell couldn't risk creating a mirror image catastrophe, they had used cryosleep to reach Deathlands. Their first time jump—to the past—would be their last, with a minimal disruption to the time stream, at least theoretically.

They did not dare return to the year 2001, or anywhere near their own era. Their conclusions about the laws of s-t/s were derived from a model and therefore not one hundred percent certain. While ninety-five percent reliability was close enough for science, this wasn't an experiment that could be repeated over and over, this was the whole ball of wax. If they had somehow miscalculated, dropped a decimal point, added instead of subtracted, failed to convert from metric, that one-in-twenty chance of being wrong could come back to kick them and the hope of humankind in the ass. Forever.

Because of the unacceptable consequences of failure, Kirby and Bell planned to enter Tanner's newly unfolding time line a century after 2001, roughly the same year as in Deathlands. The hundred-year delay would give Bell's children a chance to grow up no matter what happened, and it would give science a chance to prepare itself for their arrival, and any potential unforeseen consequences.

To this end they had prepared a special blast-proof, heat-proof, radiation-proof capsule for Tanner to take with him. The inch-and-a-quarter-long canister, worn on a neck chain, was not to be opened until the year 1997, before the time-trawling experiments began, and then only by Operation Chronos whitecoats. The freezies had decided not to use computer technology for their vital message to the new past. CD-ROM disks or tape minicassettes or memory chips were too easily damaged and the information lost. They had chosen microfilm, a universal, optically based, hard technology, primitive but virtually foolproof. On the tiny strip of film were details of their work, of the fledgling Chronos technology, of the consequences unregulated time-trawling had wrought, and their planned reappearance down the time stream.

Some of those consequences they had purposefully kept back from Tanner. According to their s-t/s model, a third jump by the same person in the same time line would literally vibrate that string of existence apart.

After Doc Tanner made the next jump, Deathlands would suddenly and violently cease to exist; not just from his perspective—from all perspectives. There would be no sound of a tree falling after he departed because there would be no tree, and nowhere for it to land.

The sound of a heated argument down the beach made Kirby, Bell and Tanner turn and look. The trainers and uniforms had surrounded a small group of recruits against the base of the cliff. What was being said was impossible to make out. Too many people were shouting at once. Then the uniforms took point-blank aim at the recruits' heads and reluctantly, angrily, they started to hand over their blasters.

The rest of recruits got their backs up in a hurry.

"What the blazes is this about?" one guy demanded.

"You can all keep your blades," the captain of the uniforms told them, "but the blasters stay here until after the training exercise. It's part of the drill. They'll be safe. You'll get 'em back."

"Like fucking hell…" the man countered.

There were shouts of defiance up and down the beach. In Deathlands, blasters were the last thing surrendered and the first thing reached for in a pinch. A violent confrontation seemed imminent.

"It's time to go, Tanner," Bell told the old man. "While they're busy with the others…"

Doc slowly rose to his feet. One by one, he looked to his old friends. Jak, the fearless wild child. Mildred, his colleague, his critic, his intellectual equal. John Barrymore, ever dependable and stalwart. Krysty, her beauty and fighting spirit like a blinding beacon. And

Ryan Cawdor, dear Ryan, a hero for the worst of times, the new Dark Ages. None of the companions looked back at him, their attention was on the scuffle and impending shoot-out. It was almost as if he had already gone. As if he had already been forgotten.

"Please forgive me, dear friends," Doc said, "but this intolerable heartache must finally end..." It was an apology they could not hear. Although Doc shed no tears at the one-sided farewell, his throat felt as if it had been pierced through sideways by a dagger.

"Now!" Bell growled in his ear.

With Tanner sandwiched in the middle, the trio ran for the cliff path, then dashed up the grade. The path was only a yard wide and the footing was slick from dripping water. Without the rope to hang on to and to pull on, speed climbing would have been impossible. The braided rail ran along the right-hand side of the zigzag track, passing through stanchion posts on the trail's outside edge and steel rings hammered into the rock on the cliff side.

"Run, you bastard!" Kirby exhorted Doc from behind. "Run as hard as you can!"

Doc groaned from the effort, his long legs driving, boot soles sliding under him. He yanked on the rope with one hand and with the other clutched his ebony walking stick.

Autofire clattered briefly from below, but no bullets spanged into the rock. The shooting was aimed elsewhere. They kept climbing, rounding the switchbacks, moving ever upward.

Two hundred feet above the beach, Kirby glanced

over the sheer edge and saw a pair of enforcers running full-tilt from the pier.

"They're on to us!" Kirby shouted.

A second after he spoke, a rain of bullets clipped the rock face above them, shattering, sparking and puffing granite dust.

"Shit! Shit!" Bell cried, still going for broke. With no cover and no place to hide, they had no choice.

After a pause, more autofire hammered the cliff face, pelting them with rock shards. The uniforms were aiming at the path above them, trying to turn them back or make them stop.

"We've got to get higher," Kirby gasped. "Higher!"

At a certain point the elevation would start to work in their favor. Unless the shooters jumped into boats and rowed offshore, they could only back up as far as the end of the short pier; after that they would lose their shot angle. The outer edge of the path would shield their targets from direct fire.

Bullets were not the only problem, though.

From the path below came the sound of rhythmic baritone grunting and heavy, scrambling feet.

The rope jerked back hard through Kirby's hand, snapping taut against the stanchion rings. The trainers were already catching up and the cloud bank that concealed the mountaintop was still far above them.

"Gotta stop them!" the mathematician cried. "Keep going! Keep going!" Kneeling at the point of a switchback, he flipped the M-16's fire select to full-auto. He didn't have to wait long.

The first of the two trainers rampaged up the grade

toward him, pulling on the rope with both hands. Kirby put the sights on center chest and let it rip. The autorifle's butt surged against his shoulder as he poured half a mag of tumblers into his target.

Every bullet hit the ten-ring but the mutie didn't stop. It didn't even slow down.

Doc stepped behind Kirby, put a steadying hand on his shoulder, then cut loose with the LeMat's blue whistler barrel, aiming for the head. A split second before he pulled the trigger, the creature turned away, averting and thus protecting its eyes. The heavy pistol boomed and flashed, loosing its load of hot metal scrap. The trainer lunged through the plume of black-powder smoke, one side of its face torn to shreds, the skin scraped off to the bone.

"Sweet Jesus!" Kirby moaned, then he shoved Doc ahead of him, up the grade.

They ran past Bell who had already unsheathed his blade and stood with one hand gripping the rope.

The rail jerked taut, singing from the strain as six hundred pounds pulled on it.

"Go on! Do it!" the black man cried. "Do it!"

When the rope snapped tight again, Bell struck and the heavy blade parted it cleanly, in a single slash. With a hiss, the severed rail shot back through the stanchion rings and vanished around the turn below. They heard the sound of massive bodies sliding, scrabbling. Then silence.

There was no time to make sure what had happened. At once the uniforms opened fire again, and a delaying action was no longer on their agenda. They were shooting to kill this time. With slugs sparking all around them, the trio struggled upward, through the maelstrom. Just when doom seemed inevitable, the howl of auto-fire dwindled to a few intermittent pot shots. Glancing over the side of the cliff, they could see the uniforms retreating on a dead run to the pier to try to flatten out their sight angle.

It was all the break Kirby, Bell and Doc needed.

Pushing even harder, they drove themselves up the slick grade, around the last two switchbacks and into the impenetrable cloud bank. The swirling gray mist was ice cold and there was so much water vapor it was difficult to breathe. It was so dark they couldn't see four feet in front of their faces.

# Chapter Sixteen

Ryan Cawdor leaned back against a beach log, his arms crossed, the heavy barrel of the scoped Steyr resting in the notch of a stripped branch within inches of his hand. He was relieved to see that Doc seemed to have recovered his senses. He was no longer babbling to himself or making emphatic gestures in the air. The black and white mutie hunters were hovering around him in a way that did concern him, though. They had definitely taken a keen interest in the old man, for unknown reasons.

As he watched the hunters speaking earnestly to Doc, Ryan caught a rush of movement out of the corner of his eye. Working as a strike team, the trainers and uniforms confronted and isolated a small group of recruits standing nearer to the cliff.

The uniforms demanded the men give up their blasters.

An immediate shouting match ensued.

From what Ryan gathered, it was the beginning of a blaster by blaster confiscation campaign. Every recruit on the beach was to be disarmed before the first phase of training started. The initial bunch of surrenderees had no choice in the matter; the uniforms had the drop on them. They handed over their weapons while glaring into the flash-hiders of a dozen shouldered assault rifles.

Everyone else in the camp was forewarned by this, and blasters came out all around.

Ryan stood, SIG in fist, with the others.

The odds were tilted in the favor of the recruits, who numbered about seventy in all, versus thirty uniforms and now eight trainers—a couple more of the sweating muties had popped out of the woodwork when their backs were turned.

With their blasters at the ready, the recruits grimly faced down the uniforms and the trainers. They weren't going to give up their weapons without a fight.

The uniform captain stepped forward and assured everyone the confiscation was only temporary. That as soon as the hand-to-hand training was completed, they could have their blasters back. He said everyone could keep their blades.

Of course he didn't make a single sale.

The standoff continued.

"Everybody has to play by the rules here," the officer told the crowd. "And the rules say the blasters stay behind this afternoon."

"Nobody takes my piece," crowed a grizzled ex-mercie. His long, tattered black overcoat flapping around his shins, he waved a worn Soviet TT33 Tokarev in the air like it was Excalibur.

It wasn't a gun worth dying for in Ryan's opinion. The Soviet ammo was nuking hard to find in Deathlands. And even if the blaster had been converted to the widely available 9 mm, it still had clumsy feel in the hand, not to mention the problem of the barrel bushing wearing out.

"You want to eat again?" the captain demanded of the mercie. "Or do you want to starve?"

The grizzled man never got a chance to answer.

Ryan missed the officer's hand signal, but there had to have been one because five of the uniforms opened fire simultaneously. The full-auto impacts lifted the guy off his feet and sat him down five feet away, his chest so riddled with holes it looked like a cheese grater. The uniforms didn't stop there. This was supposed to be an object lesson. They kept on firing, hosing down the men who'd been unlucky enough to be standing close. Three other recruits got caught in the ravening onslaught. Chopped down before they could return fire, they followed the grizzled guy on the last train west.

The trainers surged forward and seemingly without effort, batted random ex-sec men and mercies off their feet. The muties loomed over their fallen victims, amber talons exposed, ready for gutting. But they stopped without drawing blood.

Because the attacks were so tightly focused on a few and over so quickly, the recruits didn't respond with answering fire. Instead, most moved to whatever cover they could find.

Ryan had his SIG pointed at the captain's head as the man spoke again.

"Get this straight," he shouted. "Neither you nor your blasters are going anywhere. You're stuck on this pile of rock in the middle of hell. If you want to get off, if you want to get back to the world still breathing, you've got to play by the rules."

Although the recruits grumbled and cursed, there was no denying what he said made sense. Taking over the camp, even if they could do it, wasn't the answer. Most would never survive the battle, let alone make it off the island. If the ship's crew died in the fight, they'd be stuck here without food.

It wasn't trust in the wisdom and honor of the uniform captain that made the recruits relent and start giving up their precious blasters. It was submission to circumstance, a situation temporarily out of their control. Things could always change.

Intent on keeping his blasters as long as possible, Ryan slung the Steyr and slipped to the back of the pack, near the waterline. The other companions did the same. J.B. looked over at him and shook his head, the barrel of his M-4000 shotgun cradled in the crook of his arm. It was a bad scene. Risk piled on risk.

Like it or not, they couldn't make their move—yet. A major gunbattle would spook Magus for sure. They had to get close, inside his guard, before they showed their cards.

It was a typical Magus production. Just when you thought things couldn't get worse, they did. And by then it was too late to retreat. As Ryan watched the uniforms take the recruits' weapons, his scalp began to crawl and prickle. He sensed an impending, out-of-control crescendo. He felt the companions' vulnerability and his own.

The trap's jaws were already snapping shut.

Like a wet dog, he shook off the doubt and the name-less, faceless dread. Seize the small moment and forget everything else—that was the one sure path to victory. The companions were as skilled with edged weapons as they were with blasters. Losing their blasters was a setback, but not a fatal one.

At blasterpoint, the recruits lined up and yielded their sidearms to a couple of uniforms who carried them to one of the barracks' rooms. Another pair of uniforms frisked their clothes to make sure they weren't hiding anything. Disarmament was moving right along when a sudden shout brought things to a halt.

As Ryan turned toward the noise, the uniforms sent a clattering volley of autofire at the cliff above. Sparks and puffs of dust erupted along the rope-railed path, thirty-five feet above the heads of three sprinting men. Ryan was shocked to see Doc among the deserters. He was running at top speed between the two mutie hunt-ers, up the steep grade.

And it didn't look like Doc was being kidnapped. He was moving under his own power. There wasn't a blaster stuck in his back. It looked like he was ducking out, bailing on the companions, which was the last thing Ryan ever expected.

To Ryan's left, Jak reacted instinctively. That the uniforms' bullets were landing laughingly wide of the mark didn't have time to penetrate his consciousness. All he knew was that his friend was in jeopardy. He swung up his .357 Magnum Colt Python, prepared to put an end to the uniforms' turkey shoot, but was shoved from behind by a trainer before he could fire. The albino's feet left the ground and he went flying headfirst into the barracks' stone wall.

The uniforms abruptly stopped firing as two trainers started hauling themselves up the cliff path in pursuit of the deserters. The smoking muzzles of the assault rifles were aimed at Jak as he pushed up from his knees, blood smearing his teeth and chin.

Jak gave up his sidearm, butt first, but the look in his red eyes said murder.

The trainers could really move. Using both hands on the rope and driving with their massive legs, they rapidly closed on their quarry.

Realizing he was about to be overrun from behind, the black mutie hunter knelt and opened fire with his M-16. The range was no more than forty feet. He couldn't have missed if he'd tried. Then Doc followed up with a blast from the LeMat's scattergun barrel. The combined bullets and shrap had no effect. The trainers absorbed the punishment and kept on coming.

Doc and the black man turned and ran, rounding the uphill bend and slipping past the white mutie hunter who stood poised with knife in hand.

Ryan could see the way the rope jerked every time the trainers yanked on it. They were pulling with their full weight. It didn't surprise him when the mutie hunter cut the rope. It was exactly what he would have done.

Still holding on to the slack and useless rope, the trainers lost their footing and fell backward, off the edge of the path. They tumbled down the cliff, like two very ugly, very large rag dolls. One trainer managed to grab the lip of the trail as he flew past. He clung to it with a taloned hand, swinging and kicking his legs, trying to get a grip on the rock with the other hand.

The recruits on the beach sent up a cheer as the other trainer cartwheeled to earth. It landed on its back on the rocks with an awful thud. Immediately, it began to stir its legs and arms which put an end to the celebration.

Cheers were replaced by gasps of astonishment and dismay. The straight drop had been almost two hundred feet. If trainers could survive that kind of fall, they were virtually unkillable.

Quivering from head to foot, blood pouring from its open maw, the trainer managed to get to its feet. It took one step then staggered and pitched forward onto its face, stone dead.

Ryan unslung the Steyr and flipped up the scope caps. As he shouldered the longblaster, he dropped the safety. Cheek pressed against stock's rest, he acquired the target, then compensated for the up-angle bullet rise by holding a good foot and a half low.

From behind someone shouted at him to stop. Before anyone could intervene Ryan touched off a round. The rifle barked and bucked.

He already knew where the creature's weak point wasn't, so he hadn't aimed for the head or chest.

Riding the recoil wave, Ryan reacquired sight picture in time to see the trainer's lone supporting hand blur in a puff of red gore and gray rock dust.

Maybe he couldn't chill it with a single bullet, but he could sure as hell make it let go.

Grip broken, the trainer dropped. It was a thirty-foot straight fall to next level of path. The creature landed with its feet half on, half off the trail. It flailed its arms, but it couldn't keep its balance. The trainer fell over backward, falling down the cliff face. It landed square on its head, which promptly disappeared between its shoulderblades, skull and neck pounded into its torso by three hundred pounds of pile driver.

That one didn't get up.

The uniforms immediately poured a torrent of lead on the escapees, trying to cut them down before they reached the cover of the cloud bank. Their firing angle was getting close to vertical; their targets barely visible along the edge of the path.

A hand gripped the Steyr's barrel and jerked the weapon to the side. Ryan stared nose to nose with the uniform captain.

"I'll take the longblaster," the officer said.

"Sure you will," Ryan said. "You probably want this one, too."

The captain glanced down and saw the SIG's muzzle aimed at his heart. Then he looked up at the one-eyed man's fierce smile. Ryan had to give the guy credit, he hardly flinched.

As Ryan relinquished his blasters, the firing squad broke ranks and started running for the pier. They had lost their shooting angle and were trying to get it back before the AWOL recruits escaped into the clouds.

Meanwhile, another trainer had started up the treacherous cliff path. Without the rope to pull on, its progress was slow and intermittent. It slipped and scrambled on the slope of wet rock, falling to its knees, getting up, falling again.

After a couple of minutes of steady clatter, the auto-fire from the pier stopped. From the sour expressions on the uniforms' faces, Tanner and the other two deserters had gotten away.

Ryan was relieved that Doc had made it. He had no idea what was going on in that scrambled brain, whether the old bastard had gone delusional as he had on other notable occasions, thinking he was back in Victorian times, addressing his peers in the Royal Academy of Science, or some such crap. It was also possible that with the help of the mutie hunters Doc had come up with a plan to flush out and chill Magus.

Shit, anything was possible.

The uniforms started sweeping the beach, herding the recruits at blasterpoint back onto the pier and into eight waiting rowboats. The boats were crewed by the recruits and commanded by the trainers. As Ryan stepped into his boat, he looked at the faces of the other conscripted rowers. Haggard, dirty, exhausted. But above all, afraid. Every step they had taken since leaving Morro Bay was a step farther from safety, and deeper into a bottomless pit. Only the islanders held their heads high. There was no fear in their eyes, just cold seething anger.

Mildred, Krysty and J.B. weren't afraid, either. But they were disconcerted and even hurt by Doc's abandoning them, as he was. As Ryan took a seat beside Jak on the thwart, he could see that the albino was troubled over the loss, too.

The trainer stamped his foot on the gunwhale and made a motion with both arms. Universal sign language: get rowing.

As they pulled away from the picr, uniforms in four other boats tagged alongside, keeping guard.

"Doc gone," Jak said in a hushed tone. His lip was split and swollen from the slamming he'd taken. "Two mutie hunters followed from Vegas pie shop to coast."

Ryan gave him a hard look. "But that means—"

Jak didn't let him finish. "Yeah, means used same gateway we did. Been after Doc long time."

"You're right. I saw they way they were hanging around him. Doc's been a popular guy lately. Question is, what do these guys want?"

"And why he go along?"

The two men rowed in silence for a while, falling into the rhythm of the work, watching the bleak landscape glide past as they angled toward the cove's eastern point.

"Doc no coward," Jak said at last. A statement of hard fact.

"I know that," Ryan said. "We all know that. He's proved it to us over and over again. He had to have had a good reason for taking off that way."

"Mutie hunters tricked him?"

"Maybe. He was acting funny after we got off the ship."

"Doc no triple stupe."

That, too, was true.

Living in Deathlands a person either acquired a feel for picking out the bullshitters and the con artists, or he or she didn't live past age ten. It was guaranteed that every third human being you came across was going to be some variety of shit hook, hell-bent after your blaster, your jack, your jolt, or the hole in your ass. Surviving to breeding age wasn't a question of smarts; it was a question of gullibility.

"Scrub mission?" Jak asked.

"No way," Ryan said, leaning into his oar. "We don't even know where he went."

"Top of mountain."

"Maybe. And maybe there's a gateway up there and he's already long gone. Without blasters we can't follow him and find out. The uniforms would cut us down, or the enforcers would catch us. We're going to do this training, whatever the hell it is, and hope to get our shot at Magus before it's over. If we live through all that, we'll see about catching up with Doc."

Under the leaden, oppressive sky, the flotilla of small boats steadily worked its way around the island. Ryan was sweating from the effort, but not as much as the trainer who just sat there on the stern, looking ugly and smelling like new fallen chem rain. At the extreme eastern tip of the island there was no beach. The sea lapped up against a vertical wall of rock, four hundred feet of it without so much as a fingerhold. As they rounded the corner, another, much smaller island came into view.

A flat, buff-colored plate of volcanic rock. Topped at its southern end by a low cinder cone. Not a twig, not a blade of grass grew on it.

The training ground, Ryan had no doubt.

He looked up at the larger island, which loomed above the islet like a skyscraper. Its back side was even more sheer than the front. There was no path, no rope rail up its face. No dwellings along its narrow beach, just wag-size boulders of fallen granite.

As they approached the islet's shallow northern shore, the uniforms and trainers ordered their crews to run the bows of the boats up onto the rock shelf. This done, the uniforms forced the recruits out of the boats and onto the shore. Ryan and Jak jumped down and moved closer to Mildred, Krysty, and J.B. Without a word of explanation, all the boats were relaunched, stranding the recruits. The uniforms rowed the trainers away, stopping about fifty yards off the beach. Because they were in the big island's lee, the boats didn't drift after the oars were shipped. They just hung there, dead still on the flat gray sea.

The uniform captain stood on the bow of his boat and shouted across the water through cupped hands. "There are weapons waiting for you over the rise. Help yourselves!"

There was no headlong rush to do that. The ex-mercies and sec men hung back, wary of what might be waiting unseen on the other side.

The companions and the islanders took the initiative. Astride the lip of the shallow bowl, they looked down on a big pile of edged weapons had been dumped there.

Ryan recognized some of the bayonets: AK-47, L1A1/F, M5-A1. But there were much older ones, too, designed for turn-of-the-twentieth century Mauser and Enfield bolt guns. They were like short swords, handguards and all.

Most of the other stuff was flashy crap meant to hang on a wall. Nothing you'd ever want to bet your life on: a Khyber knife, the base of its wide blade chipped out at the choil; sword canes with bent and hand-re-straightened double edged blades, absent their scab-bards; nicked cheapie Tanto knives and Bowies; thirty-five-inch-long, Calcutta-reproduction 1860 Ca-valry sabers with ten-karat-gold-plated handguards. There was even a tomahawk/peace pipe with a triangu-lar splitting point.

Except for the collection of sledge hammers, hand axes and splitting mauls, it looked like an import cut-lery house's garbage bin on pickup day.

The companions and islanders without edged wea-pons, or those who wanted bigger ones, started rooting through the pile.

Eng and his crew went for the sabers. The weapons were bloody and sticky, their edges nicked by impacts on bone and rock. The islanders didn't seem to care. A yard of steel was a big selling point. They carried their swords back to the sea and carefully rinsed off the gore.

Ryan was surprised when J.B. beelined for the toma-hawk. He took a couple of practice swipes with it, look-ing very pleased with himself. Ryan had to admit, the pointy end was triple wicked. Krysty and Mildred picked up the circa 1900 bayonets, excellent choices because the blades were respectively fifteen-and-a-half and seventeen-inches long, and made of high-quality, tempered steel. Jak tested the eight-inch blade of the AK bayonet on the ball of his thumb. Satisfied with its edge, he tucked it away.

The companions stared across the bowl at the cinder

cone on the opposite side. Smack dab in the middle of it was a pair of steel doors.

"The volcano's dead," Mildred said. "That's the good news."

"The bad news is," J.B. went on, "the only 'training' we're going to get is in how to die."

Ryan turned toward the big island. He drew his panga from its leg sheath and pointed. "Up there," he said. "Magus is watching. You can be sure of that."

On cue, the sepulchral music boomed down on them from the island's cloudy heights. A raging, funereal storm of strings, brass and drums. Ryan didn't recognize the piece, but Mildred did.

"Wagner, now that's original."

Nobody said how much they missed Doc at that moment.

They didn't have to.

# Chapter Seventeen

"Louder!" Magus entreated his spin doctor. "Make their fucking bones shake!"

Silam cranked the redoubt's sound system up to the max. The "Flight of the Valkyries" raged from massive speakers concealed in recesses all along the cliff face. Even inside the bosom of the mountain the thundering, rhythmic vibrations could be felt. A fine dust of rock filtered down on them, shaken loose from the sky box's chiseled granite roof.

Magus stood with his back to Silam, looking out the broad, floor-to-ceiling window. The silhouette was all lopsided, with odd angles where struts and braces supported or replaced its limbs. The half-steel head was studded with electrical inputs and hose bibs, festooned with brightly colored wires and silicon tubing filled with pink fluid. Even with the Wagner playing at top volume, Silam thought he could hear him ticking, like a box of cheap clocks.

If the bulletproof window hadn't been there, would he have risked all to step forward and give the monster a push? About four strides and a shoulder strike and the reign of terror would have been over, as would his nightmare of fear and loathing. The short answer was never. Never. Never. Never.

His paralysis had nothing to do with panic or lack of resolve; it had everything to do with status. Without Steel Eyes, Silam was just another con man/itinerant poisoner, traipsing the hellscape with a hokey statue in the back of his oxcart.

Like it or not they were joined, though not at the hip as equals. Silam was an addendum to the master, a footnote, a big-headed mole on what little remained of Magus's human backside.

Or perhaps a festering boil nestling in the hairy crack.

The propagandist accepted the relationship's precipitous downside to keep from becoming less than a boil.

Moving to the extreme edge of the window, as far from Magus as he could get and still see out, Silam gazed down upon the training ground from a lofty height. Beyond the flat patch of sea, he surveyed the spotted beige dish of rock, the recruits milling on the shore, still ignorant of what was to come, the mini-battlefield, its array of monsters hidden, waiting, ready to attack. He thrilled to a sense of godlike power.

This was what it was all about.

Thanks to Magus's patronage, his dark fantasies came to life, fantasies of revenge against a cruel world, against a cruel people. It allowed him to recast himself as dead gorgeous, dead smart, dead creative. Magus had given him an army of coldhearts and turned him loose to work his worst. Deathlands was his canvas, his marble, his ream of blank paper.

The sad truth was, Silam had only one painting in

him, one sculpture, one bit of verse. And he painted that same picture, sculpted that same statue, wrote that same epic poem over and over again. Only in his narcissistic fantasy did the work mature, evolve, outdo itself.

If Magus was aware of this, if he even cared, if it was part of his plan, there was no way of telling. Steel Eyes was inscrutable; trying to read his mind was like trying to read the mind of a wag engine. His goals, his pleasures, were never quite what they seemed. At times he appeared to be running amok; at times he seemed completely calculating.

With Magus, appearances were always deceptive.

Silam could not make out the faces of the recruits; they were a bit too far away. With his enhanced, artificial eyes, Magus didn't have that problem. He could count their missing teeth.

"My goodness!" he exclaimed. "What have we here?"

"What is it, Magus?"

"A very special guest," Steel Eyes replied. "You have outdone yourself, today, Silam."

The PR man accepted the compliment without knowing why it had been given. "In what way, Magus?"

The half-man–half-machine turned on him. Silam took a step backward and his shoulders hit the skybox wall. There was nowhere to retreat. The pinhole pupils in the chrome eggs dilated, peering deep into his soft and squishy soul.

"You don't know, do you?" Magus said.

"Know…know…know what?" Silam stammered, as panic clawed up into his throat.

"You have delivered Ryan Cawdor to me," Magus said. "Him and his companions."

"Cawdor?"

"One-Eye."

"The butcher of Willie ville!" Silam exclaimed before he could stop himself. "He's among the recruits?"

"This is a most glorious day, Silam. There will be no escape for the cyclops this time. I have him and I will crush him."

He raised his steel hand to Silam's face. It was less a hand than a motorized vise. The metal fingers closed in a tight fist, their servos whining. That inhuman grip could turn rock to powder.

"Open the gates," Magus said. "Let the games begin."

# Chapter Eighteen

J.B. cleaned his spectacles on the tail of his shirt, slipped them back on, then screwed down his fedora until it was touching the tops of his ears. He picked up the tomahawk from the ground at his feet and slipped his hand through the wrist thong. It had a nice balance. And once it started moving, it sang through the air. The handle was made of very hard wood, hollowed out its entire length. A small bowl was machined into the ax head. A replica peace pipe, tribe of origin lost in the thirty-five-hundred-degree nuke wind.

The Armorer took another whistling cut with the ax. He wouldn't be smoking tobacco with it. He'd be smoking heads.

The stains on the rock and the bloody weapons told him that whatever was coming through those twin steel doors was triple bad. That rad-blasted music made his head ache and his skin crawl. It reminded him of the carny chilling tent they had barely escaped in Bullard ville. Old Steel Eyes liked to score his slaughter fests with what Mildred called "predark, symphonic classics." He thought it was rollicking good fun to mix great oldies with great butchery. Magus was a disease, a blight on the landscape that had to be cut out and burned. J.B. gave the tomahawk a quick forehand-back-hand slash and smiled. The weapon had some real heft to it.

Skull-cracking heft.

J.B. glanced at Ryan. His old friend stood with panga in hand, relaxed, his breathing even and slow, conserving his energy. Most of the other recruits were doing just the opposite. They were yelling obscenities at the uniforms and trainers in the drifting boats, stomping around the shoreline, waving their blades, working up their shrinking courage and venting their pants-pissing, mortal fear of what was in store for the rest of the afternoon.

Like Ryan, the islanders held their own counsel and let no emotion show. The way they gathered behind their scar-faced captain, sabers poised, gave J.B. the feeling they knew exactly what they were going to do and how they were going to do it.

If Magus had a crew armed with full-auto blasters hidden behind those steel doors, the recruits were about to be mowed down, as helpless as a field of corn before a thresher. The Armorer immediately pushed that unpleasant idea out of his head. It didn't fit at all with what he knew about Steel Eyes. Most times Magus liked his entertainment to stretch on and on, for the suffering of the players to build, for his victims to die pleading for his mercy. An attack with blasters against blades would be more like a mass execution. And he could have done that on the campground beach, and saved a lot of bother.

Whatever was coming it was going to be something special.

Spectacular, but not in a good way.

And thanks to Doc, they were one man short.

Though it was difficult, J.B. refused to let himself dwell on Doc's apparent desertion. This wasn't the time or the place to waste energy getting bent out of shape over something that couldn't be changed. He tried breathing slow like Ryan, from deep down in his lungs, letting the tension ooze out through the soles of his boots.

He thought it was just starting to work when the music suddenly stopped. The echoes of string section and kettle drum died away, leaving a terrible void. No one moved as the long silence dragged on, no one spoke as they waited for the ax to fall.

When the steel doors banged back, the music started up again, from the beginning. A shrieking fanfare of Valkryies.

J.B. squinted hard, trying to see inside the shadowy opening.

Dark brown, long-necked, featherless creatures burst through the doorway. They leaped into the air, their seven-foot-long wings flapping.

Wazls. Full-grown Wazls. Five of them.

A shudder rippled through the massed recruits.

Half gator, half condor, Wazls usually dropped out of the night sky like precision-guided bombs upon the unsuspecting, the slow, the sleepy. Though they preferred to hunt after sundown, when starved they took their meat any time they could find it.

Dark night had become dark day. Their blood curdling screams ripped through the intertwining layers of Wagner like a rusty knife.

Instinctively, the fighters closed ranks as the Wazls struggled to gain altitude. After climbing to about fifteen feet above the ground, they began to circle around and around the islet.

J.B. saw the ragged rents in their wing leather, crude mutilations that prevented the lizard birds from flying higher. Normally they would have used their seventeen-foot wing spans to catch the thermals off the cliff face of the big island, riding them, spiraling up through the cloud bank and out the other side. Like condors they were master gliders, capable of rising to impossible heights, then coasting on the wind currents for hundreds of miles.

These were landlocked Wazls, and they were not happy about it.

As they flew past, the wind they made buffeted J.B.'s face. They shifted into an attack formation, with the biggest bird in front, then three abreast, and the smallest one bringing up the rear. Their reptilian heads pivoted on their long necks as they sized up their prey. They screamed a final warning.

Death from above.

The recruits screamed back. They cursed. They booed. They shook their weapons in defiance. Some threw knives, which either missed their targets or hit sideways, or were deftly plucked out of the air by the Wazls' long beaks. Flying lower, circling closer, the lizard birds dipped and darted, wheeling, snapping, clawing at the unprotected heads without actually making contact, almost in a teasing, testing way.

Under the pressure, many of the recruits withdrew

from the perimeter, moving down into the depressed center of the bowl, edging closer to the cone and its open doors.

A bad idea.

The companions and the islanders maintained their distance from the cone, ducking under the reach of the halfheartedly slashing, black tri-talons as they swept overhead.

The music stopped abruptly again, but only for a moment this time. When it restarted, booming out that same, nerve-grating introduction, a torrent of pale, two-legged forms poured from the doorway. Stickies by the dozens rushed down the shallow slope, waving their skinny arms, making the frantic kissing sounds that always signaled a mass chilling.

At that moment the Wazls attacked, diving into the fringes of the crowd, their talons outstretched.

Knives and even short swords were of little use against the lizard birds. They were too fast, too agile, and the reach of their necks and claws was too long. In their sweeping circuits of the islet, in the seemingly playful feints and mock slashes, they had picked out their victims, the easiest meals.

Not ten feet in front of J.B., the lead Wazl slammed into a sec man's back. The impact drove him to his knees, sending his blade skittering across the rock. The recruit shrieked as the talons sank into his shoulder blades, and shrieked louder as the Wazl tried to carry him off. Wings beating, it raised him a yard or so off the ground. With slashed wings, it couldn't lift him higher. Then a second bird joined the attack, sinking its claws into the man's chest. Together, the Wazls bore him up. The sec man kicked and punched to no avail. As they climbed to fifty, sixty, seventy-five feet, they fought, snapping, dodging, flapping, pulling and twisting their prize in opposite directions. If they'd had some decent leverage to work with, somewhere solid to plant their feet, they might have torn him in two, but as it was, the second bird ripped out a double helping of pectoral muscle and abandoned the rest, leaving the first bird to bear the man's full weight. The overloaded Wazl hurtled downward like a faulty parachute, then its grip slipped and the struggling sec man fell free.

The hovering bird screeched in fury as its prey plummeted onto the rocky shallows, landing with a tremendous full-length splash. The sec man didn't move after that. His head was submerged facedown, past the ears. The water around him turned cloudy red.

In the middle of the bowl, norm and stickie collided in a howling, screaming din. The muties drove an eight-abreast column into the middle of the mass of recruits. A wedge intended to split the norm force. The recruits gave ground, yielding to the pressure and then tried to flank and surround the headlong charge. The stickies' rampage was unstoppable. While the muties along the wedge's front row did battle, the ones behind jumped over their backs and onto the stunned recruits. Once a stickie grabbed hold with those sucker fingers and its adhesive secretions, it never let go. By the sheer weight of numbers, the muties pinned their foes to the ground.

The battle turned into a melee.

No field commander could have kept order. No battle plan could have survived that first head-on impact. The stickies' frenzy was such that they felt no pain. They withstood wounds to their heads, arms, torsos and kept on pressing forward, driving their wedge deeper.

The norms who were pulled down were dragged by their faces from the ranks of their own kind, dragged into the stickie fold, where the serious tearing began. Though stickies were generally of small stature and wiry build, they were hellishly strong. With their suckers and brute strength, they split open bellies, with their needle teeth they ripped out hearts in chunks. Those that disappeared under the wave of pale bodies never rose again.

The recruits answered frenzy with frenzy, stabbing, slashing and clubbing. White limbs fell severed to the ground, sucker hands, arms, legs. Blood gushed and flowed, mutie and norm, indistinguishable to the naked eye.

It was the brand of warfare practiced in the Stone Age, before the invention of body armor or battle shields. Brute bludgeoning power against brute bludgeoning power. Foes trading blows, exchanging gaping wounds. Bloodied men stumbling over the gray loops of their own spilled intestines. Stickies hacked apart with dull swords, their bodies broken, pulped by sledge hammers.

The hand-to-hand fighting pushed back and forth in the middle of the volcanic bowl, a grinding, clanking, squealing counterpoint to the awful clamor of the music.

"That bastard tin can's up there laughing at us!" Ryan shouted at J.B. "Laughing!"

"Aieeeeeee!"

At the sound of the scream they both pivoted to the right, weapons up and ready to strike.

Another Wazl had stooped, dead-falling from a height of twenty feet, and struck. Only this time the quarry was an islander. The lizard bird frantically flapped its long wings, dragging 250 pounds of violently resisting prey along the shoreline. Its black talons were buried in the flesh of the islander's tattooed shoulders, the points curving deep beneath his collar bones. The man's flesh puckered, stretching under his body weight, his bare feet scrabbled and slipped over the rocks.

"*Patu ia! Patu ia!*" the islander cried in a high, shrill voice, his eyes huge with terror and pain.

J.B. and Ryan sprang forward at the same instant, hurling themselves on the bird before it could gain any more altitude. They grabbed the long, bony, whiplike tail and held on for all they were worth, digging in their heels. As they pulled the Wazl down, Krysty, Mildred and Jak joined the fray, jumping on the wings, the back, seizing hold of whatever they could. Together, they brought the great bird crashing to earth. To properly defend itself, it had to release its victim, and when it did so, the islander rolled away, bleeding profusely from inch-wide holes in his chest and back.

The companions gave the Wazl as much mercy as it had shown its victim.

They tag-team hacked it to death.

Over and over, Krysty and Mildred thrust their long bayonets deep into its sides, searching for its vitals with double edges of cold steel. Ryan pinned its hindquarters to the ground with his body weight and plunged his panga to the hilt into its back. The bird flapped and screeched, and tried to crane its neck around and bring its wicked teeth to bear on Krysty and Mildred. Before it could do that, J.B. leaped in with the tomahawk. A two-handed, overhead swing split the flat, leather-upholstered skull like a coconut. The Wazl dropped flat to its stomach, wings outstretched and quivering, brains oozing between plates of fractured bone.

Whether it was the smell of the liberated gray matter, or some message in the dying bird's scream, the other four Wazls swarmed in. The islander who the companions had just saved, who had staggered away, clutching his grievous wounds, was their sole target. Talons raked his head and slashed the back of his neck. Moaning, he fell to his stomach and the biggest bird landed on his back, sinking its claws into his flesh. The islanders rushed forward to try to rescue their kin, but the Wazl immediately let go of their shipmate's buttocks and shifted position, lunging, snapping, keeping the attackers off balance and well out of sword range.

The poor wounded bastard was still alive, yelling at the top of his lungs when the Wazl took his head sideways in its jaws and, bearing down, crushed it like a raw egg, making the juices squirt out between its jaws. Then it started sawing with its serrated teeth. In an eyeblink the islander's headless body dropped free, blood gushing from the tattered neck stump. Gulping down its prize, the Wazl jumped into the air and flapped away.

Captain Eng bellowed in rage as the other Wazls

flirted with him, mocked him, flying just beyond the reach of his slashing saber.

LIKE THE OTHERS, Jak had to stand and watch while the Wazl chilled the helpless islander. The sailors were bunched up so tightly, trying to get their own stabs in, that there was no room for him to strike.

Then the damned thing just tore off the islander's head and flew away.

Funny how the birds could be half chilling each other over dinner one minute and fighting to avenge a fallen nestmate the next.

Avenge it, they had.

And now they were rubbing it in, flying low, swooping, making cackling noises.

The Wazls were still a problem, but Jak knew the stickies were going to have to be dealt with pretty quick. Down in the bowl, the muties were pushing the recruits in reverse, blades flashing, scuffling feet raising rock dust. Behind the blur of arms and heads, in the wake of the stickie advance was a slick carpet of red. As the battle sawed back and forth, crumpled bodies, norm and mutie, were revealed, then hidden again.

The wildness of the scene, the sounds of combat energized the albino like a double line of prime jolt. Jak felt the call to battle, big time, and there was nothing close enough to chill.

From behind came a whip crack of leather wings, a hard gust of wind, then a woman's desperate cry. It was Krysty.

A Wazl had her gripped from behind by the shoulders of her fur coat. Because she didn't weigh more than 150 pounds, the flapping bird was able to drag her away. The toes of her boots skimmed a few inches above the ground. Krysty couldn't bring her bayonet to bear. Her arms were trapped in the sleeves of her coat by the downward pull of her own body.

Ryan turned toward her a second too late, and his jump for her ankles missed by inches. He crashed flat-out onto the rocks, arms outstretched, hands clutching nothing.

Jak was even farther away. The albino wheeled, shaking a leaf-bladed knife from his sleeve. The blade found its natural place in his hand, like a steel ball rolling into a precision-drilled hole. There was no hesitation. No thought. No aiming. Jak whipped his arm forward and let the weapon fly.

The flat-black leaf blade sang through the air, curving left and diving toward its speeding target. Jak's throw arc and the Wazl's head intersected. The point slammed into its left eye, the steel thorn driven in so deeply that it almost disappeared into the socket.

Jolted by the impact, the bird dropped Krysty, who landed lightly on her feet and raced out of the way.

Less gracefully, the Wazl skidded to the ground. Flapping its wings, screaming, it shook its head this way and that, clawing at its own head, trying rid itself of the excruciating pain.

Captain Eng launched himself at the wounded bird, his saber cocked at his hip. He drove the blade into its torso with every ounce of his three hundred pounds behind it. The Wazl reared up, its wings stiffly outspread as thirty-five inches of cold steel slid into its guts.

The bird tried to claw its tormentor and found it couldn't reach him. Eng held it fast to the ground with main strength and the skewering blade. Unable to use its talons, the Wazl tried to tear his head off with its beak.

Eng dodged the rapidly weakening strikes with ease. Then he laughed and with both hands on the sword's grip twisted the curving blade. The tendons in his massively scarred forearms jumped as he cored out a deeper, far more devastating wound. Gore and intestinal contents spewed over Eng's arms and bare chest.

With the last of its strength, the night hunter drew in its leathery wings, a look of surprise in its surviving eye. That it would meet its end at the hands of a hairy, grinning earth-bound creature had to have come as a shock.

As it shuddered and died, Eng hawked and spit in its face.

Which reaffirmed Jak's belief that there was much to like about the islander captain.

# Chapter Nineteen

Rish hung well back from the cone's doorway in a small, protected alcove. The menagerie's exit was completely blocked by rolling cages full of highly agitated Wazls. The enforcers used steel mesh nets to cover the four-foot gap between the cage tops and the underside of the double doorway. This prevented the muties from reversing course and attacking the enforcers once the cage doors were flung back.

When the cages were opened, the enforcers used prod poles to encourage the birds to exit. It didn't take much prodding to get the desired result. The Wazls flapped away, onto the field of battle, screaming blue murder.

Rish marked off item number one from Silam's checklist with a savage flourish.

Even in Deathlands, at the bottom of human culture's ash bin, behind every successful, incompetent twit there was a creature such as Rish, a diligent, hardworking, unrecognized soul. Rish was no longer stunned when Silam took credit for his ideas.

"I know you won't mind if I use that" was a phrase he had come to loathe.

Of course, it wouldn't have mattered if he had minded.

All glory went to Silam. All homage went to Silam. While Rish was sucking up, salaaming to the poet laureate, what was he really thinking?

Blockhead.

Drooler.

Pompous ass.

If he had to listen to that Hammurabi story about how Silam had chiseled a dirt farmer into giving him a free ride on all his daughters one more time, he thought he was going to go berserk.

There was another side, a hidden side to Rish. He had dreams of his own. He knew he could do Silam's job because he had been doing it for months, virtually by himself. Magus's head liar was a burn-out case. And Rish knew he could do the job a million times better than Silam ever had.

Rish realized that some of his feelings of rage and bitterness were fueled by natural jealousy over his own physical shortcomings. Silam was tall. He had normal-size hands and feet. Although he had a very strange-looking forehead, Silam wasn't cursed with a face that radiated perpetual misery. Even when Rish was deliriously happy, he looked like his dog had just died.

What infuriated him most was that he was often mistaken for a western swampie, an ankle-biter, even though he was not filthy, bearded or hairy. The resemblance in stature had made him scrupulous about his toilette. He scraped his jowls twice a day and buffed his little hands until they were pink. If his arms had had more than a fine, pale down on them, he would have shaved them, too.

Rish would never be any taller, never have manly hands and feet, never be looked upon by women with anything but revulsion, but he could orchestrate mayhem with the best of them.

After the Wazls' cages had been rolled back, he waved the enforcers over to the stickies' cells. They followed his commands immediately and without question. Rish didn't even know if the enforcers could talk. If they could, they certainly never did it in the presence of a norm.

He could list what he knew about the enforcers on the fingers of one tiny hand. They hated fire. They could see perfectly in the dark. They sweated in their sleep, and they slept in big piles, like cats. Big, sweaty piles. They never seemed to eat or drink. If their race had a culture, it was locked away in their heads. They had no tools, no books, no written language. No clothes. Yet they understood and obeyed those in Magus's chain of command.

It filled Rish with a dizzying sense of power to be able to order around such terrible destructive forces. But he was no fool. He knew the limits of that power and the extent of his own vulnerability.

Before he gave them the signal to release the stickies, he stepped into an empty cage, then shut and locked the door.

In the cell next door were two female scalies. Naked from the waist up, hugely, intimidatingly mammalian, the hems of their long skirts dragged through straw already fouled with their waste.

Safely behind bars, Rish nodded to the enforcers,

who threw open all the stickie cells. Kissing and moaning, the pale, skinny muties flooded into the menagerie corridor. They threw themselves upon the other cages and cells, trying to get their hands on the muties still prisoner.

Rish jumped back as they reached in for him with greedy, sucker fingers. Dead black eyes in excited faces coveted his soft flesh. Nose holes and needle teeth-lined jaws dripped with mucus and saliva in anticipation of smelling and tasting his fresh blood.

The stickies hurled themselves upon the unprotected enforcers. They tried to pull their watchdogs apart, but their suckers wouldn't stick to the sweat-slick, knobby skin. The enforcers started throwing stickies, picking them up around the waist and chucking them at the exit. That got the muties headed in the right direction, toward the light streaming through the doors and the sound of music, which made them coo and scatter frantic kisses.

They had learned that Wagner meant party time.

It had occurred to him before that all he had to do to get Silam's job was to keep quiet. To just agree with whatever idiotic plan the spin doctor set out. To refrain from offering subtle suggestions and advice, to stop posing key questions that revealed fundamental, grievous errors. To stop personally altering programs after the fact to correct the head liar's bonehead mistakes.

In his little, hairless hand he held the sword of Silam's destruction.

Along the side of the cheap ballpoint, emblazoned in gold paint were the words Sunset West Motel, Bloomfield, N.M.

There was nothing wrong with the scheduled order of attack, but as usual, Silam hadn't bothered to read the careful win-loss odds projections he'd done. If the spin doctor had even glanced at them, he would have seen his battle plan was badly flawed. Including the islanders in this afternoon's festivities had been Rish's bright idea, not Silam's. Although Silam had quickly adopted the clever twist as his own, he hadn't thought through some of the obvious consequences. That core of seasoned, organized fighters needed to be dealt with first, singled out, targeted and destroyed. Instead, they were ignored, treated as run-of-the-mill mercies. Silam had signed off on the choreography. It was his baby. There was no way for him to pass the blame.

Rish had a choice, to save Silam or let him flame.

He chose flame.

Rish had never actually seen Magus angry. Seeing him pleased was scary enough.

The scalies in the adjoining cell started banging their slops buckets against the bars.

"We're hungry. Feed us!" one of them snarled in his face. "This is torture!"

"Feed us, you stumpy little bastard! We're wasting away!" the other cried.

Between massive, drooping dugs, their wrinkled bellies sagged a good two feet over the waistbands of their flowing, raggedy skirts. Even though these two were relative lightweights for the species, they still weighed close to four hundred pounds. Their monumental appetites were what made them a regular feature of Magus's little military melodramas.

"You're up next on the program," Rish assured them. "You'll get all you can eat in a few minutes."

The scalies' expressions immediately brightened.

# Chapter Twenty

Doc Tanner clung to the rope rail, gasping. There was so much water vapor in the cloud that it was difficult for him to breathe. It felt like he was drowning on dry land. The condensing moisture beaded on his hands and dripped down his face.

A few more volleys of wild autofire whined off the rocks around Doc and the freezies. Then the shooting stopped. Apparently the uniforms had given up the hunt.

"We've got to keep moving," Bell said. "On the double."

They trudged blindly upward. It got even darker as they climbed. Four feet of visibility dropped to three, then two. If the rope rail hadn't been there, they would have mostly certainly blundered off the cliff to their deaths.

"The mist is getting thicker, Antoine," Bell said. "You're sure we haven't passed it already?"

"We couldn't have," the black man replied. "This trail's a dead end, like I said. It's the redoubt's emergency exit route, and the only way out of the place from the north side. The main entrance and exit is on the far side of the mountain."

"You've been here before, then?" Doc said.

"Yeah, but the secret installation hadn't been built when I visited," Kirby said.

"Then how do you know so much about it?"

"I used the data banks in our redoubt to access the site's physical layout," Kirby said. He patted his pants' pocket. "Pulled a hard copy of the setup here. Super-detailed. Floor by floor. Room by room."

Doc stopped listening. He was as lost in self-doubt as he was in the swirling, choking grayness. Questions that he couldn't answer kept popping into his head, over and over. Had he done the moral thing? Wasn't it his natural right to return to his own time? Would he be able to hold his dear children to his bosom and not think of the friends he had turned his back on? Would that precious reunion moment, so long sought, be soured, ruined by the betrayal that it had cost?

To have thrown his lot in with these two strangers, all or nothing, was a measure of the depth of Doc Tanner's desperation and spiritual exhaustion. He wanted to believe that what they were offering him was real. He wanted it with all his soul.

Bell stopped short. "I think there's something ahead…" he said over his shoulder.

Doc thought he saw the man reach out a hand.

"Metal," Bell said. "Feels like a door. Yep. There's a keypad lock beside the frame."

Kirby carefully stepped around Doc to get closer.

Doc couldn't see the door at all. From a distance of three feet, he could barely see the two men's backs.

Something beeped in the mist. Something hissed. Then the swirling cloud that surrounded them was sucked away, drawn into the redoubt by a humidity or temperature gradient. Doc stared at the open doorway that had gobbled up the fog like a hungry mouth. Beyond it, banks of fluorescent lights flickered and came on, illuminating a long corridor.

"Never a doubt," Kirby bragged.

"Shh," Bell said. "Listen..."

A scraping, grunting sound came from the path below them. The rope snapped hard against Doc's grip. After a momentary pause, it jerked again. Pause. Jerk. Something was pulling itself up the trail. Something big and sweaty, no doubt.

"Come on, Tanner," Kirby said. He grabbed hold of Doc's shoulder and pulled him into the redoubt. When all three of them were inside the entrance, the black man tapped the keypad on the interior door frame and the vanadium steel barrier slid shut.

"That should keep the bastard out," Kirby said.

"Unless it knows how to use the lock," Bell said. "Maybe we'd better shake a leg."

This redoubt was similar to all the others Doc had seen. It was furnished in a grim institutional style: gray-tile floors and walls, broad rooms with low acoustic ceilings, rooms that were divided into a maze of cubbyhole offices by chin-high, moveable partitions. Unlike most of the other redoubts, this one hadn't been looted and ransacked. The deserted workstations and tables were neat under their thick coating of dust. There were no papers strewed over the floor. The computer screens were unsmashed.

There was evidence of heavy foot traffic, though.

Big footprints tracked through the dust along the main hallway. And there were dark, muddy places where falling drips of sweat had mingled with the unswept dirt of more than a century. The corridor smelled faintly but distinctly of acetone.

"Trainers have been here," Bell said.

"There's been no audible alarm," Kirby said. "Think they're looking for us already?"

"Count on it."

Kirby referred to his printout map of the installation. "We've got to go down again," he said, tapping the paper. "The mat-trans gateway is eight floors below us."

"Then we'd better use an elevator," Bell said. "No way can we control the stairwells against the trainers."

"Where we are going, if I may ask?" Doc said.

"We're about to jump from here to our redoubt," Kirby told him. "That's where the Chronos machinery is."

The black man figured out the direction they had to travel and hurriedly led them onward.

As they trotted around the eerily empty room, Doc wondered if anyone had ever worked here. There were no personal items at any of the workstations. Just blank, gray corkboards, bookshelves with neatly stacked, spiral-bound technical manuals, a forest of identical ergonomic chairs. It appeared that all this effort, all this expense, had been for nothing.

When Kirby located the elevator, he pushed the button to summon the car, then stepped back. He and Bell shouldered their autoblasters and aimed for the middle of the doors. Doc held the LeMat in a two-handed grip, hammer cocked. They were ready to unleash an all-out barrage, but when the doors opened, the car was empty.

As they ducked into elevator, Kirby jabbed the muzzle of his assault rifle at the muddy floor. "Bastards have been in here, too," he said.

The chemical fumes in the car's enclosed space were dizzying. Like a paint factory.

"Phew, that's some high-octane sweat!" Bell said. "Do you think it's safe to use the elevator? Something in the motor could spark off on us and wham! We got ignition."

"If it didn't fireball when I hit the up button, it probably won't now," Kirby told him.

From the far side of the redoubt came the sound of a pneumatic door sliding back. From the direction and the sound, it was the same one they had used. Then heavy, running footsteps, getting louder and louder.

"It would appear the risk of descent has been superseded by the risk of staying here," Doc said.

Kirby punched the down button. A spritely bell dinged.

The trio waited but nothing else happened.

There was a courtesy delay in the automatic closing of the doors. Kirby punched the button again. Dingdingdingding.

Still nothing.

Which gave the Olympic-sprinting trainer enough time to close the gap.

"Get him!" Bell cried as the mutie burst into view down the long, straight hall, like a shooting gallery target. He and Kirby opened fire with their M-16s, a little wild at first. The spray of 5.56 mm tumblers brought down tiles from the ceiling, shattered computer monitor screens and exploded light banks. The ricochets whined around the room.

Doc braced himself against the door frame and carefully aimed for the trainer's eyes. Boom and flash. Boom and flash.

The creature held its taloned hand in front of its face and advanced at a dead run. Bullets and pistol balls smacked into it. It soaked them up like a sponge, and kept on coming.

Though it spurted some blood, it seemed to have no vitals to hit.

"Shit, shit, shit," Bell snarled as he dumped an empty mag on the floor. He slapped home a full one, gave the charging handle a quick flip and resumed firing, all in a single fluid movement.

The trainer was ten feet away when the doors finally whooshed shut. Before it could pry them apart with its thumb talons, the car dropped.

Again the freezies braced themselves and took aim at the doors. As Doc had no time to reload the LeMat, he drew his sword. He was unsure what if anything that weapon could do against the trainers, but it made him feel better to have a blade in his hand, ready to strike.

When they arrived on the mat-trans level, the doors opened onto a deserted hallway. A profusion of muddy tracks ran down its center.

Before Kirby left the car, he pressed the buttons for the six lower floors, sending the elevator to the bottom of the shaft, giving them a little more time to work before the car could be called up.

The hum from nuke generators vibrated through the floor. Doc could feel it in the soles of his feet and halfway up his legs.

As they advanced, Bell and Kirby checked the rooms on either side of the hall to make sure they were clear.

"Oh, man, have a look at this," Bell said, waving over Doc and Kirby.

There weren't any sweaty footprints in the long room. It was a different sort of mess.

The concrete floor was stained with blood and caustic chemicals, littered with boxes full of parts: medical, automotive, computer. Along one wall was a virtual machine shop with lathes, computerized drill presses, punch and milling machines. Low shelves were stacked with bar stock. On the opposite wall was a walk-in refrigerator and dozens of opaque fifty-five-gallon plastic drums containing shadowy, fetal position human forms. The barrels were topped off with formaldehyde, which acted as a room freshener.

In the center of the space, under powerful spotlights, was either an operating table or a mortuary slab.

It was occupied.

"What the hell is this?!" Kirby said.

Doc had the answer. "It's Magus's private laboratory. He fancies himself something of a virtuoso."

"Come again?" Bell said. "He's a musician?"

"No, virtuoso is an archaic term, from the seventeenth century. He's a dabbler in things scientific or pseudoscientific. A talented amateur."

The thing on the operating table might have debated

that last point. It lay on its back, wrists and ankles belted in place. It had been flayed, opened up, layer by layer. Each layer was pinned back with stainless-steel surgical clamps. Its chest cavity had been split wide and its organs opened to the air and the hard light.

Much of what he or she had been born with was missing. The eyes. The top of the skull. The genitalia. Muscle had been removed from both calves. Inside the red chasm of torso, a heart still beat laboriously, glistening lungs heaved.

"God, it's alive!" Bell groaned.

"Do you think it's conscious?" Kirby said. "Do you think it knows?"

"If so, it will thank me for this," Doc said. With that, he thrust his sword point through the middle of the pounding heart and out the other side. The muscle pumped rapidly twice, squeezing around the double edged blade, then it stopped. As Doc withdrew his point, the gaping cavity began to fill with oozing blood.

"One less toy for the monster to amuse itself with," Doc said. "Rest in peace, poor soul."

They left Magus's play room and continued on to the end of the hall. It turned out that Kirby's downloaded map was accurate. Before them was the entrance to the redoubt's mat-trans unit.

The control room was unoccupied, but its bank of computer drives were chittering, and every monitor screen was lit. Doc immediately picked out the massive metal door set in the far wall. It had an inches-thick, circular, gasketed window.

Kirby stood by while Bell bent over a monitor, surveying the system status and calling up the destination program's GUIs.

Kirby walked to the chamber's door, pressed the lever and pushed it open wide, revealing a small, low-ceiled gateway. The armaglass panels on the walls were marbled red and black, and shot through with seams of gold.

"The system is good to go," Bell said from the consoles. "The coordinates are input."

His last words.

They never heard it coming.

There was no slap of wet feet in the corridor. No rasp of breathing. No grunt of effort in the final lunge.

The trainer caught Colonel Bell from behind, pulling him away from the computer bank. Before he could reach the pistol grip of his M-16, an amber talon flicked out and stabbed into his earhole with a loud crunch, like a stake driven into a crisp apple.

As Doc backed toward the mat-trans unit doorway and the black man swung up his assault rifle, the trainer used its other amber gut hook to draw a line of red across the front of Bell's throat. The freezie's eyes bugged out, his lips moved as he frantically tried to speak. Blood gushed out over his tongue, pouring down his chest.

The trainer tossed Bell aside with one hand, like a wet trash bag. As the dying man crashed into the rows of monitors, the mutie lunged for the mat-trans gateway and more victims.

"Motherfucker!" Kirby howled. He shoved the muzzle of his M-16 at the onrushing mutie's chest. When he pinned the trigger, the longblaster stuttered full-auto. Orange flame spewed from the muzzle onto the trainer's sweat-slick skin.

Everything went white.

First ice cold.

Then blistering hot.

The explosion lifted Doc off his feet and sent him flying backward through the chamber door. The sword-stick and its ebony sheath clipped the edges of doorway and flipped out of his hands, across the control room. As his backside hit the plates, all 250 pounds of Dr. Kirby landed sprawled across his legs. Ears ringing, Doc rolled out from under the scorched mathematician, slammed the gateway door shut. The jump mechanism didn't automatically start when the door closed. He could see the trainer through the thick window glass. It spun around and around, the fire that billowed from its torso sheeting up over its face and head, black oily smoke staining the ceiling. Like a drunkard, the flaming mutie stumbled out into the hall, leaving the control room full of smoke.

Not of this earth, Doc thought.

He was stunned that the realization hadn't come to him before this. But Bell and Kirby, also trained observers, hadn't seen it, either. Sometimes the obvious was the most illusive. No creature born of this planet could evolve with the trainers' limitation, their fatal flaw. Copious flammable perspiration was nonadaptive, which meant the trainers had to come from elsewhere, or as a doomie hag once described it, *elsewhen,* a place where the physical laws of earth did not apply, a place where the combustion of volatile materials occurred at a much higher temperatures.

"Good God, Graydon's gone," Kirby moaned, his head in his hands. "After all this, and he's gone."

More trainers appeared in the control-room doorway. They peered in, leery of the smoke.

"You didn't know him," Kirby said, tears racing down his mahogany cheeks. "You didn't know his incredible brilliance. Graydon Bell was one of the greatest minds in the history of humankind. He was a second Einstein. And on top of that, a truly valiant and courageous man. He gave up everything to turn back the clock."

"We must leave now," Doc said.

"Agreed. The mission must succeed." With that, Kirby keyed in the jump sequences.

The ambient hum got much, much louder. The metallic floor plates beneath his boots began to glow softly, growing brighter and brighter as the power level climbed. Doc smelled ozone, and when he looked up at the ceiling he saw the tendrils of jump mist beginning to form, drifting down around them. The armaglass walls started pulsating as if alive. The seams between the floor plates at Doc's feet appeared to part, to spread wider and wider. And then he was falling through the yawning gap, falling into blackness at terrific speed.

# Chapter Twenty-One

Krysty Wroth's spine tingled from the base of her skull to the small of her back. Her breathing was shallow and quick. It felt as if she were only using the top inch or two of her lungs, right under her collarbones. She had come very close to meeting a very bad end. She could still see the underside of the Wazl's jaw as it dragged her along, its serrated overbite, still feel the hot, fetid huff of its breath as it flapped its wings. If the lizard bird hadn't been preoccupied first with escape and then with Jak's throwing blade, it would have chewed off her face, or readjusted the grip of its claws to bite into her flesh instead of the shoulders of her coat.

There wasn't time to brood on the near miss, even if she had wanted to. Magus had sprung his lethal trap, and the companions were caught in it, up to their eyeballs. Swimming to safety was out of the question. The uniforms with autorifles in the boats would put a quick end to any attempts to reach the big island. There was only one option: when the time was right, to put their heads down and go for broke.

By choosing to stay back on the rim and battle the Wazls, Ryan had given stickies time to fully commit themselves. Only when the muties had almost split the norm force in two did he shout and wave the companions on after him. As Krysty charged past Captain Eng, the islander realized what was happening and ordered his men to follow and join in the attack.

The idea was simple and straightforward, pure Roman Legion: meet the point of the stickie wedge with as much power as they could muster. Break the wedge apart so the recruits already in the bowl could encircle and chill the fragmented groups of stickies.

First, however, they had to push through the ranks of their own kind. They jumped over the bodies of the fallen, of the wounded trying desperately to pull themselves away. These were nothing like the casualties of Great Caesar's army. This was altogether different sort of hand-to-hand meat grinder. The wounds were not clean-edged cuts and punctures from blades and spears. They were ragged holes, divots where skin and muscle had been ripped—or bitten—away.

Krysty ran on Ryan's right, close on his heels. Around his broad shoulder she could see waving pale arms and swinging blades, and a red mist rising up from the hellish field of combat.

Mildred sprinted on her left; J.B. and Jak were right behind them. Before they reached the killzone, the islanders bringing up the rear started a war chant, or perhaps it was a death chant. Strange words shouted to the beat of their running footsteps, defiantly, grindingly out of sync with Magus's barrage of predark music. The last recruits in their way saw what was coming and gave ground. Ryan was the point of attack, the tip of the norm wedge. His panga flashing, he hurled himself into the enemy line.

His fists and feet and blade sent bodies flying to either side.

Right behind him, Krysty faced the screaming mutie horde, a yammering, jittering wall of dead eyes and drooling mouths. To keep her bayonet from getting stuck in bone, Krysty slashed and hacked with it, using the double-edged point and razor-sharp edge rather than the full length of the blade. To get the most power while continuing to move forward, she swung overhead, adding her grunts of effort to the roar of battle. The bayonet point drew lines of red down the middle of the pale faces, dividing them from forehead to chin. Clutching the split seams together, blood gushing between their sucker fingers, the wounded stickies twisted away and dropped to their knees.

The chanting islanders finished the job she and Ryan had started, slashing the fallen with their sabers, widening the column's breach.

The term "bloodbath" was invented to describe a scene like this. From the tips of flashing swords and bayonets, from the heads of falling hammers and axes, sprays of gore flew in all directions, falling like hot, copper-scented rain. The ground underfoot was crimson and slick, like it had been lubricated with axle grease.

The muties that melted to either side of the wedge point found themselves caught under islander steel or trampled by islander feet. It wasn't in the stickies' nature to ever take a step back. They lacked the hardwiring for retreat. Or to put it another way, they couldn't think that far ahead. Once they got their chill lust up, they pressed on, to victory or death. Nonfatal wounds didn't stop or even slow them. Missing arms, hands, parts of their heads, they threw themselves forward with snapping jaws.

As one already wounded mutie jumped at Krysty's face with arms and sucker fingers outstretched, she pivoted and bracing her back leg, as she let it slip past, thrust fifteen-and-a-half inches of steel into its exposed side. The blade slid in to the hilt, stopping with an elbow-jarring impact. It didn't stick in the rib cage or vertebrae; when Krysty jerked back the blade, it slipped right out. As she turned back to meet another adversary, out of the corner of her eye, she saw the stickie she'd just stabbed popping up from the ground like it was on springs, just in time for the top of its bald head to meet J.B.'s tomahawk downswing.

The impact made a hollow, wet sound, but the skull shattered like a dinner plate.

Forward motion was the key to Ryan's strategy, a strategy that Doc's swordstick would have furthered immeasurably. In the back of her mind, Krysty was still stinging from the way he had abandoned them. She was still furious, and not just at the old man. She couldn't imagine what the two mutie hunters could have offered that could lure him away. Maybe they hadn't offered him anything. She knew how vulnerable Doc was when he was having one of his spells. Sometimes the companions had to tie a rope around his waist just to keep him from wandering off. They should have seen the breakdown coming, and done something about it.

Caught up in the headlong advance, Krysty didn't

look around to see how Mildred was doing. Because the woman was keeping up the pace, Krysty figured her friend was using the same technique she was, for the most part cutting rather than stabbing with her predark bayonet, slashing throats instead of trying to pierce hearts.

Krysty could hear the swish-swish of the islanders' sabers behind her. And what sounded like cabbages being chopped in two, one after another. The crisp crunch wasn't from cabbages, of course. Nor from anything vegetative, for that matter. The islanders' sword slashes were sending bald heads leaping from necks, arcing away into the melee.

Ryan's strategy worked like a charm. The shattered column of stickies found itself caught between gauntlets of norms. The recruits attacked them from one side and the companions and islanders from the other. Three deep, the trapped muties were battered front and rear by blades and ten-pound hammers. In panic, with nowhere to go, they leaped straight up in the air. Steel rang on steel as they were chopped down.

Krysty joined in the slaughter. She could see the blood-spattered faces of the recruits on the other side of the stickies' wildly jerking bodies. The eyes of the ex-mercies and sec men were full of triumph—at last they were getting the upper hand.

As she whipped the blade point across the neck of the stickie facing her, a sledge hammer came down on its head from behind. The weight of the impact drove the mutie instantly to its knees. The rounded top of its head had become a concavity, all the way down to its earholes. The dead black eyes stared at eternity while a long strand of drool swayed from its chin. Then it fell on its face.

Another mutie side-hopped inside her guard, straddling the one who had just been dropped. If it hadn't been for the wide stance, it would have had her by the throat.

Before it could grab her, Krysty jumped off her left foot to gain momentum, then snap-kicked with her right leg. The toe of her boot connected solidly with the point of the stickie's chin. With a loud crack, its head whipped back and the chin aimed not just skyward, but somewhere over its right shoulder. The body toppled backward.

As she brought her blade up, on the other side of the gauntlet, she saw stickies jumping on the backs and heads of the recruits. The forces at the rear of the mass of muties had broken ranks, circled around the norms, and were pulling them down from behind.

Rapidly the neat battle lines blurred and the companions' forward momentum slowed. As knots of fighters, norm and mutie, tried to surround and isolate each other, combat became chaos.

Krysty and the other companions moved into a back-to-back position. No command was necessary. No discussion. It was standard protocol, the only way to survive under the circumstances.

With Ryan on one side and Jak on the other, the tall redhead fended off her attackers, striking with blade and boot. Overhead, the Wazls swooped, snatching at their heads with claws and beaks. The lizard birds didn't seem to care for the taste of stickie. They ignored the muties and concentrated on the norms. It was an instinctive choice. Wazls couldn't be tamed or trained to hunt. The wounded recruits who managed crawl away from the stickies were subject to savage attack from above.

Under the leaden sky, with music written for dead heroes hammering their ears, the companions valiantly fought on.

RYAN PUSHED between the shoulders of the norm fighters, heading for the tip of the stickie spear, the point of their deepest penetration. He knew he couldn't turn back the muties, but he could force them to either side; with his size and momentum, his chilling power, aimed a small focal point, the enemy had no choice.

The last of the recruits jumped out of the way and Ryan drove into the pale, writhing mob. He literally stomped down the first few stickies in his path, cracking their long bones under his boot heels.

When a mutie jumped at him, its needle teeth bared, Ryan punched instead of stabbed with his panga hand. The hard straight right had every ounce of his body weight behind it. His fist landed just above the nostril holes and he could feel the crunch of yielding bone all the way up his arm. With two hundred pounds of moving mass behind it, the blow jolted the stickie off its feet and sent it helicoptering sideways into the chests of its fellows.

A row of pale dominoes toppled. More bones yielded—sternums, ribs, skulls, pelvises—to the one-eyed man's crushing boots.

Another mutie leaped from the left. Ryan down-blocked it with the edge of his forearm, and as the body swept past him to the right, he ripped the panga blade across the front of its throat.

Then it was back and forth with the eighteen-inch panga, cutting down the stickies who didn't step aside. As Ryan charged and hacked, pushing deeper into the mutie ranks, he could hear the islanders' rumbling baritone war chant behind him.

*"Patu! Patu! Whakangaro! Patu! Patu! Whakangaro!"*

Under the circumstances, Ryan didn't need a translator to get the drift. The three-hundred-pound, tattooed warriors were bellowing, "Chill 'em all! Chill 'em all!"

The war chant was punctuated by the whoosh of Calcutta steel. It didn't matter that the blades were dull and nicked, that the metal had been forged more than a century ago in a dirt floor foundry. The islanders' swings were so powerful they could have beheaded their foes with three-foot lengths of unmilled bar stock.

As Ryan plowed into the muties' midst, he saw that some of them were otherwise engaged. The stickies farther back in the column, separated from the hand-to-hand by their brethren, were kneeling or squatting, taking the opportunity to feed on the fallen recruits. They raised gory mouths from the whipsawn carcasses as he bore down on them. They looked up at him with dead black eyes, still chewing.

Ryan would have had to lean down to strike them with the panga, which would have cost him time. Instead he kicked them in the head with his heavy boots. The impacts sent shock waves to his hip sockets. His bootprints branded their vacant faces. Vibram, stamped in reverse.

Because the feeding stickies farther along could see him coming, they were forewarned. Ryan rammed headlong into multiple attackers. He fired off a straight kick into a stickie's chest, knocking it sprawling. Then he backhanded the panga, side-slashing across an undefended throat, opening yawning second mouth under its pale chin. The forehand stroke that followed hacked into the side of the next mutie's neck. As the stickie spun away, its arterial blood spurted in a fine spray.

This was slow-mo war, combat as brutal and primitive as it could get.

Fighters crashing together, bone on bone, for the viewing pleasure of a jaded audience of one. Blaster chilling at eleven hundred feet per second and ranges of a hundred yards was warm milk and cookies by comparison. In this savage brand of warfare you had to look into the eyes of the thing you were butchering. You had to watch as the power of your muscles unzipped a kissing face from ear to ear.

Ryan been in the eye of this hurricane many times before.

He knew its secrets, its pitfalls—and its allure.

Being turned loose with a sharp blade or a heavy bludgeon on a mob of inhuman murderers, without rules of engagement, with no limitations of honor or respect for the enemy's innate right to life, imparted a terrible freedom, the freedom to act without conscience or regret. At some point under such conditions, after the fear of death vanished in adrenaline rush, when the fighter was no longer battling out of desperation for the sake of survival, an unholy desire took hold.

The desire to do his or her worst.

Not simply to win, but to devastate.

Ryan saw that urge as part of his animal nature. It was something that couldn't be denied, or altered. Without that deeply buried spark, he could never have become the warrior he was.

Perhaps the stickies felt the same thing when they blew kisses to their intended victims, when they chased down defenseless prey, when they pulled it apart with their sucker hands. In their case, however, the primal urge was right there on the surface. Whoever or whatever had created the stickie race, human bioengineer or forked-tail devil, it had fanned that awful ember and made it all-consuming. A bonfire of chill lust. Stickies enjoyed no camaraderie. They had no villes, they farmed no land. They were a predatory swarm.

In all his past entertainments, Magus had created a mirror of the world, a funhouse mirror, rippled and distorted by contrived situations, by intricate slaughterhouse tableaux that laid bare the darkest secrets of the species that had spawned him.

Gassing people in a circus tent.

Mocking their terror with Mozart.

Staging combat to the death on a scrap of rock.

Mocking the fighters' heroism and pain with the melodramatic strains of Wagner.

If the other recruits believed they would be all right once they wiped out the stickies and Wazls, they were in for an unpleasant surprise. From past experience with

Steel Eyes, Ryan knew the stickies and Wazls were just the beginning.

As he saw it, there was only one hope for the companions' survival. After fracturing the enemy point and dividing its column, they had to continue to drive their own spear through the stickie ranks, all the way to the cone's double doors. If they could reach that gate and control it, they could stop the flow of mutie reinforcements and control the field of battle.

If they failed to reach those steel doors, he had little doubt that they were all going to die.

With that in mind, Ryan cut a six-foot-wide swathe through the mutie forces. After hammering the skull of a stickie with the pommel of his panga, he hurtled the unconscious body onto those coming up behind. Before they could get out from under the tangle of limbs, he was on them. As he stomped their pale necks, he caught a blur movement around the edge of the bowl, above the sea of bobbing heads and waving arms. Stickies were sprinting to the rear, trying to outflank the norms.

He shouted a warning, but his voice was lost in the clamor.

Ryan had to watch as the stickies pounced on the shoulders of the recruits, sucker fingers grabbing for the eyes, dragging them backward onto the ground, then ripping off their skin and muscles.

How many norms had they lost already? In the confusion of battle, it was impossible to tell.

How many stickies were left? The way they jumped around, there was no way to count them.

One thing was for sure—all the freshly spilled blood,

and the promise of more to come, was making the muties go even wilder. Their frenzied counterattack forced Ryan to slow his advance or risk being cut off from the others. As the norm flanks buckled around them, the companions pulled together, fighting for their lives.

J.B. JOGGED ACROSS THE DISH in the three-spot behind Ryan and Mildred, on the left. The stickies who moved out of the one-eyed point man's reach, who survived the slash of Mildred's bayonet were his responsibility. Undeterred by their narrow escape from death, or perhaps energized by it, the muties lunged back into the fray with a vengeance, hands groping for the Armorer's face. J.B. tomahawked them as he ran by, swinging only at the heads he knew he could hit squarely. His sizzling, backhanded ax blows sent the muties crashing face-first onto the rock.

As the companions thrust deeper into the column of stickies, backed by the sword-wielding, shouting islanders, the other recruits regained their courage. They pressed the attack on the momentarily distracted muties, hamstringing them with low chops of their knives and axes, clubbing them over the head with their hammers.

Stickies dropped like ten pins. While they twisted and thrashed, unable to get up, the islander sabers scythed necks, and the Cawdor juggernaut kept rolling forward.

J.B. knew where Ryan was heading, and he recognized the importance of speed in getting there. Like his old friend, the Armorer had acquired a handle on

Magus's modus operandi the hard way. From experience, he knew that what they were facing now was just prelude. There would be new beasts to fight soon enough, new beasts aplenty. Short of a complete turnabout, the wearing down of the norm forces was inevitable, as was their defeat. He knew there would eventually come a point when he wouldn't be able to lift the tomahawk, let alone swing it with chilling force. Unless they could shut those double cone doors, permanently.

The window of opportunity for that was short.

Between the companions and the goal stood a savage, utterly fearless and unpredictable enemy.

With Ryan on point, the stickie column split and kept on splitting, like water under the bow of a streaking ship. Running in his wake, the companions moved forward so quickly that they couldn't avoid stepping on bodies, alive and dead, and on parts of bodies, norm and mutie.

One of the badly wounded stickies jumped from the ground just as Krysty passed by. The redhead expertly dodged and deflected the attack across her body. As she did so, her long blade flicked in and out of the stickie's side. J.B. saw the mutie was going to land to his right, inside the wedge, and too close for comfort.

Automatically, he switched the tomahawk to his right hand. He thought the stickie was probably dead meat, but he intended to give it a whack in passing just to make sure. When the stickie immediately sprang up, its mouth open, its needle teeth dripping, J.B. had already begun his compact, powerful downswing. Falling steel crunched through rising bone. J.B. skipped around the halo of backsplatter.

Although the expression in the black eyes did not change, the way the skull caved in, it was lights out. Permanently.

J.B. had only turned to the right for a second, but that was long enough for a poised, crouching enemy to find a clear lane of attack. Before he could completely turn back, a pale shape flew at him in a flat-out dive with arms outstretched.

J.B. couldn't bring the tomahawk to bear across his body, so he squatted, making the attacker miss. The mutie dragged a hand as it flew over J.B.'s head, trying to snag hold of his face with its suckers. Moist fingers slammed into the side of his skull, then cool air hit sweaty hair. His head felt light. Fedora gone, his wire-rimmed glasses dangled off one earhook.

"Shit!" J.B. growled, glancing back over his shoulder.

The stickie had landed on its feet behind him. Clutching his treasured hat, it coiled to hurl itself on Jak's unprotected back.

"Look out, Jak!" he cried.

Captain Eng was already on the case. In two long strides, he closed the distance. Swinging with both arms and putting considerable snap into the strike, the islander brought his blade down at a forty-five-degree angle, from right to left. With three hundred pounds of tattooed fury behind it, the saber's heavy middle section sliced cleanly through the stickie's eyes and eye sockets. Eng's hip-pivoting follow-through took the sword all the way through the soft skull and out the base of the neck. Freed from the body beneath, the entire back of the bald head sloughed off. As it did, blood geysered up from the arteries that fed the brain pan. Stepping neatly around the mutie's falling body, the captain snatched the fedora out of the dead hand.

Still running, the islander grinned down at his prize. For a second, J.B. thought he was going to try on the hat—a ridiculous prospect considering the size of his head. Then, with a snap of his wrist, Eng sailed the hat back to the Armorer, who caught it with one hand and screwed it back down on his head, swearing a blue streak.

The fucking thing had stickie on it.

The advance slowed as the norms reaped the rewards of mutie confusion. Their formation broken, the stickies found themselves surrounded. J.B. waged point blank war on the dead-eyed monsters, clubbing them to the ground with full power blows. As he brought his tomahawk down in a coup de grâce on an already mortally wounded stickie, he saw rapid movement at the fringes of the battle that was counter to the flow.

The flanking maneuver was perfectly timed and executed. The recruits facing J.B. were pulled down by dozens of pale hands. In the blur of flying bodies, in the screaming din, he saw men pinned to the ground and bitten, bald heads savagely shaking, needle teeth tearing out chunks.

Under the weight of the counterattack, the recruit gauntlet collapsed. In arm-waving droves, stickies broke through the holes they'd torn in the ranks. J.B.

was forced to back up or be overrun. Cutting the toma-hawk left and right, he kept the snarling muties at bay.

The Armorer sensed the companions were pulling in behind him, battle mates drawing together, shoulder to shoulder, for mutual defense. It was the last-stand for-mation. Out of the corners of his eyes he saw Jak's flying white hair on his right and Mildred's strong brown arms on his left. Their blades flashed dully in the weak daylight. Blood varnished the steel.

Overhead the Wazls dipped and dived, buffeting them with wing-wash and snatching at their heads with black tri-talons. The lizard birds knew the game was just about up.

J.B. could see the islanders had moved into a simi-lar back-to-back fighting formation a short distance away. The huge men circled right to left, chanting their war chant, stomping their bare feet, their saber points out. They were a human-powered cutting machine. Anything that came within thirty-five inches fell to pieces and died.

Under any other circumstances the sight would have made the Armorer smile.

With an overhead chop, he cleaved a charging stickie's shoulder, separating white bone socket from red flesh. It wasn't a lethal blow by any means. After a split second pause, the attacker lunged at him with its good arm. J.B.'s second strike clipped the front of the mutie's throat, sending it staggering to one side, trying in vain to keep its life blood from spurting out between its fingers.

Jak snap-kicked the gasping stickie in the side of the

head, driving it to the ground, unconscious. Blood poured onto the rock in a sheet of red, the porous stone soaking it up like a sponge.

At that moment, the thundering music stopped.

And the scuffling, groaning, ringing, shrieking sounds of the battle that surrounded them became horribly clear.

J.B. knew what was coming. They all knew.

The grinding clamor, the brutal hand-to-hand stretched on and on, and still the dreaded noise they were waiting for, the signal for the beginning of the end, didn't come. Magus was having his fun, making his victims wait.

When the double doors slammed back, the companions were nowhere near them.

# Chapter Twenty-Two

In order to restrain himself from delivering a running commentary on the battle, Silam dug his fingernails into the palms of his hands and bit the tip of his tongue. Although the urge to point this out, and to jump up and down while doing it, was powerful, he knew better than to intrude on Magus's enjoyment.

As always, when his fantasies unfolded in the flesh, Silam saw new connections and profound depths heretofore hidden. In his own savage choreography was the poetry of the spheres. The beauty of what he had wrought made him want to shout for joy. He saw the mindless hacking and hewing on the islet below as nothing less than the inescapable drama of all humankind, its hopes, its potential, its Achilles' heel. Tragedy. Comedy. Futile strivings. Glorious aspirations. Heroism. Cowardice. It was pitifully, shabbily mundane, and at the same time noble, even spiritually uplifting.

Who else in Deathlands could have dreamed a nightmare so gravid with meaning? What other genius, artist, prophet of his caliber existed? Compared to him, they were all grubby parasites and posers, the sorry, self-poisoned Uncle Lesters of the world.

This time Silam had surely skinned back the fibrous

husk, peeled away the scales of ignorance, revealing the squirt and squeal of life's underlying mechanism. He looked upon that raw red truth as a father looking upon his newborn child.

With exaltation.

His eyes brimmed with tears at the wondrous potency of his talent.

At moments like this it didn't matter to him whether Magus was amused or not, although from his tie-rod-throwing laughter, he clearly was.

As the opening act of the staged battle progressed, the horrid clanking noises became less frequent. The growing weight of his master's silence smothered Silam's understandable exuberance. And as he began to fret over the dire consequences of a failure to amuse, all the mystery and pageant of his creation seemed to slip away.

Because he hadn't carefully read the program he'd signed, he had trouble remembering the precise order of battle. He couldn't be expected to have every tiny detail at his fingertips. Of course he had a vague idea, but he had devised so many of these dance macabres that they had started to blur a bit in his memory. He relied on his ever-loyal Rish to keep the continuity straight and to remind him when he was treading familiar ground.

Silam's heart began to pound as he took in the scope of the unfolding problem. Two of the Wazls, almost half of his air power, his command of the sky, had been hauled down in short order and promptly slaughtered on the edges of the fray. The stickie column was well on its way to dividing the recruit force until the wedge of norms crashed into them, spearpoint against spearpoint, with that one-eyed bastard Cawdor leading the charge. Silam watched in disbelief as the stickie formation melted into disarray.

Those damned islanders! he thought. Whose idea had it been to recruit them? Not his, surely. Had Rish or the fumbling Jaswinder somehow planted that bad seed in his head? For the life of him, he couldn't recall. It was true that his sublime flights of fancy sometimes required serious revision. Silam knew he was not a practical thinker; no true artist was. His mind was a churning mass of ambition, jealousy, frustration, rage and fear, an engine constantly revving to redline.

A new noise echoed off the walls of the skybox, distracting him from the spectacle below.

If he hadn't known better, he would have thought someone was sharpening a hoe with a rattail file. Silam recognized the sound, of course. Magus was grinding his teeth.

Steel Eyes had never shown impatience with a performance so early on.

It was natural in a life-and-death military drama for control of one side or the other to wax and wane. For a seemingly inevitable defeat—or victory—to suddenly reverse itself. Magus's enjoyment depended in large part upon giving the intended victims the illusion that they had a chance, right up to the big finale when all hope was crushed. So why was Magus concerned already?

The answer was simple.

Ryan Cawdor.

The one-eyed man wasn't just in charge of his own crew, he was leading the islanders into battle and in the process, wreaking devastation upon the stickies.

Because Silam hadn't realized Cawdor was among the new recruits, he had failed to take his influence on the outcome into account. Generally speaking, the spin doctor tended to ignore past history if he hadn't invented it. Now it was too late to work the back story into the drama, to devise something extra awful for Cawdor to endure. Something that would give his master the ultimate in payback, and put an end to lingering frustration and fury.

Ryan Cawdor was a fly in the ointment, a pebble in the boot.

He was significant because he was a spoiler.

Silam had never seen Magus frightened, and he didn't appear frightened now. Safe in his high tower, protected by enforcers and uniforms, he had no reason to be concerned for his safety. Steel Eyes could have easily ordered the uniforms to land on the islet and slaughter the recruits. All he had to do was to turn off the music and give the command through the speakers for it to happen. But he didn't want to cut his afternoon's entertainment short unless it was absolutely necessary.

Silam had never before staged two bad performances in a single day. The consequences of such a lapse in quality made his blood run cold. This morning's fiasco wasn't his fault by any means, but he knew better than to make excuses to Magus.

Already the stickie losses were starting to mount up. From his high vantage point, Silam guessed about forty or fifty had been chilled. Losses on the norm side amounted to half that. Just the opposite of the morning's disappointing show, Silam thought. Although he wanted to point that out to his master, he dug his nails deeper into his palms and kept silent. Magus screwed the world, his foreplay terrible to behold, but there was such a thing as putting up too good a fight.

Silam tried to remain calm. After all, the tide of battle wasn't turning, he assured himself. It hadn't even really begun, yet. The stickies and Wazls' only purpose, he recalled, was to reduce the recruits' numbers and break them into small, vulnerable groups. That done, the less mobile scalies and swampies would be released to take advantage of the surrounded and stationary norms. They would be followed by the smaller creatures that were triple-fast and triple-hard to chill, with the screamies doing the final mop-up.

Long before the first act had reached its scheduled climax, Magus did something he had never done before. He called down the curtain.

In a gear-box grinding growl he said, "Send in the clowns."

# Chapter Twenty-Three

Jak would have followed Ryan Cawdor into the jaws of hell, so he didn't even blink at driving headlong into the middle of the stickie column. At last they were moving, and about to make solid contact with their main opposition. Long shadows and hard gusts of wind swept over them as they ran down the slope and into the volcanic bowl. The shadows and gusts seemed to single out Jak in particular. Again and again, the cruel black talons snatched out, trying to rip off the top of his head. Perhaps the lizard birds knew which one of the companions had taken out their kin.

The albino ignored them. The Wazls' swoops were furious but nothing close to all-out attacks. The birds had small brains, for sure, but they weren't triple stupes. They had seen what he was capable of and kept well out of his range.

Something the stickies could not do.

Using his fists, his feet and his AK-47 bayonet, Jak laid into the muties like a white-maned whirlwind. Though sharpened and resharpened so many times that its true edge almost met the blood gutter, the dagger-pointed Soviet steel had many more deaths left in it.

He lashed out with the predark bayonet, plunging it

four inches deep below an oncoming stickie's sternum, then he ripped the blade down and out. The blindingly fast strike left the gutted monster on its knees, mewling.

Holding back on his foot speed, Jak loped along behind Krysty's right shoulder. The ground underfoot was slick with gore and cluttered with dropped weapons and broken bodies. He was actually skating on the gore in places. Painful death was just a slip of the boot away. To go down was to be set upon and torn apart.

Jack could feel the momentum of their charge building. He let himself be sucked into the maelstrom of close combat. Reacting, blocking, thrusting. But always moving forward, always advancing. The chilling wasn't the most important thing. What was important was the capture of territory, breaking the back of stickie control. It was his kind of fight. He shifted his hands and feet into overdrive.

He was so quick with that sliver of ComBloc steel he didn't have to slash his opponents like Krysty or Mildred. In a blur of white, silver and red, the AK bayonet flicked over the top of the stickies' guards, stabbing, twisting, darting in and out.

Jak wasn't counting kills. He was hard focused on keeping his position in the formation and on taking out the muties that entered his range. The ones he missed were targets for the islanders.

Captain Eng ran on his right flank, wielding the replica cavalry saber. Along with his crew, Eng was bellowing some islander gibberish. Jak liked the sound of it—rhythmic, deep, resonant and menacing. He found himself chanting along with the islanders, even though he didn't know what the words meant or exactly how to pronounce them.

*"Pah-two! Pah-two! Wha-kan-garo!"*

To the beat of the war chant, Jak slapped aside an outthrust sucker hand and rammed the bayonet into an undefended windpipe. The blade darted in and out, the point just grazing the interior spine. In cross section, the Soviet steel had a diamond shape. When the bayonet stabbed, it opened a wound that would never close.

The lids blinked shut over the stickie's black shark eyes. Dark blood squirted out the corners of its mouth and jetted between the gaps in its clenched teeth.

Ryan's spearpoint pushed into the heart of the stickie column. Ahead lay a field of the fallen. When Jak saw the muties crouched over their victims, his fist tightened on the bayonet's cross-hatched grip. As the companions bore down on them, the stickies straightened, reluctant to leave the feast. Some of the fallen men were still alive, helpless, already horribly mutilated. Thrashing, moaning, howling, they begged for death. But there was no time for mercy chilling. At the last moment, the stickies scattered to either side of Ryan's blade, moving low and quick, giving up ground.

Jak saw J.B. crack open the skull of the stickie that Krysty had deflected, but missed the second mutie paying J.B. back by yanking off his fedora. At the Armorer's shouted warning, he glanced over his shoulder and caught Captain Eng slicing off half the stickie's head in a single blow.

From the way the islander was grinning at J.B. with those sharpened teeth of his, Jak figured he was going to try to put on the recaptured hat. an act that would have stretched it beyond any use, except maybe as a chamber pot.

After a couple of strides Eng relented, returning the hat to its rightful owner with a flip of the wrist.

J.B. caught the fedora, and jammed it back on his sweat-matted head, his lips moving in an unbroken string of curses.

As the stickies shuffled out the companions' path, they blundered into the blades and bludgeons of the recruits. Jak and the others spread the wedge wider, trapping the muties between hammer and anvil. What was left of the cohesion of their column disintegrated as individual stickies were ruthlessly chopped down.

The survivors had no exit, and no time to regroup.

Jak waded in, kicking and stabbing, his frenzy forcing the muties to sidestep under the falling hammers.

The collapse of recruits came even faster. One minute they were holding their own, the next they were down, buried under heaps of pale bodies and frantically ripping hands.

As Jak began to pull back, a lunging stickie managed to grab him by the arm. The sucker hand felt like a tourniquet around his bicep. It shut off the flow of blood and made his fingers go numb. Jak's skin burned under the rows of squirming suckers.

The albino plunged his knife through the middle of one dead black eye. The eight-inch dagger came to a sudden stop as its point rammed into the back of the stickie's skull. The mutie tried to twist and get at him, snapping its needle teeth. The ooze of adhesive was starting to take hold. Savagely, Jak worked ComBloc steel back and forth in the mutie's eye socket, giving its brains a good brisk stir.

The sucker fingers dropped away without attaching, and the stickie slumped dead to the ground.

Continuing to retreat, Jak bumped backs with Mildred. The good doctor looked like holy hell. The beads of stickie blood on her face, arms and plaited hair had mixed with sweat and dripped down the front of her OD T-shirt. Her BDU pants were likewise striped and spattered with gore. Her eyes were wide, and she was panting hard through her mouth.

Jak fought beside his friends, protecting their flanks with his feet and blade, as they protected his.

The music suddenly stopped, but the battle raged on.

Forty feet away, the islanders were stomping and chanting, circling around in a wheel of death.

Under his breath, Jak was chanting, too.

Then the cone doors banged back and the grim music started up again.

Whatever was coming next, it was on its way.

A Wazl dive-bombed the islander circle, catching one of the sailors across the forehead with a claw. As blood gushed out, the lizard bird smelled it and immediately reversed course for another pass. As it flapped and turned, it hung stationary for a split second.

That was all the time Jak needed. In a move too fast to follow, he shook another throwing blade out of his sleeve and launched it at a slight up angle. The knife slammed the Wazl in the side of the head, right behind its earhole. It wasn't a killing strike, but it brought the bird down hard.

For a moment or two the wounded Wazl struggled to stay in the air, violently shaking its head and frantically threshing its long wings. In the process it drifted from the dead center of the battlefield, clearing the waving islander swords, crashlanding on the stickies who were attacking them.

The lizard bird's wings batted down the muties. Its legs churned, talons clawing as it tried to jump back into the air. Whatever was beneath it as it thrashed about, it tore to ribbons. Unable to fly off, the Wazl took out its insane fury on everything in range of its jaws. The serrated teeth made short work of the stunned muties. And when there were no more stickies within reach, it turned upon itself, bending its long neck, ripping into its own breast, biting out its own heart.

# Chapter Twenty-Four

Ryan had come across plenty of suicides in his time, most so long gone that he'd located them by the perfume and circling buzzards: gun eaters, vein slashers, neck stretchers, cliff jumpers. The hellscape had a bottomless appetite for human souls. For some the only escape from hopeless lives of hardship, toil and tragedy was death by their own hand. Ryan had happened onto some triple-bad botched jobs that the scavengers large and small had finished, but he'd never seen a creature eat its own heart before.

After the grounded Wazl twisted its long neck into a U, it tore through the leathery skin on its chest in a couple of snaps, and kept right on biting, through layers of muscle, through bone. It bit until its head was buried past the eyes in its own chest. That's how it died, looking inward.

Was the lizard bird able to separate its lust for blood from the pain it was causing itself? Was inflicting pain so pleasurable that it could ignore the pain it was suffering?

Interesting questions. Ryan would have studied the spectacle more closely if the situation had been less grave.

Having taken out about half of the norm recruits in their counterattack, the stickies swarmed closer to the survivors, stopping just out of blade reach. They cocked their bald heads this way and that. The kissing and cooing sounds they made couldn't be heard over the loud music. Four and five deep, they ringed the companions, waving their arms.

The other surviving recruits had quickly circled up like the islanders and the companions. It was the only way to successfully fend off stickie attacks. The norms that tried to go it alone or in pairs were immediately overwhelmed and pulled apart by sucker hands.

Ryan guessed the number of norms still able to put up at fight was close to thirty-five. There were at least three times that many stickies jumping around the bowl.

Over the tops of the bobbing bald heads, Ryan saw Magus's second wave making its exit from the cone. Swampies marched to the gloomy fanfare, four abreast and maybe ten deep. He could smell them coming, even over all the spilled blood and guts. The stumpy little men waved wooden clubs studded with long steel spikes, short-handled battle-axes and half-size broadswords. The ankle biters' favorite tactic was to cut for the legs, bringing their foes down to size, revenge on a too tall world.

Following the swampies out the doors, and towering over them, were fifteen or twenty scalies. They waddled forward in a ragged single-file line, males and females naked to the waist. They carried no weapons. Scalies were not a particularly courageous species, except when hungry.

These looked hungry.

The mass of stickies that encircled the companions feinted and juked, sometimes knocking one another down in their excitement, but with a few exceptions they held back their attack. They were waiting for reinforcements to arrive.

The scattered clumps of recruits closer to the cone were the first to feel the sting of the combined mutie force. Stickies and swampies rushed them in unison. It was a high-low affair. The norms fighting stickies left their lower bodies unprotected. The swampies cut hamstrings with their axes and swords, and shattered kneecaps with their spiked clubs. The norms trying to beat back the swampies had to bend over to reach them, which allowed stickies to leap on their unprotected backs.

The small bands of recruits lasted a minute or two before being penetrated and overrun.

Their job completed, the swampies moved on, all business. The sour-faced muties didn't eat human flesh, perhaps because they themselves were too close to human genetically, or too smart. The swampies didn't look smart with those heavy brows and block-shaped heads, but they were a crafty race. They knew the flesh of some men had a hell-blasted, turn-your-brains-into-goo taint and avoided partaking of it.

The scalies waddled onto the scene seconds after the swampies and stickies had left. They moved through the heaps of wounded with their little pig eyes alight, like it was an all-you-can-eat buffet. Squatting, they throttled the few surviving norms with their bare hands, then started pulling off warm snacks, snapping spines and sucking out the living marrow.

Ryan could see the handwriting on the wall. The companions couldn't hold out for long against a joint mutie attack, either. It was a matter of reach, and sheer numbers. If one of the group went down, the formation would be broken and they would all go down.

The music blaring from the big island stopped, then restarted after a short pause. More enemies were on the way.

The swampies marched toward the companions, shaking their bloody weapons in the air. They trooped through the ranks of the stickies, who sensed the nearness of victory and cavorted accordingly, dancing on the bones of the dead. Ryan turned toward the islanders' fighting circle and bellowed at the top of his lungs.

"Eng!" he shouted. "We've got to hook up!"

The scar-faced captain nodded. He had seen the same disastrous turn of events and had come to the same conclusion. Eng immediately ordered his crew to close ranks with the companions. The two groups of fighters merged and blended together, shoulder to shoulder, facing outward, forming a larger and stronger defensive ring.

When the swampies attacked they were again joined by the stickies, but this time the outcome of the mad rush was different. The sabers of the islanders kept the stumpy muties from getting close enough to fracture kneecaps and slice tendons. The swampies that tried to duck under the sweep of the long blades lost limbs.

As they had done before, the stickies leaped onto the norm fighters, but with no exposed backs to take advantage of, they ended up falling on swordpoints, skewering themselves to the hilt. Their feet a yard off the ground, they squirmed like worms on a hook.

Captain Eng had his own savage technique for disengaging a skewered enemy. Instead of pulling his sword out or booting the mutie off its point, he drove down with his shoulder, leaning on the handle with both hands. He rammed the stickie's feet flat into the rock, putting all his weight behind the slam, which forced the saber's blade to slice through the mutie's pelvis and come out cleanly between its legs.

As much as Ryan liked the captain's efficiency and style, and the fact that a stickie with a split pelvis had jumped its last jump, he couldn't duplicate the maneuver himself. His panga's blade was half as long as the saber and the islander had a good hundred pounds on him. Ryan used his blade point and edge to hack down the pale creatures that threw themselves at him.

Despite being outnumbered, the companions and islanders held their own, and turned back the muties' initial charge.

When the swampies retreated a little to regroup, the stickies pulled back, as well. Behind them, the scalies waited in the wings, mountains of flab sitting on cushions of the dead, conserving their energy. The pendulous, drooping folds of their skin gave off an iridescent sheen. Their expressions were alert, expectant. They weren't satisfied with what they had already eaten. They were never satisfied. There was always room for more.

A half dozen of the swampies turned on one of the larger scalies, a five-hundred-pound bull. They surrounded it and began to prod it with their weapons. They shouted for it to get up and fight. The seated behemoth tried to swat them away, and when it couldn't, when the swampies started to draw blood with their edges, it howled and its face turned red. The swampies kept on poking the scalie and yelling until it rose to its feet and started lumbering toward the circled defenders.

As it lumbered, it picked up speed.

And all the swampies and many of the stickies fell in behind its vast bulk.

The strategy was simple. Break through the ring with an unstoppable, living battering ram, then attack and chill the norms from two sides at once.

The plan would have worked if it hadn't been for the Calcutta cavalry swords.

"Let him in!" Eng screamed to his crew.

As the captain stepped out of the way, so did Ryan. The circle opened, then it closed, slamming shut right behind the scalie.

The swampies and stickies trying to ride on its coattails found themselves too close to sharp steel. Those that couldn't jump back were chopped down and stomped flat.

The scalie had closed its eyes a split second before it made contact with the circle. After taking four strides forward, when there was no resistance, it stopped and opened its eyes. It looked around and saw it was surrounded. And all alone.

Eng shouted a command and four of his crew turned away from the edge of the circle, which instantly closed ranks again. The four formed a second circle, this one around the stock-still scalie.

"As you can see, I have no weapon," it said, holding out its blood-rimed hands, making the gross flesh of its upper arms ripple and sway. "Those little swampie shits made me attack you. I had no choice. They would have chilled me. Please protect me from them. I mean you no harm."

The gore and bone marrow smeared across its cheeks and chins made the last statement suspect, to say the least.

One of the crew pivoted from the hips and swung down his saber in a tight, downward arc. Bright steel cut through baggy, tentlike pants, and slammed into buttery-soft flab. The scalie shrieked as it lost thirty pounds of excess weight from its backside. The clean slice exposed a thick rind of white fat, and bloodred flesh beneath. The other crewmen spun to build their momentum, then struck the huge mutie again and again. The blows rained down on it from all sides. Swords flashed and the scalie's monumental load of flesh sloughed from the bone.

It was the islander diet. It made you thinner in a hurry, but it also made you dead.

A much reduced, virtually unrecognizable scalie collapsed amid mounded hunks of his own flesh.

Above their heads, Ryan heard the buzzing of insects, loud enough to be audible over the music. Flies to the feast, which struck him as odd as they were so far out at sea.

Then an islander to his right let out a scream. He backed into the middle of the ring, clutching at his bare

stomach with both hands. The man was shivering head
to foot, every tendon clenched, like he was about to
shake apart. As he turned, Ryan saw a thick lashing
shape trapped between his hands, a black segmented
tongue jutting from the center of his impressive belly.
As the sailor tried to pull the thing out of his stomach,
a thousand bristling legs along its underside were frantically burrowing in.

Captain Eng stepped forward and slashed down with
his sword. The well-aimed blow struck the black-
shelled creature's twisting rear. The blade bounced off
its back without cutting. The shell didn't even dent.

*"Patu ia!"* the man squealed as the mutie squirmed
through his white-knuckled grip, disappearing into
his torso.

Under the circumstances there was only one way he
could be helped.

Eng lifted the sailor's thick, black braid out of the
way, and with a single swing of the saber cleanly cut
off his head.

A FEW MINUTES OF CLOSE combat confirmed Mildred's
belief that the companions had landed themselves
smack in the middle of a death camp. The little pile of
volcanic rock was an amphitheater, a natural Coliseum,
and the ex-mercies, the former sec men and the mutie
hunters were slaughtering and being slaughtered for
the amusement of an emperor who sat in safety high up
in the royal box seats. Undergunned gladiators were
pitted against the most terrible and terrifying beasts of
the hellscape. Mildred knew that with Magus playing

Caesar, there would be no winners in the contest. It was going to be thumbs-down for everyone.

Like the other companions, Mildred was still struggling with the sudden loss of Doc Tanner. It was like losing a finger from her right hand. The old man had been fighting by her side and covering her back for quite some time, and she had done the same for him. That he could leave just like that, with no word of explanation, no goodbyes, was very hard for her to take. She and Tanner had had their headbutting moments in the past, he could be an infuriating, pedantic old fart at times, but they had come to respect each other in the end. Knowing Doc as she did, knowing his courage, his integrity, his intelligence, she knew he had to have had a good reason for running off. But for the life of her she couldn't guess what that reason could have been.

Doc had left before Magus revealed the real destiny of his "army," so he had no way of knowing that it would come to this. The sheer, grinding weight of the chilling was unspeakable, and she had a sense that it would end only when the last norm fell.

Mildred was not a "blade person." She much preferred to do her chilling with centerfire cartridges, from a distance of at least ten feet. Even with a seventeen-inch Enfield bayonet, there was more personal contact than she found palatable. It wasn't just a matter of the backspray flying from the blade's long blood gutter, or the matter of the stabbee's last foul breath gusting into her face as she pierced it through the heart. There was also the problem of the dying party releasing the entire contents of its bowels at once. In the case of the stickies, who came mostly naked into battle, the problem was not only apparent, but underfoot. Mildred wasn't the least bit squeamish about taking lives, as she couldn't have survived very long in Deathlands if she had been, but she knew enough about the ways of hostile bacteria and viruses to be concerned about blood and other biological materials flying into her face and eyes and open cuts. As with the *taua* onboard ship, she had to forget everything she knew about infection and get the chilling done.

The killing field had begun to be less crowded—at least with vertical bodies. Drawn back into a fighting circle, she could see the swampies and scalies exit the low cone. She saw the other circled recruits fall to the muties' combined attacks. The swampies spiked and slashed the norms, then piled on after the stickies pulled the victims down. The grubby bastards jumped on the recruits' chests and bashed their brains out with bludgeons and battle-axes.

The two mutie races were definitely cooperating to chill their mutual enemies, but only up to a point. Once sucker hand touched flesh, once nail-studded cudgel slammed into kneecap, the rules of the game changed. It was every creature for itself. The competition between the Wazls and the stickies wasn't so evident because the lizard birds were few and they worked the fringes of battle.

The swampies left their battered victims and advanced in formation toward the companions and islanders. Mildred could barely make out their squinty little eyes under the bone-shaded sockets and fright-wig eyebrows. The swampies pushed between the milling, excited stickies. The tallest of the little bastards only came up to the middle of the pale chests. The shorter swampies, presumably the females or immature males, were waist high, if that. They all had short, powerful arms and legs, and their weapons were well matched to their size and strength.

By far, the quickest way to chill anything was to put a 125-grain hollowpoint .38 slug through an eye socket, an option no longer available to the good doctor.

The blaring clamor of overamplified Wagner stopped again. Mildred had figured out what that meant. It was a signal from Magus to whoever was stage-managing the show that it was time to let out more muties.

Mildred was very relieved when the islander crew joined forces with them, and she found herself bracketed by a pair of three-hundred-pound men with swords. Their cheap reproduction sabers had already landed so many blows that they were starting to look like kris, either that or they'd been run over repeatedly by a back-hoe.

The stickies and swampies attacked the entire perimeter of the circle simultaneously. As she had done before, Mildred handled the stickies with ease, but she couldn't cut swampies' throats in the same fashion. They were too short for a clean strike, and their long chins and matted steel-wool beards protected their Adam's apples from her blade's edge. In addition, their necks were too stumpy for her to get a good angle on the sides. When she tried slicing downward to sever the carotids and jugulars, she ended up chopping through their collar bones, which only disabled them on one side. And made them very angry.

Mildred had to let the islander bookends deal with the ankle-biters and concentrate on the stickies.

One of the smaller swampies ducked under the slash of the cavalry sword and, side-hopping two feet to the right, rushed at Mildred's legs with a cocked-back battle-ax. Before it could swing at her shins, she swept the point of her bayonet down, then up, driving hard, skewering the attacker and lifting it from the ground. The ax dropped out of its too large, too hairy hand. A blade thrust clear through its chest, the ugly little creature spit and fumed and bared its mossy-green teeth. It reminded her of something out of *Snow White*, only *Snow White* on jolt.

And all the dwarves were named Psycho.

With a swampie in such close proximity, impaled to the hilt of her bayonet, Mildred realized that these creatures never washed their entire lives. The aroma was a combination of armpit, smegma and unwiped bum. It was hard to believe that the one she had just stabbed hadn't just rolled on a two-week-dead, sun-baked possum. Swampies died as triple bad as they smelled, foaming at the mouth, eyes bulging, fighting to get in one last lick. Mildred gripped the knife with both hands, braced her legs and extended her arms so it couldn't claw her face and eyes.

The islander to Mildred's left reached over and grabbed the mutie by a shoulder and with a snap of his arm gave it a spin on the blade. Three, four, five times the swampie pinwheeled around the hilt of bayonet, its arms and legs outstretched, yelling its head off. When it stopped spinning, it was both limp and silent. Mildred flung the corpse over the heads of the oncoming stickies. She didn't see where it landed.

Around the perimeter of the circle the muties were either chilled or turned back. Not one of them made it through the norm lines alive. The swampies retreated a dozen steps, viewing their quarry with a new, grudging respect. The stickies drew back, as well.

A handful of swampies surrounded one of the bull scalies and goaded it to its feet. Though the creature complained mightily, it submitted to the swampie demands and began to charge at the norms. The islander captain shouted an order and the ring perimeter parted just wide enough to let the mutie in. Then it closed, shutting out the swampies and stickies that were following on the behemoth's heels.

At a second command from the captain, the man on her right peeled out of the formation, his sword up and ready to strike.

Caught in the open ground, the scalie tried to talk its way out of the predicament, but islanders weren't having any of it. With their sabers they cut the mountain of flab into bushel basket-size chunks in the middle of the ring, then retook their fighting positions.

The islander on Mildred's left said something to the other crewman as he returned, freshly blood-spattered.

The man on Mildred right grinned and replied.

Then they both laughed.

"What did you say?" Mildred asked them, curious about what an islander would find funny about the situation. She had to repeat the question before she got an answer.

"Harawira say, 'Plenty fat.' I say, 'Plenty dead, too.'"

As she might have guessed, the big joke lost something in translation.

When she first saw the scagworms coming at her, she thought she was imagining things. They looked like shadows flying across the ground as they slithered and snaked over the battlefield's scattered bodies and through the standing puddles of blood. Their domed, eyeless, antennaeless heads reminded her of the business ends of Redeye antiaircraft missiles. Their segmented armor backplates looked slick, like they'd been greased, and there were all those scrabbling yellow bug legs underneath.

Scuttling at high speed, the worms weaved erratic trails through the dead to reach the living. One creature shot along the spine of a dead stickie and hurled itself at her foot. She jumped aside or it would have gotten her. If she'd had her ZKR 551 in her hand instead of the bayonet, she could have blasted it in the head end as it rushed by her. The bayonet was too slow and the worm was running too low to reach, no more than ten inches above ground.

As it slithered between her legs she yelled out a warning that was lost in the din. The scagworm crossed the ring, its thousand legs a blur, ran up an islander's leg and bit him in his belly. Blue-black, horizontal jaws snapping, it ate and scrabbled and twisted into his torso. Despite the islander's efforts to stop it, the tail end disappeared through the four-inch-wide hole above his navel. Once the scagworm was inside him there was no way to remove it. To spare his crewman an agonizing death, Eng mercy-chilled him.

Mildred would have done the same.

Other black shadows shot out from among the dead, and suddenly the norms had their hands full. There weren't that many of the worms, but trying to chop them up with swords and tomahawks was more challenging than it looked, thanks to the muties' rapid sinuous movement and their slick armored shells. The norms fended them off with blows to the head, but they couldn't seem to chill them.

The swampies, stickies and scalies watched the unfolding chaos, but did not join in. They were waiting for something else to happen.

Mildred caught a high-pitched whine overhead, which quickly became a buzzing so loud it half drowned out the roar of the Wagner. Looking up, she saw a widely dispersed cloud of flying insects. As the bugs swirled around and around, they flew closer and closer together until they were a churning black mass that instilled fear and dread in the stickies and swampies. They backed up in a hurry. Even the scalies got off their butts. Mildred didn't like the look of it, either, but had nowhere to back up to.

The cloud of insects zeroed in on two islanders standing shoulder to shoulder. The set-upon crewmen tried to beat the bugs out of the air with the flats of their swords, to no avail.

The swarming flies landed all over their heads and tattooed torsos, and then they started stinging. Death-

lands had some wicked biting bugs, but from the way
the islanders screamed and hopped these were triple
extra nasty. The crewmen slapped themselves, squashing
the insects with the flats of their hands, but the stingers'
poison was already taking effect. Their flesh began to
balloon up, eyelids squeezing shut, great angry welts
popping out everywhere. The bugs clung doggedly to
their skin, letting themselves be crushed rather than
withdraw their pumping stingers.

Blinded, the sailors staggered backward. They managed only a few steps before they fell to the ground, and
lay there gasping for breath. Unable to defend themselves, they were easy pickings for the scagworms
which homed in on their feeble struggles. Before any
of the norms could intervene, the islanders' ribs were
snapping between bolt-cutter jaws and the two-foot-
long worms were boring into the dark warmth of their
bellies.

No one tried to end their torment. There wasn't time.
A new hazard was almost on top of them. Moving much
faster than the worms, and leaping in high, energetic
bounds, was a chill pack of gray, hairy creatures.

They were jumping like they were on springs.

Only when they got closer did Mildred get a clear
look at them. They were the size of a terrier dog, with
a vicious set of fangs and a naked, ratlike tail.

These rat muties leaped horizontal distances of
twenty feet or more in a single bound. Mildred saw one
go airborne much closer than that and just had time to
raise her bayonet point to catch it. She speared a fat two-
pounder through the middle; the true edge of the blade

had clipped its spinal cord. Its back legs hung down limply, the front legs were going to beat the band. It had bulgy red eyes, shaggy mouse-gray fur tipped with yellow, and pointy ears. Though it was half paralyzed, bleeding and crapping, its naked tail wrapped around the blade, it snapped its fangs, trying to get a piece of her. She flipped it off to one side.

Down the perimeter, things weren't going nearly so well. Two rat devils were tearing out an islander's throat while a third rode the back of his neck, trying to bite through into his brain. Ryan and J.B. tried to kill the things with panga and tomahawk, but their blows never made contact. The little muties were too quick, and they could jump too far. The islander was beyond help, bleeding out from massive wounds to both sides of the neck.

To her left, Harawira let out a shrill cry. A rat devil had sunk its fangs into his thigh, just above the knee. The mutie was hanging on, shaking its head, trying to tear out a hunk of flesh. The islander reached down and snatched hold of the creature, squeezing on its neck until it opened its jaws. Harawira then hoisted the rat devil up and, gritting his teeth, squeezed some more. The mutie's torso popped like a rotten tomato in his fist, turning to bloody scrap of hair with legs.

When another islander went down with a terminal case of scagworm, the stickies and swampies surged forward. With the norms reeling, their formation shaken, the time had come to close the deal.

"Pull in, pull in!" Ryan shouted. "Close ranks!"

Mildred saw him glance over his shoulder, back the

way they had come. Something in his expression, a realization, perhaps, made her look in that direction, too. The path they'd forged from the rim of the dish led nowhere but the water's edge.

And there the boats full of uniforms waited.

They had drifted much closer to shore, perhaps so the passengers could get a better view of the show. They were within forty feet of the beach and all the oars were shipped. Men with autorifles looked on the carnage and smiled toothlessly.

There was no way to win.

No place to retreat to.

No way off the stinking rock.

Even so, Mildred would not admit defeat. She was an optimist, first and foremost. She believed that where there was a will to survive there was a way to survive, especially in the company of courageous warriors. She knew she was getting tired, that her reactions were slowing down. The bayonet felt like it weighed ten pounds. She didn't know how much longer she could effectively fight, but she clung to the belief that she could fight long enough to get through this.

Then the music stopped again.

The steel doors banged back.

And Mildred felt her hope sputter and fail.

# Chapter Twenty-Five

Rish was still wearing his protective gear when the music from the big island stopped again, giving him the signal to release the next wave of combatants. He had just turned loose the rat devils and Silam was already calling for the screamies.

The diminutive man stripped off his heavy leather gauntlets and the screen mesh, full-head, fencing mask. A smile twisted his hangdog jowls.

Things were going wrong, just the way he had hoped.

A cohesive, seasoned fighting force was much, much more difficult to deal with than onesies or twosies. Not that the individual recruits were triple easy to chill. They died taking muties with them, which reduced the mutie numbers and increased the odds in favor of the organized norm units.

It appeared that even the self-deluded, king of pomposity was beginning to see the scope of the problem. Rish got a warm feeling as he imagined Silam trapped in the sky box with the likes of Magus, helplessly watching the disaster unravel, which spelled his own doom.

Was the poet laureate trying to repair the damage?

Of course, he was. The screamies were Silam's mutie trump card. They were also the next-to-last resort before he called in the uniform death squads.

The screamies had only been released into combat once before, and that had been a limited field test. The consequences of that release gave everyone pause. Only the enforcers and Magus himself could withstand their hypersonic attack. From the test, norms and other muties had no chance against them. Turning the five wraiths loose on the islet was tantamount to admitting that things had gotten out of hand. Once they were released, they were uncontrollable, indiscriminate chillers. The idea of losing all his muties in one fell swoop wouldn't sit well with Magus. There was the cost and the trouble of restocking his zoo, and of course the lost time.

If the screamies failed to bring down the curtain on Cawdor and the islanders, it would be up to the men in the boats, using their assault rifles on foes armed with blades and axes. It wasn't the kind of high-quality entertainment Magus sought. If it all came down to blasters versus knives, Silam might as well pick up blade himself and cut his own throat.

Question was, would he live long enough to cut Rish's throat first? The man he had relied on to edit his art, to fine-tune his inspiration. The spin doctor's spin doctor.

"Why is he calling for the screamies?" Jaswinder said as he removed his fencing mask and threw down his gauntlets. He mopped the perspiration from his balding pate with the palm of his hand, then shook it off. He seemed struck by the strange expression on Rish's face and his forehead furrowed in concern. "What is going on out there?"

Rish let his smile melt back into the drooping, down-turned folds around his mouth. "I think Silam may have miscalculated the resilience of some of the recruits," he said. "The afternoon show isn't going exactly as he planned. There's no time for questions, Jaswinder, not unless you want to die today. Come on, give me a hand, and be quick about it."

With Jaswinder on his heels, Rish trotted down the menagerie corridor to the screamies' cell.

The five muties turned to look up at him as he reached on tiptoes for a stone shelf beside the door. From the shelf he took two pairs of Bull's Eye Ultimate 10 Hearing Protectors and two pairs of Lexan, wrap-around goggles. It was the gear they used during feeding and periodic hose downs.

After he and Jaswinder put on the muffs and goggles, Rish waved over the zoo's contingent of enforcers.

When they opened the cell, the gagged and bound screamies just glowered at them from the straw. Seeing the ear and eye protection, they didn't bother giving voice. They looked like five very unhappy teenage girls, though what they really were Rish had no clue. Were they even human? Based on their abilities, he guessed not. They appeared to be related and the same age. They could have multiple births, sisters or even clones. The screamies had just turned up in a cargo of muties, already bound and gagged, with written instructions on their care and handling. There were specific instructions on safety procedures, lethality ranges and the like. Rish had heard the rumor that Magus had paid dearly for them in wags and high-test fuel.

At Rish's signal the enforcers entered the cage and, gripping the girls by their upper arms pulled them to their feet. The wraiths visibly recoiled at the creatures' sweaty touch.

Rish found himself looking up at them, and they looked down their pert noses at him, radiating contempt for the gnarly runt who had control of their destinies. The screamies were a good head and a half taller than he was.

"You're going to be good girls, now," he said in an affirmative tone. He couldn't tell whether they understood him or not. Their pretty faces seethed with rage. He made a calm down gesture with his tiny hands. "Take it easy. Just take it easy. We're going to let you out for some fresh air. And a little choir practice."

They didn't respond to him, but they looked at one another, sharing a sisterly moment.

Rish and Jaswinder cut the tape loose from their hands, then they removed the tape wrapped around their heads, sealing their jaws shut. The norms stepped back as the screamies pulled the wet, wadded rags from their mouths and threw them down onto the straw.

Then two things happened, very quickly.

It had all been planned, of course, while they'd sat bound in their cell. Rish could see that from their triumphant expressions, a plan worked out in eye movements, head nods, perhaps even mental telepathy.

One of the screamies reached out and with a single swipe of her hand tore the ear muffs and the goggles from Jaswinder's head.

All five of the muties opened their mouths, showing the black lining, and cut loose with a ten-megawatt, super-high-frequency chorus.

Rish didn't actually hear the noise. But it hurt, oh baby. It hurt like a steel bit drilling up through the roof of his mouth. The side of his body facing the muties was blasted by heat, like he had stepped too close to a bonfire. He tasted blood.

Not his own.

It was Jaswinder's.

Poor Jaswinder jolted backward, thrown against the bars as if hit by a wag.

"Stop them!" Rish cried to the enforcers as the wraiths' nubile bosoms heaved, gathering air for a second blast.

Before they could intervene, blood gushed from Jaswinder's ears, eyes and nose. Not in pulsing arterial jets, but fountaining like a busted water pipe. The skin of his bald head rose up in great, watery blisters. Jaswinder took one breath, choked and spewed gore halfway across the cage.

That breath was his last. The screamies moved in and wreaked close-range devastation. Their assault cooked his brains like a microwave oven. Jaswinder's eyeballs bulged, smoking, then they exploded. Brains bubbled out his emptied eye sockets like pink gravy. He slumped to seated position on the floor, chin resting on chest.

Rish could feel and smell their sweet breath on his face as they aimed a torrent of destruction at him. Despite the protection he was wearing, the drill bit spun faster, bored deeper, augered wider. Rish whimpered

and backed away as the enforcers grabbed them from
behind and clapped hands over their open mouths.

Sweaty fingers squeezed off pert noses, as well.

The muties kicked wildly and tried to scratch the
knobby skin. All they managed to do was break their
nails. Slowly, their faces turned red, then purple, then
they stopped struggling.

Only when they went limp did the enforcers let them
breathe through their noses.

Rish looked down at Jaswinder. His face was a
bloody mess. Steam rolled out of his eye sockets and
ears. Rish couldn't imagine what it had to have felt like
to die that way. The building pressure and heat inside
the skull. Eyeballs bursting. The explosion of pain that
was not a release but a door opening to even greater
agony. Jaswinder hadn't deserved such a horrible
death.

"Let them go," he told the enforcers.

When the creatures obeyed he saw that the pressure
of their hands had left red marks on the milk-white skin
and glistening smears of sweat.

Despite himself, Rish was taken aback when the
wraiths started laughing and giggling, pleased that their
affronted dignity had been revenged, for the moment.

They flipped their long braids over their shoulders
with a practiced toss of the head. Again the small, perfect noses went up in the air, the blue eyes flashed behind cornsilk lashes. So haughty. So defiant.

So infuriating.

Jaswinder still lay twitching in the straw, his brains
running into his lap.

Rish had the urge to order the enforcers to regag and rebind the screamies and send them out into battle. That way, the other loosed mutie species would pull them apart. As powerful as the impulse was, he thought better of it. His hand could not be apparent in the disaster.

"Get those bitches out of here!" Rish shouted at the enforcers.

# Chapter Twenty-Six

Doc Tanner fought his way up a curving, narrow passage. While the steeply angled floor had substance—it looked like black marble—the walls and ceiling did not. They were smoke, impenetrable gray smoke that churned around and under the free-floating platform. It was like being inside the belly of a tornado. He touched the wall with his hand and the smoke swallowed it up. Though the air appeared to be moving in a clockwise swirl, he could feel no wind.

Above him was the strange passage's end. A single floor-mounted spotlight shone on a wooden door thickly painted apple-green. As he continued to climb toward that goal, the effort caused his legs and solar plexus to ache. Ignoring the pain, he put one unsteady foot in front of another.

When Doc reached the barrier, he turned the knob. The door slammed back on its hinges from a powerful suction, sending him skidding in reverse. He had to drop to his knees and put his hands flat on the marble to keep from losing all the ground he had gained. The wind through the doorway was blowing directly into his face, and it was so strong that it was difficult to breathe, so strong that he had to lean forward and drive with his legs to hold his own against it.

As he hung on there, things began blowing past him, swept downward by the rush of air.

Maple leaves in fall colors, red, gold, orange.

Shreds of paper.

Browned rose petals.

Dead birds, sparrows and robins somersaulted limp winged around his ears.

Dropping lower to his belly, he crawled forward, pulling himself to the door jamb. When he reached over the jamb, he could no longer feel the floor. It ended on his side of the jamb.

Before him, beyond the reach of the spotlight was pitch darkness. After a moment a pinpoint of brightness appeared in the center of the black, growing wider and wider, like the iris of a great eye opening.

Doc choked on a flood of tears, certain that he was looking at the backside of very same oculus that his daughter Rachel had glimpsed November of 1896, glimpsed more than once and could not forget. How it had frightened her. An eye hanging in space. God's eye, she had called it.

At the time Doc had been very concerned by the girl's reports. He had enough medical knowledge to realize that hallucinations were not always the result of an overactive, childish imagination. They could also caused by tumors of the brain or poisons in the environment. He had no way of knowing that what Rachel had witnessed were tests of the time-trawl machinery from the distant future, a maw opening and closing.

Through the iris he could see bright gray, but it wasn't fog and it wasn't smoke. It didn't drip like a mist; it had no moisture to it. It didn't burn his nose and eyes; it held no choking ash. When he turned his head, the blur of gray moved with it. It seemed to be something internal, like his own vision was failing, clouding over with cataracts.

More stuff was sucked or driven past him.

A St. Charles spaniel with leash.

A lady's hat, widebrimmed with gray and white feathers. With a start, he recognized it as Emily's.

Then came an open parasol.

A wicker baby carriage tumbled sideways over his back, followed by the spilled contents of a trash can: wads of greasy newspaper, half-rotted vegetable matter, empty tin cans, broken bottles, beef soup bones. All of it rattled past him.

Then something much larger shot by. Though he saw it only for a fraction of second, the image stuck in his consciousness. It was the image of himself sucked headlong down the churning tunnel. He saw the terror and disbelief in his own eyes, the long frock coat with small gold buttons, the diamond stick pin in his cravat. The hair not yet streaked with gray.

Gone.

To a future that didn't want him.

To a landscape of pain and regret.

A moment or two later, the wind currents changed, like a tide going slack. As he rose to his feet and stood on the edge of the jamb, the fog parted and he saw his little family standing huddled before him on the misty

Omaha street. They were just as he remembered them—Emily holding their infant son Jolyon, Rachel standing close to her.

Heart soaring, he stepped out of the doorway, out of the great eye of Chronos, and knelt with arms out-stretched.

"Oh my darlings," he said. "My dearest, most precious darlings."

The faces of his wife and daughter radiated shock, absolute white-faced shock.

"Where's my daddy?" Rachel cried.

"It's all right, Rachel," he said. "Daddy's here. He's back with you and safe."

Rachel started screaming over and over again, "Where's my daddy? Where's my daddy?"

Emily drew her closer with a protective arm, her dark eyes full of anger and dread. "How do you know my daughter's name?" she demanded. "Who are you, old man? What do you want? Where's my husband? What have you done with him?"

Before he could frame an answer, Emily grabbed the little girl by the hand and, clutching Jolyon to her breast, took off in the opposite direction. As she ran she shouted, "Police! Help! Police!"

"Wait, Emily, dearest!" he cried.

Doc raced after her, but his legs had no strength left in them. He couldn't catch her. Emily and Rachel vanished into the fog ahead. Doc took a few more steps, then stumbled and fell. The ache in his stomach suddenly became unbearable. His entire body convulsed. He vomited until he had nothing left, until he tasted blood.

When he raised his head, he saw that nothing was as it seemed. He was in a mat-trans chamber. Sitting on the floor across from him was Dr. Antoine Kirby. His tall topknot of dreads had completely flopped over to one side. Puke stained the lap of his BDU pants.

"God, that was awful," the black man groaned. "Got to get some air or I'm gonna dry heave again." He crawled to the door, opened it from his knees, then crawled out of the unit.

Doc looked around the chamber floor for his sword-stick, then remembered he'd lost it at Magus's redoubt. Without the help of the cane to get to his feet, Doc had to crawl out, too.

The gateway control room was one of the largest he had ever seen. It had three times the normal number of workstations. One wall was made up of massive, tape-drive computers, and another wall was line with what looked like power transformers and boosters. Everything was humming and clicking; the air smelled of ozone and warm plastic.

On the fourth wall were a pair of gasketed vanadium steel doors, side by side.

Doc pointed at them and asked, "Are those gateways, as well?"

Kirby looked over. "No, those are temporal transfer chambers."

"Two of them?"

"You and I will be transferring simultaneously."

"Why is that necessary?"

"It conserves energy. It takes a tremendous amount of power to get the system online. In fact, it will pretty much use up all of this redoubt's nuclear reserves. We have to jump simultaneously. There won't be enough energy left for another power-up. When the system's operational energy level is reached, two jumps, perhaps even a hundred jumps are possible if they take place in the same instant. There's another reason for simultaneous transfer, too. For us both to slip back into same time line, our jumps must be coordinated to a fraction of a nanosecond."

Doc couldn't help but notice that the mathematician's grief over the loss of his colleague seemed to be under control.

On the verge of a great experiment, the culmination of a life's work, the salvation of the known world, there was much to occupy and distract Kirby's mind. "How do you know any of this for a fact?"

"It's not fact. It's predictions derived from our computer models of supra-time/space."

"Do your models tell you what we will experience when we go back in time?"

"No. That's something impossible to predict. We assume it will be similar to the mat-trans experience. Disorientation. Unconsciousness. Vivid dreaming. Nausea after the fact. What was it like when you traveled forward in time?"

"The lower depths of hell."

"We can hope for better than that."

Remembering a fragment of his mat-trans jump nightmare, Doc asked, "Will I see myself?"

"Perhaps. Perhaps not. The door you are about to exit through is not the same one you were drawn into two hundred years ago. It will be close, but the locations will not overlap."

"What must I do?"

"All that's required is that you open the door and step out of the chamber. You won't be home until you leave it. You must exit within a minute or so of reaching the terminus."

Doc had sudden awful suspicion, also fueled by his nightmare. "Will my family even recognize me? I am older than when I left. The trawling has aged me, too."

"Say you were struck by lightning."

"I beg your pardon?"

"A joke. Pretend to be taken gravely ill. As far as they're concerned you won't have left at all, you will just have disappeared for a moment. Trust me, they will accept you with open arms."

"But I am different," Doc said. "It is going to be like stepping out of a room and returning a minute later scarred physically, and perhaps mentally. My young Emily will be suddenly be married to a sixty-year-old man."

"Your teeth are still fine."

For the first time, Tanner got the distinct impression that Dr. Kirby didn't care what happened to him, as long as he stepped out of the time chamber on cue. Perhaps that was understandable. It wasn't his problem.

"I have a lot of preparations to make," Kirby said. "It will take twice as long to set up the computers without Graydon's help. Why don't you go have a wash? The showers are through the door and down the hall to the right. There are some clean clothes laid out for you."

Doc found the washroom, stripped out of his clothes and got into the white-tiled stall. It was the first hot shower he had had in a long time. Using plenty of soap and a small brush he found, he scrubbed out the ground-in filth of Deathlands. When he toweled the steam off the mirror afterward and looked at himself, he decided that without the dirt, he looked even older. Late sixties, perhaps. The grime had plugged the seams in his face like Pancake makeup. There was a light in his haggard face, though. He was to be released from prison after serving an unjust, two-hundred-year sentence.

He thought better of changing his clothes. Appearing in a light blue, Air Force-issue jumpsuit would have been yet another shock for his loved ones. He pulled on the threadbare coat and trousers, the worn, patched knee boots.

When he returned to the control room, he saw that Kirby had washed and spruced up, too. Gone were the massive dreads. He had shaved and waxed his head and discarded his Deathlands' clothing. He wore a sparkling white lab coat. Clipped to the pocket was a plastic photo ID from Livermore Labs.

"I'm still running system diagnostics," Kirby told him. "We have time to eat."

"My last meal in Deathlands."

"The redoubt is well-stocked, equipped with subzero freezers. Government money paid for it all. Our tax dollars at work. What's your pleasure, Dr. Tanner?"

He didn't have to think about it. "A well-aged T-bone steak. Scalloped potatoes. Steamed, buttered asparagus. And an appropriate wine."

"Been a long time, huh?"

"I have to admit, it has been a while."

"I can provide everything but the wine. Colonel Bell popped a bottle of predark Cabernet Sauvignon after we came out of cryogenesis. There was stuff floating around in it that you wouldn't believe. The cork had failed. All the corks have failed. I do have some interesting Scotch. One hundred fifteen years' mellow."

They retired to the redoubt's fully automated mess hall. While the dinner was cooking itself, they drank liquid amber silk from crystal tumblers.

"Are you trying to get me lubricated?" Doc asked as the mathematician refilled his glass for the third time.

"Relaxed," Kirby said. "And I'm drinking as much as you. A mat-trans and a time jump in the same day could be rough."

"Is all that fine food I smell going to come out my nostrils?"

"Live for the moment, Tanner," Kirby said. Then he raised his glass. "Here's to Colonel Graydon Bell."

For a second, Doc thought the man was going to lose control again, but he recovered, wiping his eyes with the back of his lab coat sleeve.

"To Colonel Bell," Doc said. "And to my companions."

"Salute," Kirby said, downing his drink. He reached into his side pocket. "I have something I want you to take with you. It's more important than you can imagine. The survival of our world depends on it."

He put a tiny metal capsule and a neck chain onto Doc's open palm. "Inside the capsule is information that must fall into the hands of the heads of Operation Chronos before the first time-trawl is performed," he said. "You must find a way to insure that this happens, and that the contents remain intact."

Doc slipped the chain over his head. "I will do my best to honor that request," he said.

As they began to eat the food, Doc changed the subject to the trainers and their unique attributes and peculiarities. "How could a creature have evolved on this Earth?" he said. "Nothing about them makes sense."

Although Kirby's grasp of evolution was less than perfect, he saw the problem. "If they didn't come from here, then where?"

"Precisely," Doc said. "Rumor has it that Magus time travels."

"No, that's bullshit. He can't be jumping back and forth in time. S-t/s says reality would fall to pieces."

"Time is a dimension, correct?"

"Of course, the fourth dimension."

"What if some other kind of dimensional travel is involved? Beyond the fourth, I mean. If there are four, might not there be ten or a hundred?"

"Or a million."

"If the travel in this case was between parallel universes, would there be catastrophic disruption to the current existence?"

"There's no way to tell. Our experience with consequences of temporal transfer is limited to what happened to you. A single case. Certainly parallel universes have been predicted, theoretically."

Doc could verify those theories, but chose not to.

"Is it conceivable that he could be looting parallel worlds and returning to this one?"

"No. The kind of dimensional travel you are talking about is impossible. No such technology existed prior to the Apocalypse, and I seriously doubt it could have been developed since. There are fundamental insurmountable problems. Even if Magus could move between universes, how would he ever find his way back? How would he know where he would end up when he stepped across? There is no up or down in what you are describing. Just a vast otherscape. We're not talking about a map of Georgia here. It's a random number crapshoot. One universe is just as likely to be next door at one moment as any another. And the consequences of travel would be just as destructive. Bringing things into a time line from elsewhere…"

"Else*when*…"

"Sure, whatever. It would have the same destabilizing effect."

"So, where did the trainers come from?"

"They could have come from outer space," Kirby said. "That's an easier sell than parallel worlds. But it doesn't still speak to a larger issue."

"Which is?"

"If Magus could go anywhere in a million universes, why would he come back to this hellhole? Even for a visit?"

Doc sipped at his Scotch whiskey. It was very, very smooth. "Touché, Dr. Kirby," he said. "Why indeed."

"It's time to get back to the control room," the black

man said. "Under the circumstances, I think we'll leave the dishes."

Doc pushed up from his chair and fell in behind.

Clearly there were some things that Kirby wasn't taking into account. Doc had seen matériel from another world, seen beings from that world arrive here not once, but twice, with his own eyes. And despite that double intrusion, the fabric of existence seemed as whole as it ever had. None of Kirby's supposed, disastrous effects had taken place.

Perhaps it was a problem of specialization, he thought. When Doc had gone to university it hadn't been an issue, but in the last part of the twentieth century whitecoats only worked in limited fields. They didn't know the rules or operating procedures of other disciplines. And moreover, they didn't give a damn. Perhaps if Colonel Bell had survived, he might have gotten a more satisfactory answer to his question about the trainers. Physicists in his experience were voluble and interesting conversationalists, less grounded in the purely rational than other whitecoats. Freer, more liberal thinkers. Not that Kirby wasn't personable enough, but he was a mathematician by training and inclination.

Somewhat tipsy from the whiskey, and sleepy from all the food, Doc felt a sudden rush of sentimentality. He was about to say goodbye to Deathlands after all these years. The actuality of his leaving had finally begun to sink in. It was no longer an abstract desire, a wistful longing. He was really going, forever.

He thought about the memories he would be taking back to Nebraska. Of the battles. Of the dangers. Of the triumphs. Of Lori Quint. Truly he was not the same man who was stolen away. He had changed into a hardbitten warrior.

Could he actually return to his own peaceful time, to domesticity, to academia?

Could he live as he should have lived?

Could he slip into the ease and safety of Victorian America as if none of this had ever happened?

To have seen so much death and suffering. To have caused death and suffering in order to survive, answering bullet for bullet, blade thrust for blade thrust. What kind of a father would such a man be in a world where violence was not a virtue, but the act of a psychopath, a serial criminal. Would he be the kind of father children would run from screaming?

Doc slumped into a control room chair, feeling the full weight and sum of his years.

Kirby tinkered with the computers and gradually the room started to get very warm. The generators' hum had become a shrill whine. They were nearly at peak power.

"It won't be long now," the mathematician assured him. "The grid is just coming online."

Doc let his gaze turn inward. Instead of joy, he felt excruciating pain over what he was about to give up. It was something he hadn't expected to feel at this moment, something he had to put aside.

What I have prayed for so long, he told himself, I will humbly accept as God's true gift. The path that lies straight ahead is the path I will not waver from.

# Chapter Twenty-Seven

Ryan had already made his decision before the grating music paused and the doors banged back for the fourth time. It was a decision forced upon him by circumstances, a decision of last resort. The army of freebooters that had sailed south from Morro Bay had dwindled to thirteen souls.

Eight islanders. Five companions.

If the survivors of the *Taniwha tea* remained where they were, in the middle of the islet, the combined attacks of large and small foes were going to grind them into stew meat.

Ryan smacked an oncoming scagworm in the side of its domed head with the flat of the panga. It made a clanking sound, like he'd swatted a steel ingot. He'd already learned that striking these muties with the sharp edge did nothing but dull the blade. The panga blow knocked the scagworm off course, and diverted its attention long enough for it to acquire another target. Instead of rejoining the attack on him, it slithered off to assault an islander who was stomping a rat devil to pulp while two more chewed the backs of his calves.

"Back to the beach!" he told the companions. He repeated himself to Eng, shouting, "Into the water! We've got to get into the water."

The captain waved his men after them.

They formed another flying wedge of sword and knife and tomahawk, and ducking under the swoops of the Wazls, fought their way through the stickies and swampies. There were fewer to deal with now, and the ones that remained seemed warier, a tad less suicidal.

As they broke through the thin mutie ranks and charged for the shore, the uniforms in the boats stood and shouldered their autorifles, but in a very relaxed, lackadaisical sort of way. Their expressions said, "This is going to be good."

"Ryan, what the rad blazes are you doing?" J.B. asked.

"Just leveling the playing field."

"But the fuckers in the rowboats—"

"If they shoot, they shoot," Ryan said as the companions joined them, splashing into the warm water. "Would you rather check out from a bullet, or die with a stickie peeling off your face?"

"A bullet, most definitely."

"Deeper!" Ryan shouted to the others. "Wade out deeper!"

The thirteen survivors trudged out until the water came up to their hips, then they turned toward shore to face the coming onslaught.

"Yes!" Ryan exclaimed as the fastest and most agile of their pursuers jumped into the water after them. The rat devils could swim, all right. They dogpaddled, their heads held above water, little legs kicking. But they swam in straight lines at a tenth of their speed on land. And they couldn't jump around to evade the falling blades.

No one needed instructions on what to do next.

Cursing and snarling, the survivors hacked and whacked the surface-swimming rat devils. The glancing blows stunned them; the well-aimed swings bisected them. Their toy-poodle-size bodies drifted by, leaking red. Some of the stunned muties came to between the shore and the boats, struggling with broken legs and broken backs to stay afloat, to keep their heads above the water. Their frantic efforts created bubbles and splash, ripples and wavelets on the smooth gray sea.

Sensing that dinner might soon be out of reach, the two Wazls grew more frantic in their attacks. The down drafts of their swoops and dives buffeted the companions' faces, and the gusts of wind propelled the floating rat devils even farther off shore.

The scagworms reached the finish line next. A half-dozen of them snaked right up to the waterline, but stopped short of getting their thousand or so feet wet. They either could no longer sense the presence of their prey, or they refused to enter the water to chase it.

Swampies had a problem with the water, too. They were smart enough to see that if they waded out far enough to reach the norms, they would be submerged to their armpits, which meant they couldn't swing their clubs and swords with any power. Not being able to finish the job they started made the ankle-biters furious. They smashed their weapons into the shallows, pounding the water to a froth.

The stickies were the immediate concern. Water didn't bother them, and once they had regrouped and gotten their numbers up, they seemed to have rediscovered their zeal for the hunt.

As with the others, the stickies were dealt with more easily in the water than on land. Again, because it limited their jumping and maneuvering ability. The stickies had to come to the norms, and when they did they were met with sharp steel. The islanders slaughtered them like pigs, with sword sweeps that practically cut them in two. Everyone got their licks in. J.B. with his tomahawk; Jak, Mildred and Krysty with their blades. Again and again, Ryan's panga cleaved soft skulls down the nose holes. Mutie gore spread in a thin greasy film on the water's surface. Stickies and parts of stickies drifted away in a swathe of blood.

Seeing the futility of attack, a few of the bald muties actually managed to hold themselves back, although with great difficulty. They blew kisses, hopping around wildly behind the irate swampies on the shore.

From over the top of the low rise came a buzzing sound, then bleating squeals. Three scalies, their heads shrouded in clouds of stinging black flies, blundered blindly toward the water, their flabby arms outstretched. The other muties stepped aside and let the behemoths pass. The scalies threw themselves into the water, submerging in an attempt to drive off their tiny but lethal attackers. It wasn't a bad idea, but it had come to them a little late. The waves they created were still lashing the shore when they popped up like dead whales, facedown, spread-eagled.

The recruits were clearly winning and yet the uniforms in the boats still held their fire. When Ryan glanced back at them, he saw they had actually lowered their weapons. A couple of men in each boat had slipped oars in the water and were rowing off shore a bit. The splash of the blades stirred up the floating blood and rat devil bodies. The rowers couldn't seem to get out of the spreading slick, or maybe they weren't trying. The uniforms and the trainers stared fixedly at the cone and the steel doors. What were the bastards waiting for? Ryan wondered.

On the far side of the boats, Ryan saw boils in the water, huge boils from red-orange shapes rolling just under the surface. They were big shapes with big mouths, moving up the chum slick of dead and dying muties, lazily gulping. Every time a struggling rat devil was sucked down it sounded like a toilet flushing. The boils got closer and closer.

With a grating, scraping noise one of the boats suddenly moved six feet sideways, nearly pitching out the occupants.

The other boats were likewise jolted, uniforms and trainers clinging to gunwhales for dear life.

Behind him, the Wazls let out a piercing shriek. Not of fury or bloodlust this time.

Of pain.

KRYSTY DUCKED HER HEAD as the lizard bird's shadow swept over her. After the close call she'd had a few minutes ago, it was impossible not to flinch. The Wazl reversed course and joined its sole surviving partner above the middle of the islet. The pair began to fly in tight spirals, trying desperately to gain altitude. With their torn wings, they could only climb to sixty or seventy feet.

Krysty didn't see the five blond girls as they stepped out of the doorway. She was looking at the birds. When she glanced down, the wraiths were already descending into the amphitheater. Krysty would have laughed at the sight of them, but she knew the kind of jokes Magus played weren't funny to anyone but him. They looked like sisters. Quintuplets. Identical heights. Tall and willowy, with perfect snow-white faces.

The young girls glided over the littered battlefield, the long hems of their white gowns dragging through the carnage, their thin arms folded under their breasts, like they were crossing a ballroom at a baron's wedding feast. To Krysty, there was something odd about the way they moved and held themselves so erect, something unnatural.

They walked directly under the desperately flapping birds and raised their heads. When the wraiths opened their mouths, Krysty saw they were black inside, like they'd been eating licorice. The teeth and tongues were black, too.

It looked like they were yelling at the birds, but no sound came from their throats.

Unable to escape, the Wazls swooped down on the newcomers. It was a big mistake. The huge birds dropped out of the sky as if hit by cannonshot, one instant flying, the next falling in a heap. The lizard birds died thrashing on the rocks while the Nordic quintet sang its silent song. The odor of cooked lizard meat wafted across the islet.

The wraiths moved on deliberately, but without haste, as if they had all the time in the world, as if they were in total command.

A few of the scalies still hunkered over their human victims. They saw the girls coming out of the corners of their eyes, but waited too long to get their feet. After they had risen from their haunches, they realized they couldn't move fast enough to escape.

Black mouths opened in unison.

The scalies held their hands over their ears, but it didn't do any good. They clustered together, dropping to their knees, moaning, bobbing their heads. Krysty saw their eyes burst, then what had to be liquid brains started running out their noses. The blond teenagers weren't done yet, though. They glided closer, sucked down a breath and opened their mouths again. Shortly thereafter, the scalies' skins began to delaminate. Between the layers of tissue on their sagging chests and backs, air pockets formed, then expanded as intense heat turned trapped juices to steam. As on a well-roasted turkey, great voids appeared under the skin, translucent bubbles glistening with fat.

It was clear to Krysty that whatever blundered into the girls' range died. Pretty heads turned, mouths opened and eyeballs exploded.

"What the hell are they?" Mildred said.

"A mutie clean-up squad," Krysty told her. "They're coming for us, and taking out everything in between."

The swampies saw what they were up against, and took off running around the islet's perimeter.

The stickies on the beach appeared confused, unable or unwilling to leave. Still hopping around, they started bleeding from ears and nostrils as the wraiths glided closer.

"They're doing everything in unison," Krysty said. "They turn at the same time, they even blink at the same time. I don't think they have the power to chill one-on-one. I think it has to be five to one."

"I can't throw a knife that far and hit anything," Mildred said. "But Jak can."

"Chill them, Jak," Krysty said.

The albino shook his sleeve and a pair of leaf-bladed throwing knives dropped into his hand. "Two left," he said.

"Just do it. Don't let them get any closer."

They were already too close. Krysty could see their blue eyes, their pale cheeks touched with roses, their nubile bodies under the gauzy gowns. Their unnatural, black-lined mouths turned toward her.

The spearing pain up through her palate was accompanied by the taste of copper and a sensation of extreme heat, as every nerve in her face, chest and arms fired at once.

"Throw it!" she cried.

With a snap of his arm, Jak fired off a knife. It sizzled through the air, arcing the last four feet, curving and diving into the front of the long white throat.

Whatever the hell it was, it shut its mouth and staggered backward into its mirror images. Thick blood dripped onto the wraith's bodice. She opened her mouth, and it was no longer black. It was red, and more red poured forth. She staggered out of formation, clutching her neck.

The other four continued to silently scream. Two of the islanders standing closer to the shore sprang tremendous nose bleeds. They ducked under the water to block out the pain.

Jak threw his last knife. Again, he aimed for the windpipe, and he hit what he aimed at. The impact knocked the mutie down. It did not get up. Its airway blocked by cold steel, it slowly suffocated.

At once the mutie attack lost its force.

Krysty and Mildred charged out of the shallows and launched themselves onto one of the wraiths. Dodging her sharp nails and teeth, Krysty grabbed her by the braid and Mildred caught hold of the backs of her arms. Together they shoved her head under water. They held it there until she stopped struggling and stopped blowing bubbles. When they let go, the limp body rose to the surface and floated slowly away.

The other two wraiths met less peaceful ends at the hands of Captain Eng and his crew. In ankle-deep water, the islanders surrounded the pair. Behind the wall of wide, brown bodies, sabers rose and fell, rose and fell. If the muties cried out in pain, the sound was drowned out by the grunts of their down-swinging executioners.

Screams, then a flurry of staccato blasterfire came from the water behind them. Krysty looked over her shoulder and saw six of the rowboats had overturned and men were splashing around in panic.

J.B. SENSED THE TIDE OF BATTLE was turning when Jak took out the first wraith with a knife. When the second wraith met the same fate, the pain in his skull diminished substantially. The field of combat was heaped with dead. Most of the other muties—Wazls, scalies, stickies, rat devils—were out of the game and the rest had scattered to escape the silent chilling. The scag-worms had taken cover by burrowing deep into the piles of bodies. The main obstacle to the companions' survival was the uniforms, and it was a big one.

The Armorer had been glancing back every few seconds, watching the approaching boils. Sawtooth backfins five feet long sliced through the chum slick. He saw thickly scaled, orange backs, and when the great maws opened to gulp stickie arms or whole rat devils, he got a glimpse of wicked canine fangs, six inches long with spike points.

As the fish began jostling and ramming the boats, J.B. cheered them on. "Get the rad bastards!" he shouted.

These were not normal pargo. For one thing they were twice as big as usual, two-hundred pounders, easy. They had absolutely no fear of human beings, and they attacked the boats with a hard-focused savagery J.B. had rarely seen, jumping clean out of the water to slam the hulls with their bony heads and backs.

As the boats were knocked sideways, the uniforms fired wildly into the water. The men who were shooting weren't holding on to the gunwhales. The impacts knocked them headfirst into the water. As they bobbed up, thrashing their arms, wide, toothy mouths came up behind them. The jaws closed on their heads, then the fish rolled, dragging them under.

The trainers leaned way over the sides of the boats, trying to cut the attacking fish with their talons. The shift in weight caused a critical imbalance. In the blink of an eye six of the boats had overturned. The uniforms frantically tried to swim to safety, but before they got ten feet they were taken down by the mutie fish. The trainers just disappeared. They sank like three-hundred-pound boulders and didn't even leave a bubble trail.

While J.B. watched, two more boats flipped. The men treading water screamed and pleaded for help from the other boats as tall back fins slashed through their midst. One by one, the swimming uniforms were pulled down and they didn't come up again.

Instead of trying to pull their comrades from the water, the uniforms in the other boats rowed in a frenzy for shore. As they leaned on the oars, their hulls were bumped and scraped, and the direction of travel veered erratically from side to side. They weren't riding over a river rapids, they were riding on a moving shoal of fish backs. Their faces were blanched, bloodless, their eyes huge with terror.

The four boats and eighteen uniforms made it to the beach. None of the trainers made it; the boats carrying them had all tipped over. The rowers drove the bows hard up onto the rocks, then they abandoned ship, jumping out and running from the water's edge.

Some of them took their assault rifles with them. Others were so scared that they left their weapons in the boats.

Ryan and J.B. quickly took advantage of the confusion. From the bilge of one of the boats, J.B. grabbed a pair of folding-stocked AKs. Ryan snatched up a short-barreled Galil and a full-stocked H&K 33 from a vacated bow, both in good condition. Without hesitation, they opened fire on the retreating uniforms. Blasters blazing on full-auto in both hands, they swept the men's backs with full-metal jackets, cutting them down before they could turn and fire.

Seeing blasters in the hands of the norms, the swampies took to their heels again, running low and fast back toward the steel doors.

The survivors had yet to face the most dangerous mutie species Magus had under his command. Across the dish, Dix saw a half dozen of the trainers jog from the cone onto the field of battle.

Before trainers could get near them, the islanders and companions raced to pick up the dropped assault rifles.

"We've got to go!" Ryan shouted. "Krysty, Mildred, Jak, come on!" He and J.B. were holding the bow of a rowboat. When the trio piled in and moved to the stern, they lifted the bow and slid the boat off the beach, jumping in as it drifted backward.

"Into the boats!" Captain Eng cried. He divided up his seven-man crew between two of the boats. Before he got in himself, Eng cut loose with his Galil, stitching holes along the bottom of the remaining craft so they couldn't be followed.

With J.B., Ryan, Mildred and Jak manning the oars, and Krysty sitting in the bow, the companions stroked away from the awful shore. The islanders were right behind them, pulling hard.

The trainers arrived at water's edge a few seconds too late. They waded in, and kept wading until the water closed over the tops of their heads.

It didn't take long for the school of giant pargo to locate the trio of boats. They homed in on the splash of oars. The hull under the companions' feet thumped and flexed inward as back fins scraped across it.

"Keep low and keep rowing," Ryan exhorted to the others.

With the wide heads bashing into the sides of the boat, it was difficult to maintain a straight course. The blades of the wooden oars were splintered and gouged with teeth marks. Every time the rowers dug in, they made contact with solid objects. Fish sides. Fish backs. Fish mouths.

Krysty raised an AK from the bow and took aim at an onrushing orange shape.

"Don't waste ammo!" Ryan shouted over his shoulder. "Stay down!"

Over the middle of the reef the attack reached its peak. A huge fish jumped into one of the islander boats. Two hundred pounds of blind fury slapped its tail and humped its body, breaking legs and battering out the boat's bottom.

The craft immediately swamped and began to sink.

More orange monsters lunged at the foundering boat, easily clearing the gunwhales. Already waist-deep, the crew fought back with blasters and swords at point-blank range.

Standing on the bow of the second islander boat, Eng looked like he was about to jump in and take on the fish with his Galil.

"No, dammit!" Ryan yelled at him. "Don't do it! They're too far back. You can't save them. You can only take your revenge. Eng, it's Magus. Look at him! Look at him up there! He staged all this."

Behind the smoky window set high in cliff something silvery flashed.

His tiger-stripe scars flushed with blood, Eng shouldered the autoweapon and touched off a crisp burst. The bullets sparked off the rock face, rattling but not breaking the glass. "Row harder!" he snarled at his crew.

The swamped islanders put up a furious fight before they were pulled under, which allowed the others to reach the big island. Shadowed by huge forms, they ran the boats up onto the rocks.

In the lee of the towering cliff, along the narrow strip of beach, the nine survivors paused for a quick weapons check. They had no extra ammo, just what was in the blasters they'd appropriated. The companions' own weapons were on the other side of the island.

Captain Eng fumed as he replaced the Galil's mag.

"I actually thought Magus was putting together an army," he said. "How could I have been so stupe? I have led my brothers, my cousins, my uncles to their deaths. Out of sheer greed."

"Not stupe," Jak told him. "Magus find soft spot."

"He must pay, Captain Eng," Ryan said. "And not just for this. For every evil he's ever done."

Nosing around, J.B. found the path running along the base of the cliff and waved the others over. The companions and islanders followed it to the hidden redoubt entrance.

As Mildred tapped in the entry code, a dozen assault

rifles took aim at the door at chest height. When it opened, the elevator was empty, except for the sweat puddles on the floor.

Everyone piled in. All the big bodies made a very tight fit in the ten by eight car.

"There's only one way for Magus to get off this island," J.B. said as the door slid shut. "He can't use the white ship because he has no crew to man it. He's got to use the mat-trans gateway."

"If we control the gateway, we've got the bastard," Ryan said. He punched a button on the console with his thumb and the elevator lurched and started to climb.

# Chapter Twenty-Eight

Silam had the taste of iron in his mouth. The clowns—the scalies and swampies—had failed. The most ferocious, blind-chilling mutie predators had failed. Even the screamies had failed. And in the process, virtually the entire menagerie had been destroyed. It was a catastrophe.

He could feel Magus staring at him, chrome irises locked down to pinpoints, his torso clanking with irritation, like a dieseling wag engine.

The fantasist couldn't bring himself to turn and face his master's terrible wrath, yet he had an overwhelming urge to say something in his own defense, to placate. But he was unable to speak. His tongue cleaved to the roof of his mouth. He was scared spitless, which was actually a lucky break as all Silam could offer was excuses for the poor showing. Excuses under any circumstances were grounds for execution.

When the recruit survivors had rushed into the water, Silam had been confident that everything was going to turn out fine, despite the initial setbacks. And he liked the idea of a last desperate stand waist-deep in the sea, sandwiched between rampaging muties and the armed uniforms. It was a perfect, bitter counterpoint to the gushy, heroic music.

Magus never rooted for the underdog. The whole point of the performances was to see the underdog crushed. He relied on Silam to offer the participants an illusion of hope, of the power of valiant struggle, and then to snatch it away.

Leaving nothing but pain and suffering.

It had never occurred to Silam that an unlikely confluence of events might reverse the situation: the blood and bodies in the water attracting muties not on the afternoon's program, the screamies chilling muties by the score, but not a single norm, the uniforms panicking, then running their boats aground and losing control of their automatic weapons.

"You call this garbage entertainment?" Magus demanded as autofire clattered and the fleeing uniforms were chopped down. "I thought this morning's show was pathetic. Now you've gone overboard in the other direction. This is turning into a rout."

Silam wanted to say, "they call it suspense," but he kept his mouth shut. Lecturing the master on the finer points of art appreciation was yet another quick way to get dead.

"That's Ryan Cawdor doing the shooting down there," Magus said. "The cyclops is tearing you a new asshole."

Actually, the one-eyed man and his partner had already torn multiple new assholes in the backs of the running uniforms. With the help of the other recruits they collected weapons from the dead and manned the rowboats.

"They're going to escape the islet," Magus said in disgust. "If I had a switch, I would turn off this piece of shit."

Silam rooted hard for the pargo as they attacked the fleeing boats. The fish had wreaked havoc before; they could do it again. When one boat was wrecked by a fish, he thought the other two would meet the same fate. But the muties let him down.

As the recruits stroked hard for the beach in the remaining boats, Magus wheeled from the window. "They'll be at the redoubt entrance in minutes," he said. "Do you know what this means?"

Silam had a fair inkling. If he didn't think of something spectacular, he had about five seconds to live. The ideas that came to him were feeble and uninspired.

Everybody has a bad day.

Things average out.

As time dwindled away, he blurted, "Look on the bright side, now you can chill Cawdor face to face."

Magus moved in a blur, grabbing hold of his hand. Silam had never been touched by the master before. The combination of cold steel and overheated flesh made his skin crawl. He would have yanked his hand back, but the grip around his fingers was too powerful to break.

"Do you think a face-to-face killing would satisfy my needs?" Magus asked. "My needs!"

"I'm afraid, Magus," Silam said weakly.

"With good reason, you slime. You less than slime."

The steel fingers closed tighter and tighter, a vise squeezing shut with thousands of pounds of pressure.

Silam gasped as all his finger bones shattered. Pain shot up his arm into his shoulder socket. He dropped to his knees before the master who still held him fast.

"I have been your loyal servant," Silam wailed. "I

have given you everything I possess. My talent. My imagination. I have helped to build your legend for the ages."

"Silam, you know nothing about me. You only know the inside of your own head, your own pathetic strivings and petty frustrations. Like an infant you daub the nursery walls with the contents of your own diapers."

Bullets from below thundered against the panel of armored glass, making it quiver in its steel frame. Silam jerked at the sounds, but Magus didn't even flinch. He leaned closer, so close the fantasist could see the metal guy wires in his jaws and cheeks sliding in and out of their pilot holes.

"What I am, and what I am capable of is beyond your feeble imaginings. I must teach you a lesson."

"A lesson?"

Magus released his hand.

Run, Silam told himself. Just run.

But his legs had turned to jelly. Try as he might, he could not get up from his knees.

Magus took hold of him again, working quickly, used his half-mechanical hands to crush the bones of his arm. Silam shrieked.

When Steel Eyes destroyed his other hand, turning it into a bloody mangle with a single squeeze, the poet laureate passed out cold, thereby missing the shattering of that arm, of all the bones in both feet, both legs, his pelvis, and most of his rib cage. Magus proceeded with skill and precision, tackling the job in a specific sequence, using just enough pressure to pulverize the bones. This was something he had done many times before. He left the skull and spinal cord intact.

Insistent prodding and kicking returned the spin doctor to a semblance of consciousness.

"Have you learned your lesson?" Magus asked.

"What?" Silam wheezed wetly, lungs punctured, tossed on a sea of bloodred pain. "What lesson?"

"This is what I always had in mind…"

Last thing Silam saw was Magus's heel stomping down on his oversize skull.

# Chapter Twenty-Nine

It took a good two minutes for the elevator car to reach its first and only stop. The companions and the islanders had their weapons up and ready to rip as the doors opened. But there was nothing alive to shoot at.

They looked onto a broad room with a low acoustic ceiling. It was chopped up into clusters of tiny work cubicles. The dust of a century lay inches thick on the desk and computer drive towers.

Someone had passed through recently, though. There were muddy tracks in the dirt on the gray tile floor. Most of them huge, and barefoot.

J.B. knelt for a closer look. "These belong to Doc," he said. He pointed down the hallway. "They lead that way."

With J.B. on point, they followed the bootprints around the perimeter of the room to another elevator. When the car doors opened, the odor trapped inside came rushing out.

Who had last used it was not a mystery.

"Damn, those knobby bastards reek!" J.B. said.

That they could even detect spoke volumes about its pungency. The nine of them had been fighting for their lives with edged weapons, and had acquired their own skunk funk.

"How are we going to find the gateway?" Krysty said as she got in the car.

"We can't take the time to hunt around this place for a map," Ryan said. "Jak, punch all the buttons."

The albino hit the indicator for every floor below them. There were fourteen.

Every time the doors opened, the companions and islanders were ready to fight a pitched battle. No battle came. The first seven floors were deserted and quiet, except for the buzz of the banks of fluorescent lights.

When the doors opened on the eighth floor, they heard the sound of nuke generators. Not the soft throb of mimimal, redoubt maintenance output, but the grinding rumble of full power. There was nothing in the hallway before them, but that noise shouted gateway ready to transport.

"This is it," Ryan said. "Triple red."

Taking the lead, he trotted down the hall in the direction of the sound. There was only one doorway ahead, and it was on his side. When he looked inside, his H&K 33 out in front, he let out a groan. He shouldn't have been surprised by the mechanized butchery, but he was. He turned away from the barrels full of specimens, and the dead thing on the operating table, opened like a trout.

Farther down the corridor, he saw evidence of recent water damage from the overhead fire sprinklers. The ceiling and walls were wet, but the tile floor was dry, except for scattered, irregular puddles. They weren't water. They were pools of trainer sweat.

Krysty, who had moved ahead while he was checking Magus's playroom, turned back to him and said in a whisper, "Got something down here, Ryan."

What they had was a cooked enforcer. Three hundred pounds of charred corpse lay in the middle of the hallway. The wall and ceiling near it was scorched and blackened.

"Man, that was some blaze," J.B. said.

Ryan had to agree. The body had been reduced to ashes. The heat was so intense it had melted the floor.

It was obvious that the creature had come from a doorway about twenty feet farther down the corridor. The door's lintel and the hallway ceiling were stained black with soot, and there was a similar smear along the left-hand wall where it had staggered before falling.

What had set the trainer alight? Based on years of experience, Ryan figured that Doc Tanner had had a hand in it.

He skirted the body and the greasy patch that surrounded it and made for the scorched doorway. As he approached, he heard the sound of computers chittering. Ducking low, his weapon shouldered, he swung around the control-room entrance.

And immediately let out a shout of warning.

They had found what they were looking for, a strange, shambling figure cobbled together out of metal and flesh.

Companions and islanders rushed in behind the one-eyed man. The shooting started at once. Nine assault rifles spewed a withering torrent of lead. There was no answering fire.

The enforcers shielded Magus from the full-auto fusillade with their own bodies, about three-quarters of a ton worth. Dozens of slugs hammered each of the trainers, but they had little effect. Steel Eyes didn't run, perhaps because he couldn't. He walked with a decided limp.

Ryan unleashed a spray of tumblers, trying to find a gap between the hulking bastards and clip his target. But the distance Magus had to cross was short, and the opportunity was over quickly.

The door to the mat-trans chamber slammed shut, leaving two of the trainers outside.

"Shit!" J.B. cried.

As the system powered up to initiate transport, the trainers unsheathed their talons and started to advance on Ryan and the others.

"Magus's going to jump!" Mildred said. "The bastard's going to get away!"

"Back up!" Ryan shouted, waving the others out of the room.

If bullets were ineffective on the trainers, hand-to-hand combat was out of the question. The only other room in the hallway was a dead end. If they were going to escape with their lives, they had to go either up or down.

Ryan brought up the rear in the retreat to the elevator, occasionally skating on the sweat puddles. The trainers were in hot pursuit. When they reached the car, Eng hit the call button. Then everybody turned and opened fire in an attempt to buy time. Gunsmoke billowed down the corridor, the roar of autofire was deafening. The enforcers shielded their eyes from the bullets and continued to advance.

The car doors opened behind them. As they backed

into the elevator, all the actions locked back, mags empty.

The fluorescent lights shone on the puddles of sweat they had smeared across the floor, all down the middle of the hall.

The trainers were within fifty feet of the elevator when Ryan reached for the Close button.

"Wait, Ryan!" J.B. said as he dug a match out of his pocket. "Okay, go ahead."

As Ryan pushed the button, J.B. struck the match on his thumbnail. Just before the elevator doors closed, he flicked it out into the hall. It landed on the floor and ignited the smears with a whoosh. The line of foot-high flame raced all the way to the feet of the enforcers.

The elevator doors shut as the creatures exploded in fireballs. Ryan could feel the heat through the double layers of steel. A second later, fire alarms started going off.

He let the trainers cook a minute or two before he opened the car's doors again.

The hallway was choked with acrid smoke. Fine spray from the fire sprinklers pelted the walls and floor. One of the monsters was down, about twenty feet away, still alive, but barely. The flames had turned it into a cinder. It didn't make a sound with its mouth, not even a whimper. Its body hissed and steamed as the water showered down on it.

The other trainer was staggering down the corridor, a smoldering torch. The sprinklers had extinguished the fire, but too late. The creature fell heavily onto its face, and did not stir.

The stench of roasted flesh was overpowering.

From somewhere in the ceiling, powerful fans kicked in and started sucking the smoke out. Then the sprinklers and alarms stopped.

The companions and islanders hurried back into the control room.

Ryan headed straight for the mat-trans gateway window. The chamber was empty. Magus and his trainers had escaped.

"Face it, we've shot our wad, Ryan," J.B. said.

"We didn't get him," Krysty said. "But he didn't win."

Though it stuck in his craw, Ryan knew she was right. They were alive to fight another day.

Mildred walked over to a corner of the control room and picked something up from the floor. When she turned, she held an ebony cane in one hand and a lion's-head-handled sword in the other. "Did Doc leave this behind on purpose, so we'd know what happened to him?" she said.

"Maybe wants us follow," Jak said.

"You know he'd never give up that sword of his unless he was in bad trouble," J.B. added.

"Or unless somebody took it away from him," Krysty said.

Mildred agreed. "It was lying on the floor unsheathed. He could have been trying to use it to defend himself. Maybe he was taken away from here against his will."

"We can't piece together this puzzle," Ryan said. "It leads in too many directions. All we know is, Doc left from here."

"And we've got to go after him," Krysty said. "He'd do the same for any one of us."

"Go after him quick," Jak said.

Mildred sat at a computer console and started tapping the keys, trying to see if she could call up a destination log. "Bingo. I have the coordinates that Magus transed to, and the coordinates of whoever used the system before him. Looks like the previous transfer took place about an hour ago, which would put it at about the right time."

"When was the transfer before that?" Ryan said.

"Uh, four hours ago."

"Then we know where Doc went," he said. "This is a first. Punch in the numbers, and let's go."

It took her seconds to enter the coordinates.

Ryan opened the chamber door. "This way, Eng," he said. "Come on, and bring your crew."

The captain folded his massive arms across his chest and he shook his head. "We're not going in there," he said.

"What's the problem?" J.B. asked.

"If we go in there, what will happen?" Eng asked.

"It's just a predark transporation device." Mildred told him. "A different sort of sailing ship. The coming and going is as safe as mother's milk."

The captain didn't budge. He shook his head again. "We islanders travel in this world until we are called to the next by our Mother. We don't volunteer to pass on by being transported by predark devices."

"Suit yourself, Eng," Ryan said.

"Safe journey, my friends," Eng said.

"Thanks, Captain."

The companions entered the chamber and Ryan closed the door. They got as comfortable as they could, sitting on the floor, leaning their backs against the chamber's walls.

"We'll get him back, Mildred," J.B. said. "He's a tough old bird."

"Hard to chill," Jak said.

A mist began to form around the ceiling of the chamber. It grew thicker and thicker, until it was like cotton, and then it started to descend around them.

One by one, the companions slumped unconscious onto the glowing plates of the floor.

# Chapter Thirty

Doc Tanner felt the pulsing glow of the violet armaglass walls and floor. The warmth surged into the very marrow of his bones, and when it ebbed, it left behind a chill. Warmth and chill. Warmth and chill. The mist descending from the ceiling enveloped his head and shoulders. He knew better than to fight it. Fighting was useless. Once the process was set in motion, there was nothing he could do to stop it.

Every time he'd made a mat-trans jump, he'd experienced the same initial hallucination. The seams between the floor plates appeared to yawn open like earthquake chasms, sucking him in and down, into absolute blackness.

This was something very different than matter transfer. The floor remained solid, and he had no sense of blacking out, nor of free fall through an endless void.

After a moment of extreme dizziness, the mist around him appeared to lift. Gone were the colored walls. In their place was a membranous barrier, translucent but not entirely transparent, lit from without by a warm, soft radiance. It formed the ceiling, the floor under his feet, and two of what had been the four walls.

The chamber's other walls were absent. He sat in a cylinder that extended in front of him and behind him.

On closer inspection, he saw that the walls had a texture, that they were infused here and there with a crosshatching of slightly more dense fibers. It was these fibers that kept the material from being entirely transparent.

Doc pressed his eye closer still, peering through one of the clear places. Though the image was blurred, he saw colors, glowing, shimmering colors, bright points of light in long strings. For some reason he was reminded of the streets of Paris on a warm summer evening, though there were no recognizable landmarks to indicate that that's what it was. It had the feel of radiant life, of complex culture.

As he stared harder, trying to make out details, he realized that the blurring was not a consequence of the material he was looking through. The objects on the other side were themselves blurred, like a photographic images overprinted, the tiniest fraction of inch to one side. Only the overlaid images in this case were not identical, and they were moving.

Beyond his reach, objects whose outlines he could not quite decipher—great blobs of color, glowing orbs of light, city blocks—were sliding, all in the same direction, in a kind of cosmic peristalsis.

The pulsations coincided with the beating of his heart.

With everything moving to the same pulse, his pulse, for a glorious moment Doc felt the scope of eternity.

Then the membrane that surrounded him began to close in. The ceiling lowered, forcing him to his knees.

As the walls drew in, he put up his hands. He could not stop them from molding elsewhere to his form. When the next contraction occurred, he was propelled head-first down the tubule. He traveled at great speed for a short distance, then stopped. There was a pause, then he shot forward again. When the motion ceased, he tried to see through the membrane. All he could make out were vague shapes, colors, a confusion of lights.

On the fifth contraction, something on the other side of the membrane moved against him, sliding up over his feet, his legs, his chest.

He found himself palm to palm, knee to knee, with a cherry-colored being. Its humanoid features were distorted, flattened by the pressure of the intervening film.

When the next pulsation came, they scooted along together.

Whatever the strange creature was, it seemed to desire communication with its Victorian counterpart. Through the membrane, the sounds it made were muffled, garbled, a soft liquid growling.

Doc was shocked when the film that separated them dissolved and their palms touched. Not just touched, but began immediately to flow into each other, disappearing as they did so, one hand eating the other. The sensation was electric. After their hands merged, the wrists followed, swallowing each other up. Then the arms. Then chests, legs and heads, cheek to cheek. Doc and the red creature passed completely through each other, and at the moment they were entirely joined, he felt a terrible suffocating panic. In that instant, they knew each other's thoughts.

"I am lost" came into Doc's mind.

Not spoken words. Not written words. Just there, undeniably there.

And along with it, a sense of sadness more profound than anything he had ever felt, or dreamed he could feel. A tragedy deeper than any mortal soul could bear.

I am lost.

I am lost.

When the two bodies had passed through each other and come out on the other side, the membrane reformed behind Doc's back. He shot forward alone, pushed by another wave of peristalsis. Like a pistol ball down a barrel, he rushed toward the closed end of the tube.

What lay before him was not an oculus or a doorway, nor was it a shimmering split in the fabric of reality that conjoined two worlds. It was something animate and profane. A tiny circle of light, bounded by dense rolls of pink muscle.

He couldn't tell if he was dreaming this cosmic sphincter or not, if the nightmare had ended. The world shuddered and changed before his eyes. With a start, he awoke to find himself on his back on the violet arma-glass floor. The violet walls surrounded him. The door to the chamber stood widely ajar, and tendrils of gray fog coiled over the jamb. The journey appeared over, and he felt no nausea, only a slight weakness in his knees.

Doc rose to his feet and moved to the door. He couldn't see three feet in front of his face, but he could hear a high, child's voice, a voice that could have been his daughter's.

"You saw it, Father! You saw it! You saw it, did you not?"

The exclamations touched a deep and treasured memory, and brought back a flood of intense and detailed images. It was Rachel. His Rachel. A terrible burden lifted from Doc's heart, and pleasure and delight flooded in to fill the void.

Then came a man's voice, as familiar as his own.

"Aye, perhaps I did see...something."

"More eyes from heaven?" said a woman in a cheerful, mocking tone.

"Emily. Oh, Emily," Doc murmured.

"The eye! God's eye! Look, Father! Do you see it? Do you see?"

A hard wind began to blow across the doorway where Doc stood. It tugged at his coat, howling.

"Theo!" the woman cried.

"Father!" the child called.

"Thunder and damnation!" exclaimed the man. Then he added, "I love you."

Doc watched a young man tumble past the doorway, his frock coat aflutter, hair wildly blown, eyes wide with disbelief.

"Believe," Doc admonished him.

Then he heard the reply that he missed when he was trawled so long ago. The woman answered back as her husband was torn from her, "I love you, too, my dearest Theo."

As Doc braced himself against the door frame, preparing to make his exit, the fog thinned a bit. Straining his eyes, he saw two backlit dark shapes coming toward him, growing more and more distinct as they approached. One was of medium height; the other had the stature of a small child. The taller one was wearing a long dress and carrying something bundled in its arms.

It had to be little Jolyon, his precious son.

It is time, Doc told himself. Time to reclaim your beautiful life.

"Theo?" the woman said.

"Father?" the child said.

The two figures stepped out of the swirling mist, hand in hand.

Doc Tanner froze in midstep, his heart pounding in his throat. Like a gong, the words rang in his head.

I am lost.

I am lost.

I am lost.

# Chapter Thirty-One

Antoine Kirby was greatly relieved when he rose from the floor of the chamber with his stomach contents on the inside of his body and not all over his shoes. In his lab coat's side pocket, he had tucked Colonel Bell's family photos. They were all he had left of his friend and colleague.

Outside the chamber door, the fog was lifting. It was time to take the measure of their success.

Kirby waited until he could see the ground before he stepped out. It was paved. It looked like polished concrete, and it had a decided slope to it, angling down to the right. He hopped down and watched the fog disappear completely, fading into rough-textured concrete walls and ceiling.

A parking garage ramp was his first thought. It made sense. His intended destination was Los Angeles. A place choked with similar structures. This Los Angeles was a vast improvement from the one he'd seen from the decks of the *Taniwha tea*. But as he looked around, he saw it was not the L.A. he remembered.

Down the slope, attached to the ceiling was a sign that read: Slime Zone 100 Yards. The term had no meaning for him. It didn't sound like something pleasant, though. One hundred yards, give or take, from the sign, the fog still lingered, blocking the passage. A smell of ammonia wafted up from below, and it was dark down there. Uphill, it was light.

He heard noise coming from that direction—shouting, banging and what sounded like music. Yes, it was definitely music, and with a lively beat. Aside from the bass and drums, he could make out guitar, saxophone, piano, congas and the sexy sounds of a female singer.

There was no doubt about it, the world and its complex, intermingled human cultures had been restored. This was Colonel Bell's moment as much as his.

"Graydon, we did it!" Kirby shouted. Then he laughed and corrected himself, "Or should I say, we undid it."

As he walked up the ramp, he hummed along with the song. The words were impossible to pick out. Empty foil packets about the size of paperback books blew down the ramp, end over end. Littering, it seemed, was still a problem. He snatched up a couple of the wrappers. There were two varieties: Beefie Cheesies and Tater Cheesies. Obviously some kind of fast food. Curious about the diets of people in the twenty-second century, he read through the list of ingredients. At the top of the list he was stunned to find peridotite and olivine. Rock sandwiches? Clearly that had to be some kind of typographical error.

Kirby was hoping to see some skyline when he neared the end of the ramp. There was neither sky nor cityscape. Overhead was a solid gridwork of structural concrete. The ceiling was two stories high, taller than any parking garage had a right to be; mercury vapor lamps set in it, and protected by metal cages, provided all the light. It was impossible to tell whether it was day or night. From the end of the ramp, the noises sounded less happy, less friendly. Kirby cautiously peered around the corner.

What he saw was people. People everywhere. The sidewalks were overflowing. The streets were clogged, not with vehicle traffic, but with more people. All along the sidewalk, bonfires raged in fifty-five-gallon drums. Facing the sidewalks on both sides of the street were wall-to-wall two-story buildings in various states of disrepair.

Savage fistfights spilled from the sidewalks onto the street. Dirty, ragged, skeletal men, women and children were doing their best to kill each other with their bare hands. There was not a policeman in sight. Those not involved in the melee moved aside and ignored it.

Looking the other direction, Kirby saw a massive video screen and sound system hanging down from the ceiling. That was where all the music was coming from. Now he could make out the words to the catchy little song.

"Buy, buy, buy, eat, eat, eat, that's what makes life so swee-eeeet."

People on the street and sidewalk swayed to the insistent Afro-Cuban beat, staring up slackjawed at a twenty-foot-tall, impossibly beautiful, impossibly statuesque blonde woman in a green crocheted thong. She was tanned, overfed, overpampered, overjoyed, everything the spectators weren't. As she sang and danced at a sunsplashed poolside, her naked breasts with their pink bull's-eye nipples bounced and swayed, as did her smooth buttocks.

While the band took an instrumental chorus, the singer took a jumbo shrimp break. She ate from an iced dish at overloaded buffet table under gay red-and-white striped awning. Her expression said, "Yummy." She danced as she chewed, her lavish hips rolling. She washed down the shrimp with a long sip of something from a hollowed-out pineapple with a paper umbrella.

As the music returned to yet another chorus, she bounced across the gleaming white patio and opened the door of a two-seater red sports car. The engine was five times the length of the passenger compartment. She started singing again as she squirmed her bare butt across the custom leather.

"Buy, buy, buy, eat, eat, eat, that's what makes life so swee-eeeet."

The car started with a ferocious twelve-cylinder roar. Although the blonde stroked the shifter knob, she didn't put the car in gear. She just sat there and gunned it, burning fuel for no reason, her long, pearl pink fingernails tapping out the beat on the steering wheel.

This was a different kind of porno, Kirby realized.

Consumer porno.

You can't have this, but you can watch me have it.

The mathematician scanned the length and breadth of the squalor. There was no reception committee of distinguished scholars. Perhaps Tanner hadn't passed on the microfilm? But if he hadn't, all this would not exist.

It was hard to believe that this was the world he had saved.

The world Bell died for.

Perhaps it was some kind of ghetto, even a prison. That would explain everything. Determined to find out, he left the cover of the ramp and accosted the first person he came across.

"Where am I?" he said.

The answer was less specific than he'd hoped. "You're in the wrong fucking place, whitecoat."

"Whitecoat!" someone else cried. "Get the whitecoat!"

Kirby hadn't brought any weapons with him. He had figured he wouldn't need them in a world without the Apocalypse. He was wrong. As several men attacked him, the big man was forced to fight with his fists. On the first punch, he split the back of his lab coat right up the middle. He also split the eye of the grimy, greasy, ponytailed bastard who tried to club him with a roundhouse right. The blow sent the man spinning to the ground, blood spurting from between his fingers.

None of the attackers had Kirby's size. They didn't have his Deathlands experience, either. Kirby didn't mess around. He broke one man's windpipe with a karate chop and snapped another's neck with a neat, left to right twist.

The cry of "Get the whitecoat!" drowned out the over amplified strains of consumer porno.

Before he could move off the sidewalk, he was surrounded. Somebody jumped on his broad back, trying to strangle him from behind. Kirby shot a hard elbow in the man's ribs, heard the crack as they snapped, then the weight fell away from his shoulders.

There wasn't any point in trying to reason with them. They were a mob, and they were out for his blood.

When his kicking and punching opened a seam in the throng, Kirby launched himself between the gap. Covering his face with a forearm, he jumped through a dirty plate-glass window. He landed in what once had been a hotel lobby. A shabby hotel lobby. Now it was a wall-to-wall crash pad.

As he turned to engage the denizens pouring through the broken window, someone hit him in the back of the head with a two by four. Everything went black.

Kirby woke up stuffed into a fifty-five gallon drum set in the middle of the street. His wrists and ankles were hog-tied behind his back. Liquid sloshed around his ankles; from the smell, it was gasoline. Thousands upon thousands of people pressed in around him.

The chant had changed.

Now it was, "Burn the fucker! Burn the fucker!"

A tall, rangy looking man with a mane of past shoulder-length greasy brown hair was prepared to do just that. He held a flaming torch in his hand.

"Why?" Kirby demanded of him.

"Because you bastards did this to us," the man said.

"Did what?"

"Made it so there's nothing left to eat but rocks. So there's nowhere safe to live."

"What about the promise of science?" Kirby said in desperation. "It can feed the world."

"Where have you been, whitecoat? That PR bullshit

don't fly anymore. All you bastards gave us was empty promises. And when they didn't pan out you said you needed to do more research. All you wanted was to keep the fucking gravy train rolling. Hey, shithead, there's no more gravy."

The man swung at him with the lit torch.

The gas fumes were making Kirby's head spin and his stomach heave. "I saved your world," he cried. "You wouldn't be here without me!"

"That's why I'm doing this…"

With that, the greasy-haired man tossed the torch into the barrel.

Kirby ignited with a thundering whoosh and a plume of fire fifteen feet high.

Over his own piercing screams he heard the sound of cheering.

# Chapter Thirty-Two

As the five companions staggered from the mat-trans chamber, something flashed behind the porthole window in a door across the room. At the same instant, the lights dimmed, then recovered.

As the door slowly swung open, Ryan unsheathed his panga and prepared to strike.

"Easy, dear Ryan," Doc said, holding up his hands for calm. He was smiling ear to ear. "I am greatly relieved to see that all of you remain in good health."

"You are a sight for sore eyes, too, Doc," J.B. said.

"You had us sweating bullets," Mildred told him.

"I am afraid I owe you all an explanation," Doc said. No one argued that.

"The two mutie hunters I met in Morro Bay turned out to be whitecoats," he said. "Freezie whitecoats like you, Mildred. From predark times. They claimed to be in possession of certain facts. The most alarming of which was that I, alone, caused the Apocalypse."

"You?" Mildred said. "That's ridiculous! You were a victim of it."

"Not so quick, my dear Mildred," Doc said. "There appears to be some merit in their argument. They said they had detected changes in the fundamental nature of reality, the physical properties of matter after I was trawled the first time. They claimed they tried to warn the heads of Operation Chronos that a greater disaster was imminent if the trawling program was not immediately curtailed. The freezies told their masters that a second trawl would permanently damage space-time, and cause reality to collapse. They were ignored, of course, and I was sent here. Dr. Kirby and Colonel Bell were so convinced of the validity of their claims that they entered cryogenesis to find me."

"They found you," Ryan said.

"And they offered me my life back…"

"Good God," Krysty said. "That's a time machine?"

"Of a sort," Doc said.

"You left, but you came back," Mildred said. "Why? None of us would have blamed you if you hadn't. You know that for a fact."

"Yes, dear friends, I do know that."

"Did something go wrong?" J.B. asked.

"Their calculations were based on extrapolations from a single experience, mine," Doc replied. "From the consequences of that first trawl, they constructed a theory that explained the nature of existence, and defined the structure of an external dimension, that they called supra-time/space. A theoretical viewpoint outside the human experience of time. And when that was complete, they went on to devise computer models to make predictions about changing the future. According to their theory, it was possible to undo the Apocalypse by reinserting me into the past at or near the moment I was taken. They gave me this capsule to carry with me, with instructions to see that it passed to the Operation Chronos whitecoats before they attempt a first time trawl. It contains an explanation of the whole catastrophe, its cause and effect."

"What went wrong?" J.B. repeated.

"I returned to a past, all right," Doc said, "but it wasn't my past. For a brief moment I thought I was a spectator at the events of my trawling, but as I was about to join my family the veil suddenly lifted. I saw that it wasn't my Emily. It was another woman, nothing like Emily. And my Rachel was another child, not mine."

"I'm getting confused," Krysty admitted. "If they didn't send you back where you came from, where did they send you?"

"I believe I entered a parallel universe. It could have been the correct year, but it was not the same timeline as this. It was another Nebraska, a different Theophilus Tanner."

"Close but no cigar," Ryan said.

"Exactly. I never intended to desert you. I just wanted to see their faces again. One more time. And now I know that can never happen." He ripped the chain from around his neck and threw the capsule across the room. "What is done is done. And there is no way in this or any other universe to change it."

"Time travel is only possible in one direction?" Mildred said.

"Or not possible at all," Ryan said. "Perhaps all we can do is jump universes and enter new time lines."

"We would be falling into our whitecoats' trap if we

hypothesized from a single instance," Doc said. "There are many explanations for what happened, none of them verifiable."

"What happened to the mutie hunters?" Jak asked.

"One was chilled by an enforcer. The other time-jumped at the same moment I did. Because his chamber is vacant, I presume he stepped out of the machine, to another elsewhen."

The room lights dimmed again. This time they nearly winked out altogether, and they took a long time coming back up.

"I doubt the power in this redoubt is going to last much longer," Doc said. "We should return to the island before it fails us entirely. Before we do, however, there are some things in the galley we should gather up and take with us."

AFTER A MEAL OF STEAKS, ham, lobster, a wide variety of starches and vegetables and a full fruit pie per person, the companions and the islanders lingered over cups of fresh brewed coffee and predark cigars.

Ryan quickly tired of the replays of the battle and who did what to whom. He left the dining hall and, after finding a map of the redoubt floorplan, worked his way down to Magus's skybox.

Puffing on his stogie, he stepped to the wide window that overlooked the islet. He was surprised to see movement. A few of the muties were still running around over the heaps of dead. He picked up a pair of binocs from a low table and had himself a better looksee.

With closer view, he could see right away that they

weren't all muties. A pack of swampies was chasing a norm around and around the islet. The norm wasn't much bigger than the muties, practically an ankle-biter, himself, and he had a long, hangdog sort of face.

It was a race he couldn't win.

Ryan found the controls for the sound system and turned up the Wagner to max. He watched through the binocs until the little man was pulled down from behind and disappeared under falling cudgels.

Then he returned to the party.

# ROOM 59

A nuclear bomb has gone missing. At the same time Room 59 intercepts a communiqué from U.S. Border Patrol agent Nathaniel Spencer. But as Room 59 operatives delve deeper into Mexico's criminal underworld, it soon becomes clear that someone is planning a massive attack against America…one that would render the entire nation completely defenceless!

Look for

## aim AND fire

by

## cliff RYDER

GOLD EAGLE ®

*Available July 2008 wherever you buy books.*

GRM593